BOOK I

MURDER
AT THE
SPRING
BALL

A 1920s MYSTERY

BENEDICT BROWN

COPYRIGHT

For my father, Kevin,
I hope you would have liked this book an awful lot.

THE CRANLEY FAMILY TREE

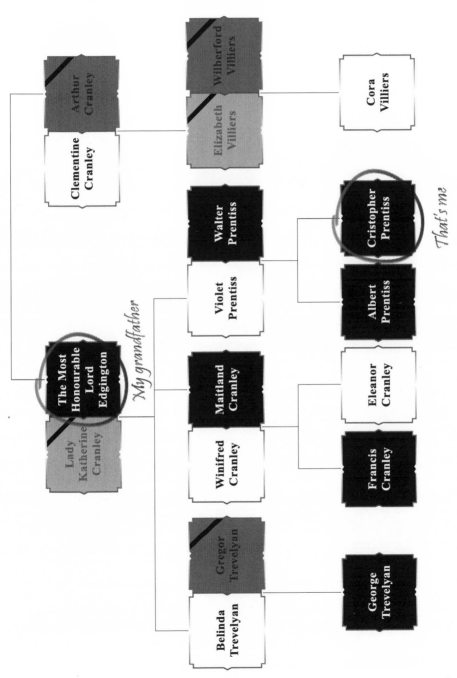

Arthur Cranley

Clementine Cranley

Wilberford Villiers

Elizabeth Villiers

Cora Villiers

Walter Prentiss

Violet Prentiss

Cristopher Prentiss

That's me

Albert Prentiss

The Most Honourable Lord Edgington

My grandfather

Lady Katherine Cranley

Maitland Cranley

Winifred Cranley

Eleanor Cranley

Francis Cranley

Gregor Trevelyan

Belinda Trevelyan

George Trevelyan

5

CHAPTER ONE

Surrey, England,
1925

It must be strange to know that everyone in the room wishes you were dead.

My grandfather sat very straight in the stiff, high-backed chair where he'd been resting for the last ten years. It wasn't just our immediate family who'd come to celebrate the old man's birthday. Every last rat had scuttled out from under the skirting boards. Every cousin and nephew, niece and nobody from within the ranks was there to pay their respects to Lord Edgington of Cranley Hall.

The unappealing collection of playboys and charlatans, spinsters and spoilt brats sat waiting for something to happen. We sipped our tea politely, hoping that someone would break the silence. Inevitably, it was my Aunt Belinda who finally did.

"Such a lovely party." She did not sound sure of herself, and my grandfather let out a huff that was only perceptible thanks to his prodigious moustache ruffling in the resultant breeze.

"Yes, quite lovely," her portly brother rushed to agree. "And it's incredible to think that you're seventy-five, father. You don't look a day over…" The sentence faded away without resolution. Presumably my sycophantic Uncle Maitland had failed to think up an age that would sound both flattering and realistic.

My great-aunt Clementine had fallen asleep in the corner and let out a single grunted snore, which made the atmosphere in the room all the more uncomfortable. Following in its wake, the only sounds were the clinking of teaspoons on porcelain and the ticking of the gigantic clock beside the door. Even Grandfather's ageing retriever wasn't enjoying herself and rolled onto her side, apparently ready to give up the ghost.

With so many expectant heirs on hand, it was a tight squeeze in the old man's sitting room. My rakish cousin George had made sure to get a seat close to the front and, as second in line to the Cranley family fortune, looked keen to discover why our grandfather had called everyone together for the first time in a decade.

There were piles of cakes and sundries on offer, but they remained largely untouched. Cranley Hall's cook was well known for the eccentricity of her culinary creations, and, while Lord Edgington adored them, it turned out that haddock and honey sandwiches were not to everyone's taste.

"Ahem...?" Our butler Fellowes cleared his throat to get his master's attention.

The birthday boy continued to stare out of the window, down past the lake and across the expansive grounds of his estate. Perhaps concerned that her father had finally lost his senses, my mother frowned, just as he turned to look at us with a sudden snap of the head.

"I'm not planning on dying just yet." His cold, grey eyes surveyed the crowd, and he spoke through resolute lips.

There was no reaction at first, except for a distracted sigh from my big brother, who was still recovering from his last ill-fated romance. A few guests looked at their neighbours to confirm that they really had heard Lord Edgington's pronouncement, but then he spoke again.

"I know what you're all thinking and you're wrong." His sonorous voice boomed through the floor like a minor earthquake. He rose without a wobble and gasps went up around the room as if Lazarus had risen for the second time. "My days are not yet numbered and I still have plenty of living to do."

As the esteemed former police superintendent stood imposingly before us, the assembled leeches failed to smother their moans of disappointment.

"Really, father," my beak-nosed Aunt interjected, "no one could possibly think-"

Our host's gaze fell upon his eldest daughter. "Belinda, I've been sitting here mourning your mother for long enough. As much as you'd like me to do the honourable thing and shuffle off this mortal coil, I'm afraid I have other ideas."

The notoriously impertinent butler let out a brief, caustic laugh.

This elicited a curl of the lip from Uncle Maitland, a squat, middle-aged man, who was forever dressed in a Norfolk jacket and hunting cap.

My grandfather didn't seem to notice and continued with his speech. "I still have a lot I want to do with my life. Starting with this place." He glanced around the room as though he were taking in the faded décor for the first time in years. "Cranley isn't what it used to be. It's high time I did something to bring the house back – back to the way it was when my beloved Katherine was still with us."

"Well, I say, jolly good!" my father proclaimed with a clap of his hands, and received several stern looks for his trouble.

Grandfather nodded his appreciation before explaining further. "I've spent the last few months wondering if I'd ever find the strength to break free from this room, but the moment has come." He tugged his waistcoat down to straighten it before announcing the first of his elaborate plans. "It's been twenty years since we had a real party at Cranley, and I'm going to throw one."

This led to a murmur of speculation and several excited squeaks from younger members of the family. Even my brother Albert looked a little more cheerful as a party meant the promise of new young ladies, who would break his heart all over again. My mother smiled up proudly at her distinguished father, but her siblings clearly did not approve of the announcement.

"Really, Daddy," Belinda began, "are you sure you've thought this through?"

Lord Edgington's voice rose to become a short poke in the ribs of everyone present. "I certainly have." He nodded to his butler, who stepped forward to place an ancient magnum of champagne on the occasional table in front of his master. "Katherine and I were given this on our wedding day and spent our lives waiting for the right moment to drink it. I don't want to be like this old bottle gathering dust anymore. I want to fulfil my potential, so I've finally thought up a reason to pop the cork."

My uncle was up next, with a sceptical question of his own. "But a party? Don't you think it's all a bit much (at your age)?" He didn't actually say these last few words, but the meaning was clear.

The look which Lord Edgington directed at his son spoke volumes. "No. I do not. Cranley Hall always hosted a spring ball when I was a child, so I'm reviving the tradition. I have a clear idea in my head of how I would like it to be, and all I need is someone to help me make it a reality."

The sedate atmosphere in the room vanished as ambitious fathers pushed their offspring forward to be the lord's assistant and mothers delivered stirring appraisals of their preferred candidate's suitability. The opportunity to curry favour with the wealthy old patriarch, in what were surely his final years on the planet, was too good to pass up.

Grandfather soon silenced them. "I've already made my decision." His gaze passed over disappointed faces, searching for his chosen relative. "My grandson Christopher will be helping me."

All eyes turned to the back corner of the room, where I was daring myself to eat one of Cook's appetisers.

"Christopher?" Father asked.

"Our Christopher?" Mother sought to confirm, her face mirroring her husband's for incredulity.

"That's right." Lord Edgington straightened his back and looked at me with a knowing smile. "Christopher will be perfect."

I froze with my mouth open and, for a moment, no one made a sound. A chunk of mustard-coated turnip made a break for freedom from my sandwich and, as it landed with a splat on the thick Chinese carpet, all hell broke loose.

CHAPTER TWO

"I don't understand it," my brother complained, once the furious crowds had dispersed and we were back in my large, opulent but blood-chillingly cold bedroom in the east wing of Cranley Hall. "I would make the most wonderful assistant. Why didn't grandfather choose me?" Albert collapsed dramatically into an armchair and put his hand to his head.

"We're not entirely sure." My father still looked puzzled on the matter. "Perhaps... Perhaps the old fellow..."

"I've no doubt there's a very good reason for why Daddy chose Christopher. Perhaps..." My mother was usually quick to smooth things over, but even she struggled to come up with an explanation. "Perhaps Daddy felt sorry for him."

They looked in my direction, but I was ignoring them. A flash of colour suggested there was a redstart in the rose garden and I had my binoculars at the ready in case he should pop back out.

"First Evangeline snubs me for 'Porky' Cumberland and now this." My brother managed to swoon even deeper into his seat.

The redstart turned out to be a plain old robin and I decided it was time to stick up for myself.

"Or perhaps grandfather saw the potential in me that you've all failed to notice." I was chomping on a banana and horseradish sandwich. I have to say that it wasn't nearly as bad as it sounds. "This might come as a shock, but it's just possible that I was the best candidate."

The two hairy caterpillars who lived on father's forehead wriggled closer together and he tried to look cheerful. "You're right, Christopher. That's the only explanation."

My mother's face brightened. "Of course. That must be it, but..." She wasn't sure where to go from there. "But you hide your gifts so well, don't you, darling? Evidently your grandfather has wormed them out of you."

I was used to such backhanded compliments from my family – and my teachers, friends and casual acquaintances for that matter. It's true that I was no genius and had yet to find the field in which I would excel, but I was still only sixteen. I was just starting out in the world and you shouldn't write a good man off before he's had the chance to do so himself.

Sitting in a Directoire-style chair beside the unlit fireplace, my father used his businessman's instincts to cut to the chase. "So, what did the old chap tell you about this plan of his?"

"Well, nothing." The truth is that I was as much in the dark about grandfather's announcement as any of them.

In contrast to my father, Mother is a poet and likes to take her time. She contemplated the conundrum before replying with, "It's very nice of you to be so loyal and keep it under your hat, but he must have said something to you."

I was fairly certain she was wrong. "No, he didn't."

Albert narrowed his eyes suspiciously. "When didn't he say anything?"

I smiled. "Quite often actually."

"Listen here, Christopher." My father walked over to the window and put one hand on my shoulder. "When was the last time your grandfather spoke to you?"

"I'd say... Yes, I think it was in 1915. Just before Grandmother died."

The three of them stared at me like I had a dollop of banana on my face.

Mother broke through their astonishment. "Ten years ago? How is that possible?"

"You're telling me you've been living here for the last six months and he hasn't uttered a word to you?" Father sounded rather angry on my behalf.

"That's right." I was grinning by now. "Since I arrived at Cranley Hall, the old man hasn't left his suite and he's never once called for me. It's awfully hard to have a conversation when, until today, we were never in the same room."

My family had returned to their gawping, but I was saved by a knock at the door.

Fellowes didn't wait to be admitted and strolled right in. "Lord Edgington wishes to see Chrissy." With his gruff delivery, not only did Grandfather's most loyal servant not sound like a butler, he also didn't look like one. Short and skinny with a scar under his left eye, he was unusually scruffy at the best of times. I once saw him wandering through Cranley Hall with his shirttails flapping loose. Still in his thirties, he was also younger than most such retainers and swaggered about like he thought he was Don Juan.

My parents' stunned reaction told me that they had no idea how to reply to such a request. Fellowes had already left the room, so I hurried out after him.

"'Ere, what's wrong with your brother?" he asked when we drew level in the corridor.

I'd spent enough time with the man to not be offended by his lack of manners, or the fact that he let his true South-London accent emerge when we were alone together.

I answered his question. "Albert's still nursing his wounded pride after Evangeline De Vere refused to go to the university ball with him."

The butler wore a perplexed expression. "Nah, not what's wrong with 'im today. Why's he always such a wet blanket? He goes about with a face like an orphaned monkey." He laughed like he really enjoyed his own joke.

"I think it must be hard being the firstborn son," I attempted to explain. "There are a lot of expectations to live up to. Or at least, that's what Father says."

The conversation tailed off as we both chewed this over. Crossing Cranley Hall can take quite some time and the quarters where I stayed when not at boarding school were about as far from my Grandfather's suite as he could have put me. We cut through the water garden, then traversed the two-hundred-yard corridor in the western wing with its black and white chessboard tiles and endless selection of Cranley family portraits. When we reached the stairs up to his rooms, we did not turn off as I'd been expecting but carried straight on.

We passed the odd, lingering relative along the way. Great-Aunt Clementine had found a new spot in the smoking room to snooze in and her granddaughter, the young, pretty, ultra-modern Cora Villiers, was puffing on a large cigar. She shot Fellowes a distrustful look as we passed and I gave her an inappropriately cheery wave in return. In the grand salon, Uncle Maitland and his two snobby children were having an argument and some chap who looked like a pigeon (plump, sallow and rather hungry) was sizing up an expensive vase as we made our way towards the ballroom.

I have to say that I was taken aback to see my grandfather roaming the house. The last time I'd seen him anywhere but his own suite was at Grandma's funeral. Her sudden death in her sixties had profoundly affected him and yet, there he was in all his brittle elegance; lord and legendary police superintendent, proudly surveying his domain.

"Fellowes," Aunt Belinda growled as she passed us in the other direction. "See if you can talk some sense into the old fool!" It was my auntie who had been the most aggressive in the ruckus that had followed Grandfather's announcement. She'd looked at me like I was trying to steal the food off her only son's plate.

Fellowes put on an innocent smile and bowed his head to her. She scowled in my direction, then slunk from the room.

"The boy," the butler told my grandfather. "As requested, Milord."

I'd often wondered exactly why it was that the renowned Lord Edgington would put up with such un-butlerish behaviour from a servant. At the time, though, I didn't have the guts to look my grandfather in the eye, let alone ask him such a question.

"Jolly good," he said, without turning around. "Fellowes, you must tell Violet that she and the family are to stay an extra night. Make up the dining room and we can eat there all together."

Fellowes looked surprised. "The dining room, Milord? Not in your suite?"

"That's what I said, man!" Grandfather's temper flashed like a cracking whip. "Now run along and do as instructed."

Fellowes squeaked back across the shiny floor, and we stood in silence, appreciating that fine spring afternoon through the French windows. A gardener was trimming the hedgerows in the distance with a rhythmic snipping of his shears, and a breeze ruffled the oaks over in the wood. If I'd been alone, I might have closed my eyes and drifted away with the music of nature, but, instead, I tensed all my muscles and waited for my grandfather to address me.

"You like birds, don't you, Christopher?" he finally enquired, his gaze twitching over in my direction, like he'd only just realised I was there.

"No, sir," I floundered. "Well, yes. But it's not as if I imagine they're my friends or..." I was never the most confident person and right then I was a jittering bag of nerves. "I actually think they'd make rather good friends, but I know that's not possible." This is exactly the kind of thing my father always told me off for saying. I braced myself for a withering look from my grandfather, but his moustache twitched upwards a fraction.

"I think you're onto something there. Birds are sensible creatures. They're focussed, hardworking, loyal to their own." He stroked the hair on his chin contemplatively. "Yes, if I was to choose an animal to make friends with, I could imagine a lot worse than a bird."

As if she'd been listening, his lolloping golden retriever, Delilah, nearly fell over herself as she bundled out from behind a row of chairs. She settled at his feet and I realised it was my turn to speak.

I couldn't think what else to say, so I went with, "Woodpecker."

"I beg your pardon?" Master and dog looked at me in bemusement.

"The lesser spotted woodpecker." His brows met at diagonals and I thought I might crumble out of existence. "That's my favourite bird. I think they look rather comical and I like their name."

He grunted his acknowledgement in a similar fashion to the way my teachers dismissed me at school. I decided it was better not to say anything more and waited for the old man to speak.

"Well, I just wanted to say…" He sighed then, as if communicating such information was simply too much effort. "… that I've spotted you dashing about in the gardens and I'm glad you've had the run of the place during the weekends. It's nice to see someone making the most of Cranley for once and you seem like a thoroughly…" He paused to find the right words. "You seem like a boy who knows how to enjoy himself."

I dared a glance in his direction. He peered through the window, out towards the grotto with its terrifying sculpture of Prometheus having his liver eaten by an eagle – a sight I'd had nightmares about since I was four.

Though he'd never been in the army himself, my grandfather had a military air about him. He was as straight as a set square, and his clothes were always impeccable. Every cuff and collar was neatly pressed and his buttons, cufflinks and watch chain looked as though they'd been arranged to the eighth of an inch by a mathematician or master painter. I always picture him in dove-grey formal attire as that is what he wore most often. On that particular day, the shiny fabric of his morning coat sparkled a little in the afternoon sun.

"Grandfather, is that why you chose me?" I asked, then immediately regretted saying anything and went back to my shaking. I won't lie, I was just as terrified of Lord Edgington as I was of poor old Prometheus's punishment in the underworld.

He looked at me as if he couldn't quite recall who I was. "Oh… No, not at all." He fell silent for a moment and there was no way I'd have found the courage to ask him again, so it was a good thing he coughed up the answer on his own. "I chose you because I knew how much it would annoy the others."

He looked me dead in the eyes and I felt like a mouse staring up at a hawk. His pale, whiskered face retained its typically stern expression. Then, for the first time I could remember, I heard my grandfather laugh. It was a staccato burst of sound which reared up out of nowhere. For some reason, when he fell quiet again, I was even more scared of the formidable ex-policeman.

Without warning, he put one foot in front of the other and set off for a turn about the ballroom. I assumed that he wanted me to follow, so I scampered along to keep up.

"I have a lot of plans, Chrissy," he announced, and I was too polite to point out that I hate it when people call me that.

I hadn't been inside the ballroom in years and the furniture was covered over with heavy, burgundy blankets. The opulence of the gold and pastel stuccoed walls was in evidence though, and a scene of devils and angels in battle floated above us on the ceiling.

Coming to a stop at the far end of the long, rectangular space, he cast his fierce gaze across the room. "I want to bring Cranley Hall back to its best before I die. I want music and laughter, discussion and joy." I could tell from the way his eyes etched out a pattern in front of him that he was seeing the place as it had once been. "But that's just the beginning. There's a litany of things I want to do and I need a companion for all of them."

His gaze burned through me once more and I was a gibbering wreck.

"Wouldn't… Wouldn't you be better off with one of the others? My cousin Eleanor can juggle and Big Francis can do a stunning impression of Aunt Belinda. They'd be much more fun. I'm not sure there's anything I can do which-"

"Stop it, boy!" he roared, and I almost jumped out of the window to escape. "You're blathering. I can't stand blatherers."

I smoothed my hair down with the palm of my hand and he waited for me to compose myself. "Sorry, Grandfather."

"And don't say sorry, either. It's a terrible habit."

I thought about apologising again but caught myself just in time.

His silver-grey hair seemed to wave at me in the breeze of the open window before he spoke again. "I chose you, not Eleanor nor Francis, but the boy who's been running around my gardens for the last six months with a pair of binoculars and a smile on his face." He put one hand on my shoulder and his confidence surged through me. "There's no doubt about it, Christopher. You and I are going to take on the world."

CHAPTER THREE

The following day was a Saturday, but I woke to the sound of workmen hammering away in the distance. I'd always thought of Cranley as the seat of luxury and, compared to our own humble manor house on the other side of the Surrey Downs, my grandfather's home was a palace. I'd spent every holiday of my childhood there and still hadn't run out of rooms to explore.

Built in a rather too flamboyant style by my great-great (plus several more greats) grandmother, it was bedecked with fine Romanesque carvings, more Doric columns than the whole of Greece has to offer and countless de-armed statues. Subsequent generations had built on to the original structure so that the hall had ended up as a big square with two rectangular wings extending off it. It was vast enough to house a small army, but, instead, accommodated one old man, his grandson at the weekend and a staff of full-time servants.

The value of the paintings in the eastern gallery alone would have paid off Britain's war debt. And yet, after the builders arrived, I began to understand what Grandfather had been talking about. The childish lens I had viewed my ancestral home through fell away and I could finally see just how shabby the place was.

It had aged over the last decade at a similar pace to its owner. As his wiry hair had changed colour, the plaster and brickwork had dulled and begun to flake. There were draughts to block in every window, (especially in my icehouse of a room) and leaks and drips wherever my eyes now landed. The gold leaf that adorned the woodwork required more than just a lick of paint, and even my illustrious forebears in their immense frames looked down at us through cracked visages.

There was also the feeling that Cranley Hall had been passed by in the technological rush of the twentieth century. Though some rooms had electric lighting and there were several telephones scattered about, the east wing hadn't been touched in years and I still had to find my way back to bed every evening by candlelight.

So, I was quite excited by the thought of workmen tackling the old place. I bounded downstairs to find out what passed for breakfast that day, only to discover that the kitchen was empty. Even Delilah was missing from her basket. I was planning to make the most of this freedom to whip up something edible, when I caught wind of a commotion outside.

"Not like that, man," I heard a familiar voice declare through the open window. "You're here to fix the place, not destroy it further."

I went to see what the fuss was about, only to encounter every last member of staff. From Fellowes and Cook to the Irish maids and gardeners, they all stood gawping as my grandfather directed a group of workers who were installing scaffolding on the façade of the building.

It was not the commencement of the renovations that had attracted the crowd, so much as the sight of a seventy-five-year-old man, who hadn't left his bedroom in ten years, jumping about in a frenzy. Not unlike the golden retriever who accompanied him, my grandfather was a whirlwind of sprightly energy as he barked orders at the labourers. It was hard to say if he was a help or a hindrance, but I felt a flush of joy to see him back to his old self. I could still remember a time, before my grandmother had abruptly dropped dead, when he'd not only looked people in the eyes, but even smiled on occasion.

My parents had heard the hullabaloo and come to bear witness for themselves.

"What on Earth is going on?" Father squinted to make sense of the scene.

"That's it, gentlemen. You're doing a fine job!" Grandfather brushed imaginary dust from his hands as if he was the one doing the heavy lifting of metal tubes, brackets and wooden planks.

My mother stood aghast. "Daddy, you mustn't strain yourself."

My brother said nothing, as he hadn't appeared. I am not a clairvoyant but I can say with great certainty that he was either in bed dreaming of Evangeline De Vere, or he was in bed crying into his pillow (over Evangeline De Vere).

"Good morning, children," my grandfather practically sang as he caught sight of us and made his way over. "And what a spectacular morning it is. There is nothing quite so beautiful as an English garden in the springtime."

"Absolutely." My father was swept along on a wave of the old man's positivity.

My mother, not so much. "I think you should be sitting down."

Her father's quick eyes clicked onto her and his tone became more serious. "Well, I'm afraid to say, you're wrong. In fact, I've done enough sitting down to last a lifetime. I might decide never to sit down again." Cold determination flashed through his voice, but he followed his words up with a jubilant burst of laughter.

Like Mr Scrooge at the end of 'A Christmas Carol' he was "so fluttered and so glowing with his good intentions" that he could barely stand still before us.

"I just want to make sure you're all right," my mother added by way of an explanation.

With a cheerful look, he attempted to set his daughter's mind at ease. "You need not worry, my dear child. I haven't felt this alive since... Well, I'm sure you know when."

The energy which coursed through him seemed to ebb and flow and I could understand why my mother was so concerned.

I was lucky to have been born into a remarkable family, and Mother was the best of us. She was an artist, a poet and a champion for under-supported causes – like universal suffrage, hospitals and child welfare. But what I loved about her most was the well of compassion she could draw upon for all those around her. She regarded her father then as if he was one of her own children.

"You mustn't take too much upon yourself."

"You're right, Violet. You're absolutely right." The old man was a decent actor, but I could tell what was coming next. "I thought you were due to head home early this morning. With all this work going on, there isn't much to keep you here."

He was already steering them back inside as he finished speaking and my mother had to shout to me over her shoulder. "Keep an eye on your grandfather, Christopher. Make sure he doesn't do anything we wouldn't approve of."

There was no time to point out that, at my age, I generally liked it when people did things which my parents didn't approve of. They had disappeared from sight and Lord Edgington was once more dusting his hands off as he turned back to me.

"This is just the first stage, Chrissy. I have so many ideas for what comes next." Well-hidden behind his impressive whiskers, his mouth betrayed no signs of happiness, but his eyes were wide. "When I was a child, this estate was the jewel of the county. My family were famous for the balls they hosted and we will be once more."

I had to ask myself what possible role I could have in any of this. Luckily, he read my mind.

"I'll be overseeing the restoration of course. If I close my eyes, I can see exactly how this place was fifty years ago and how it will be again very soon." He came to a halt and I could tell that he was away with his memories until something pulled him back to the present day. "What I need from you is to organise the party itself. You'll have to think about what food we provide and what sort of entertainment there will be."

"Can I choose the music?" My voice went up sharply as I gave away how excited this made me. As the elder child, my brother had always been the one to decide which concerts our family attended, which records we listened to on Father's gramophone and even which band played at my sixteenth birthday party.

"That's right." The ends of his ice-white moustache jerked up a little. "What sort of music do young people listen to these days? In my day it was all Wagner. I used to go crazy for the chap and my parents couldn't stand him, I…" He stopped speaking then. I think my eyes might have glazed over – as is the right of any adolescent when an older relative starts reminiscing about their youth.

"I suppose you'll want some sort of *band*." He pronounced the final word in a long, disdainful manner as if it were a terrible insult. "But I'm warning you now, I won't tolerate too much shimmying and shaking. I like to think I have a modern view of the world, but there's progress and there's outright bedlam…"

He could see that I'd faded out of the conversation again and stopped himself to affirm, "Yes, you can choose the music."

It was my turn to clap my hands together. "Thank you, grandfather. I won't disappoint you."

"Make sure that you don't." Lord Edgington was a pacer and, now that my initial duties were established, he set off in the direction of the Italian gardens to consider what else needed to be done. "We'll have to make up a list of who to invite of course. I doubt many of my old friends are alive these days but perhaps we'll be lucky."

I felt I should be taking notes as he hurried off in front of me. "Will all the family be there?"

I managed to catch up and he reflected for a moment before answering. "Of course they will. Still, I wish your great-aunt Clementine would stay at home. The woman could sleep for England and she's barely got a wit left in her head."

A thought occurred to me then which made me panic. "Grandfather, if it's not too impertinent to ask, when exactly were you thinking that we might-"

"Really, Christopher." He came to a stop in front of the large, oval reflecting pool. "You'll never get anywhere in this world by mumbling." He sounded like my father.

I fought my nerves to get the question out. "When will the ball be taking place?"

"The first weekend in June, of course. When else would we have a spring ball?"

"But that's-"

"Three weeks, yes." He sounded like he relished the challenge. "Plenty of time to get this place looking… what's that word you young people like?"

I had no idea what he was talking about. "Nice?"

"Spiffing; that's the one." I believe there was an actual smile on his face right then.

Personally, I don't think there's anything more embarrassing than when adults attempt to sound like they're still young. I was busy trying not to hyperventilate though and didn't have time to worry about such a minor detail.

"Three weeks?" I managed to exhale.

My eccentric grandfather threw his hands in the air like an over-dramatic continental type. "Exactly. And what an adventure it will be."

I steadied myself by sitting on a bench only for Delilah to immediately launch herself onto my lap. She gazed at me with a look of great sorrow and I knew that she understood exactly how I felt. I might possibly, conceivably (but probably not) have told my grandfather how insane his plan sounded but then his arms dropped to his waist and his good cheer dissipated.

"I don't understand what I was thinking, locking myself away all this time." He stood with his back to me. I didn't have to see his face to know that there was a reserve of sadness running through him.

"After Katy died and then the war took its toll, I just…"

Delilah jumped off me to comfort her master and I decided to do the same. Well, not the rubbing myself against his ankles part, but by finding a way to hearten him.

"Three weeks will be just the right amount of time to get ready for the ball." I'm a terribly unconvincing liar and my voice came out in a crackle. "Cranley Hall will be beautiful and it will be a day that none of us will forget."

He pursed his lips together, and kept his eyes on the enormous stone edifice before us. The eastern façade of the hall looked like Zeus had kicked it from the top of Mount Olympus to land in a pretty garden in the south of England.

He responded with a soothing lie of his own. "That's right, Christopher. It will be child's play. We must simply put our heads down and seize the moment."

It was around then that I realised just how much I'd missed him. I was only six when he'd retreated from the world. I'd already lost my grandmother and I think that his sudden absence had a similar impact upon me.

This was the man who, in his calm, serious manner, had taught me how to play (or rather lose at) chess, find flint to make arrowheads and tell a cuckoo from a sparrowhawk. He'd been gone for so long that just the glimpse of his re-emergence was thrilling and unnerving in equal measure.

"Thank you for choosing me," I said, not quite sure where the words had come from.

"You're welcome. You know, having my own assistant reminds me of my days in Scotland Yard, I-" There was a clang then, as a pole rolled off a wooden platform. My grandfather flinched. "What in heaven's name…?" He walked towards the house, where the workmen were assessing the fallout. Halfway across the garden, he called back to me. "We'll have to continue this later, I'm afraid. But remember, this is just the first part of my plan. I haven't even told you about the hot-air balloon yet."

It made me happy to see his enthusiasm return but then his words sank in and I called after him. "What balloon, Grandfather? What are you talking about?"

"Motorbikes and racing cars too, of course, but before long we'll be up above the clouds. You wait and see!"

I ground to a halt, unable to comprehend such dangers. Luckily, Delilah sensed my pain once more and proceeded to whimper affectionately. It was almost enough to soothe away the shock.

CHAPTER FOUR

Everything happened remarkably swiftly after that.

By the end of the day, my grandfather had hired all the contractors we would need to get Cranley spruced up in time for the ball. He had even extracted a commitment from the builders that we would see neither hide nor hair of them on the first of June.

I spent my time considering the ingredients for a successful party. My parents were forever swanning off to balls, dos and soirees, but I hadn't been to many myself. The one thing I came up with for certain was dessert; so I made an alphabetical list of the different types of cake we would need. It started like this:

Apple turnovers.

Battenberg, Belgian buns, Black Forest gateau.

Carrot cake, Chocolate eclairs, chocolate profiteroles, chocolate pudding…

In fact, the entry for C went on for a page in itself.

I was never allowed to use the candlestick telephone in my own home so it was great fun to take charge of both the mouthpiece and receiver in the petit salon and connect with the operator. I needed contacts for caterers, florists and entertainers in the local area. Sadly, they didn't have a number for any musicians and, as liberating as it was to be able to choose the band for the ball myself, the only one I knew was "Gilbert Gordon and his Cabaret Cohorts". My brother had picked them for my last birthday and it looked as though they would have to be hired again.

"Yeah, I know a bloke who knows a bloke," Fellowes informed me when I asked for advice. This is one of his standard answers. Another is, "I can get you a good price if ya like," which I'm fairly sure means he'll be receiving a cut himself. He's a little like my father, but, instead of being a stockbroker who knows all the right people in the City, he has a network of dubious contacts in every field.

He left me with a sausage and mango roulade (much better than it sounds) and I left him with the task at hand. I hadn't been able to get any more information from my grandfather about what the second stage of his plan might involve, nor how balloons and motorbikes came into it, but he had told me to spare no expense in organising the ball.

"You're the expert of course," I told the florist in our local village of St Mary-Under-Twine, "but I suspect we'll need two, no, let's say three thousand delphinium."

I heard the old lady crash down in her seat and the telephone made a buzzing pop. "That's an awful lot of delphinium. About a field's worth, I'd say. Are you certain about this?"

I had a quick think to confirm it. "Well, it's an awfully large space we'll be decorating. One field of flowers for one big room; that's the ticket. Throw in half a field of peony and a copse of lilac and I think we're onto a winner."

She swallowed hard. "And you're sure you're Master Cristopher, from the hall?"

"Yes, that's right; Lord Edgington's grandson. I bought some roses off you for Mothering Sunday. Perhaps you remember?"

She made a sort of warbling sound in confirmation and we concluded our deal. Party organisation is clearly one of my hidden gifts. Perhaps it would be the trade for me, once school and university were out of the way. Father said he wanted me to go into banking, but I've never been too hot on numbers or mathematics, or any kind of counting, really.

I was just contemplating this conundrum when I heard voices in the corridor. I instinctively ducked beneath the table, as no one had expressly told me that I was allowed to use the telephone.

"You can moan all you like, Maitland, but I'm the one who'll suffer." I recognised my aunt's voice as she berated her brother. "I'm the eldest and it will be my son who ends up destitute if Father starts giving George's inheritance away willy-nilly."

Uncle Maitland wasn't the type to point out that his sister's house was no cottage and that she'd already inherited her late husband's impressive wealth. "Yes, Belinda, and that's why I said we should do something about it. This ridiculous ball mustn't go ahead. I for one won't stand by while the old fool bankrupts us."

I inched forward under the table to spy on them.

A devious look crossed my aunt's face. "What do you suggest we do about it?"

It was hard to comprehend how my sweet, gentle mother could

be related to either of her siblings. Uncle Maitland had a nervous, ratty way about him, like so many self-serving minor villains from Dickens novels. And, though my parents said that Aunt Belinda could be charming when she wanted to, with her pallid skin and witch-like posture, it was difficult to imagine.

Maitland lowered his voice. "We should do whatever it takes to bring him to his senses."

"And if he won't listen?" Belinda was quick to ask.

As if some gossamer demon had crossed the space between my uncle and the window, darkness momentarily consumed Maitland's countenance. "If he won't listen to reason, we'll have to-"

I can only imagine what rotten plans they would have hatched together if a rasping breath hadn't broken into their conversation. It wasn't me, I'm glad to say, but Great-Aunt Clementine who was asleep in an armchair beside the door.

Recovering her nerves, Belinda let out an ill-tempered moan. "What on Earth is she still doing here?"

Maitland wore a baffled look. "I thought Todd had driven her home?"

Except for taking me to school and back each week, Grandfather's chauffeur had very little work to do and was always willing to drop off stray guests.

"I thought you'd taken her?" Like a comedy duo from a music hall sketch, the two stared at one another in mute wonder, waiting to see who would give in first.

It was down to Clementine to break the uneasy stalemate with a gentle snore.

Maitland peered at the old woman with a question mark on his face. "Surely she hasn't been in here since yesterday."

Belinda took a few steps closer to her elderly aunt and looked at her up close as though checking she was still breathing. "Auntie? Auntie, it's me, Belinda. Are you-"

Clementine suddenly surged forward. "Oh, dear. I must have nodded off." She looked at her niece and nephew and then at the room where she found herself. "Cranley? How nice. Is the party still going or has everyone gone home?"

Clementine is my Grandfather's sister-in-law. His older brother was the original heir to Cranley but died in the First Boer War. People say that it left her with a few screws loose but, as far as I was concerned, at eighty years of age, she had every right to be a little batty. She had a unique smell to her, like lavender, boiled cabbage and Christmas trees, and I think I was one of the few people in my family who genuinely liked her.

The frail old thing tottered up to standing and then fell back down for Maitland to catch.

"Why don't we get you home, eh, dear?"

Her feeble eyes shone more brightly. "Oh, you are good to your old auntie."

All the spite and cunning had disappeared from their faces and they gazed at her in apparent affection.

"Come along now." Belinda took her by the arm. "Let's find Todd, shall we? Or perhaps you'd like Cook to knock you up something first?"

Clementine's face took on a decidedly green hue. "No, thank you. I think I'd rather just go home."

The three of them toddled off and I was left to consider what my aunt and uncle had been planning.

CHAPTER FIVE

During term time, I spent my weekdays at school in Oakton and popped down to grandfather's house every Friday afternoon. Mother and Father thought it would be a good idea for someone to look after me so that I didn't get into trouble with the other boys. Of course, until that weekend, Grandfather never left his rooms and his staff got up to far more mischief than I ever could at school.

It wasn't just Fellowes the butler who had the run of the place. Cook's cooking grew wilder by the week. She enjoyed experimenting with new combinations of completely incongruous ingredients – which only Lord Edgington himself could endure. The pack of Irish maids, household staff and gardeners made sure that every night was a celebration and Todd, our chauffeur, was the only one who seemed to have his head about him. As his head was normally buried in an adventure novel, he didn't have time to play nanny.

They all made a fuss of me and fed me treats, but I can't say there was much supervision going on. The night after Grandfather's birthday was a case in point.

"Why don't you cough it up?" Our atypically skinny cook demanded as the staff sat in the kitchen, playing cards.

"It's not my place to tell ya." Despite his own humble background, Fellowes liked to believe he was more cultured than his colleagues. He loved nothing more than to lord some juicy titbit of information over them.

"What about you, Christopher?" The youngest maid, Alice, enquired. I was a little bit in love with Alice. She had a kind Irish lilt and pretty blue eyes. "Do you know why Lord Edgington decided to throw this ball?"

The atmosphere changed as I slurped at my boiled ham and anchovy soup. It was almost appetising, despite the cinnamon.

"I don't completely understand it," I replied once the scalding concoction had made its way down my throat. "All Grandfather said was that he wants to shake the place up and have a celebration. Mother and Father wouldn't tell me what he said to them after dinner last night. Though I'm sure they think he's lost his mind."

There was some laughter at this and one of the gardeners said, "Aye. That may be."

Cook threw her cards across the table in disgust. I had no idea of the rules of the game, but she always claimed they were rigged against her.

"I heard Lady Belinda in the kitchen garden with him this afternoon and she said a lot worse than that." It was her moment in the spotlight and we listened attentively. "She was awfully angry and accused him of trying to palm off her George's inheritance to young Christopher."

Fellowes let out a despondent sigh. "I hope Lord Edgington lives to be a hundred. I can't stand the thought of that harridan taking over Cranley Hall."

I almost considered telling them what I'd overheard from under the telephone table, but Cook spoke again before I could decide whether it was a good idea.

"Her father will outlive her and that's something you can bet on. Shrivelled old Belinda will have drunk herself to death long before-"

She never finished the sentence as, just then a looming figure appeared in the doorway and everyone held their breath.

"Don't let me interrupt you." My grandfather took a hesitant step into the kitchen, like a schoolboy entering the teacher's corridor. I'd never seen him look so uncertain before. "I thought I'd come down and say hello."

Todd the chauffeur bolted to his feet and a couple of the gardeners did the same. There was an awkward hush as Fellowes looked about at his colleagues in the hope that one of them might know what to say next. When none of the adults could make a decision, I decided to offer my grandfather a chair.

"Well... yes, Christopher. Why not?" He asked the question as if hoping that someone would provide a good reason. "I'm happy to see that you're being fed... Growing boy and all that."

I was taken aback by the change in him. This wasn't the same Lord Edgington who had brought the Ealing Strangler to the gallows or cracked the Bow Boys crime ring. As he sat down at the table, he was acting like a stranger in his own house.

"Please, everyone, sit down," he said and the men slowly retook their places at the long, wooden worktable. They looked as sombre as mourners at a funeral.

"Are you hungry, Lord Edgington?" Cook enquired. "Would you like some broth?"

Regaining something of his composure, Grandfather sat up straighter and shook his head. "It looks delicious, Cook, but I should really refrain. Though I'm sure Fellowes will have told you how I much I enjoy your soups." My grandfather was the only living person who could make such a claim.

He cleared his throat before continuing. "It occurred to me this evening how strange it is that there are rooms in my house that I've never visited and people who live here I've never spoken to." As he said this, he cast his gaze towards the two, normally rowdy gardeners, who looked down at their hands in reply. I was coming to think that my parents were right and old Grampapa had finally lost it.

"Would you like a drink, Milord?" Fellowes was up on his feet and had assumed his butlering pose; heels together, feet turned out, chin raised high. "We have a nicely aged whisky. I know how you like your single malts."

"That won't be necessary. Sit down, man." The vein of annoyance reappeared in his voice but died away again just as quickly. "And please, everyone, go back to your game. I didn't mean to interrupt."

On catching her master's raised voice, Delilah poked her sleepy head out of her basket before bumbling over.

"So what did you come here for, Grandfather?" I asked. He looked straight at me and I wished I could take my question back and hide in the pantry.

"I came to talk to everyone. You see, I may be the occupier of Cranley Hall, but you…" He peered around the nervous visages of his employees. "All of you, are its heart; its lifeblood. A house is nothing without humanity and that is what you provide the place with."

There was some appreciative murmuring, but the staff kept their eyes low, as if Lord Edgington was a star that was too bright to look at directly.

When the voices faded out, he continued. "I can see that my plans are going to make life more complicated over the next month, but I know you all have it in you to cope with the changes." He paused and his moustache wiggled a little like he'd heard something funny. He pointed over to his chauffeur and serving staff. "Todd, Fellowes and

Halfpenny, I'm expecting you to lead the younger members of staff in their duties and address any problems they might have."

The three men looked proud to be singled out by name, and my grandfather moved on.

"Cook, you needn't worry. We'll be bringing in a fleet of assistants to prepare the food for the party and Christopher here is in charge of the menu, so it shouldn't be any more work for you than normal."

He scanned the faces of the young maids. "To the rest of you, I'm afraid you're going to have your work cut out. We'll be using rooms in the house which haven't been opened in years. Not just the ballroom and salons, we'll have a number of guests staying the night and so the unused bedrooms in the east wing will also be required."

It was the gardeners' turn next and they finally looked up at him. "The gardens will need to be at their very best too. I know that change can be frightening, so try to stay focussed on the end result. Cranley will look more beautiful than she has in a century and I believe in each and every last one of you."

His rousing words finally seemed to have had an impact and Alice smiled across at me enthusiastically as Grandfather finished his speech.

"You probably think I'm quite mad. But I promise that's not the case. I merely want to fulfil a few lifelong dreams, while there's still time."

"Very good, Milord," Fellowes offered in reply, and his words seemed to rally his colleagues. There was a buzz of chatter as Grandfather stood back up and, like celebrants before communion, we all rose.

"I'm sure the ball will be wonderful, your lordship," Cook added and performed a little curtsy where she stood.

"That's right." The old man smiled, finally looking comfortable in his own kitchen. "Wonderful is just the word for it."

CHAPTER SIX

After Todd dropped me off at school that week, the days dragged by. I can't say I've ever been particularly scholarly (if that's the right word for it) but after my weekend of surprises, each sixty-minute period at Oakton Academy took forever. I felt just as my grandfather must have for the last ten years; held in stasis, waiting for life to kick back in.

In general, boys my age fall into two camps, the bullies and the bullied. With my love of birds, cakes and Charles Dickens, I doubt I need to tell you which one I belonged to. The only good thing about my academic career at Oakton was that I was so entirely average at science, maths, rugby, cricket, hockey and lake swimming that I never stood out among the more successful boys. But with Cranley's spring ball firmly planted on that year's social calendar, I was suddenly the talk of the school.

Who knows how these things get out to the wider world (my best guess would be that Fellowes had sold the information to some gossip hound) but there was even an article about it in the social column of The Daily Telegraph. Such provincial events rarely made it into the national papers, so you can imagine what a story it was that Lord Edgington, the wealthiest landowner in the whole of Surrey and one-time scourge of London's criminal underworld, was dipping his toe into high-society functions.

Far more interesting than that, though, was an article alongside it all about his career. I have to admit that I considered my grandfather something of a hero. Rather than staying in Cranley his whole life to live off the fat of the land, he decided that he wanted to make something of himself and so joined the police. Not only did he become one of the most celebrated officers in Britain, he shunned his family contacts and went in at the lowest rung of the ladder. Starting off as a constable, he worked his way up through the force on his own merit. I imagine that everyone at the time thought he was a raving loon.

Perhaps it was this, even more than the ball, which caught my curious peers' attention. Suddenly everyone looked at me differently, but there were still two distinct trends to their behaviour. Three quarters of my schoolmates attempted to charm me in the hope of gaining an invitation for their families and the rest… well, let's say that they were a little more hostile.

"Reckon you're something special, don't you, Prentiss!" Marmaduke Adelaide (known in the faintest of whispers behind his back as Marmalade) was a six-foot-three ape with luminous ginger hair and fists the size of megaliths. I'd lived in fear of him since we were five years old but he'd never paid me much mind, until now.

"Not at all," I told him, as he grabbed me by the cravat to lift me off the surface of our small, muddy recreational yard. "I actually think I'm remarkably normal."

"Well I think you've got a remarkable cheek answering back to me." Marmalade was as well-spoken as any lord, and his family had more money than King George, but there were unflattering rumours about where the Adelaides' wealth had come from.

"Um," I replied, wishing I'd learn to keep my mouth closed. "I don't honestly know how to reply as you might think I'm answering back again."

The fingers in his right hand flexed, then curled together. He pulled his arm back, and I closed my eyes to prepare for impact.

"Master Adelaide," a voice interrupted. "Would you please return your friend to where he was previously standing and be on your way? Master Prentiss has two perfectly good brown eyes, I doubt his mother would wish you to turn them black."

Finding myself on terra firma once more, I stared out through tiny slits. Standing up close to Marmalade was our ox-shaped headmaster.

The bully's grip relaxed and he offered a smarmy explanation. "I'm sorry, Mr Hardcastle. I was just giving little Chrissy here an astronomy lesson."

The top man of The Oakton Classical and Commercial Academy for Distinguished Young Gentlemen had more to say on the matter. "That's one thing you've never quite grasped in the years you've been here, Adelaide. You see, it is we teachers who are in charge of doling out the lessons and you boys who must learn them."

If there was one person Marmalade was scared of, it was our headmaster. "Of course, Mr Hardcastle. I don't know what I was thinking."

The trusty educator watched Marmalade rejoin his gang of equally thuggish friends then walked away smiling.

I let out the breath I'd been holding for the last minute, just as Marmalade reappeared to deliver a swift, sharp dig to my ribs. I made a noise like a bellows with a hole in, as he delivered the complementary warning.

"You got away with it for now, but next time even Hardcastle won't be able to save you." I was doubled over with my hand to my stomach, so he grabbed my hair and yanked me up to look at him. "Don't forget it."

He released me to stagger away, then disappeared off to class.

For some reason, I couldn't help feeling sorry for Marmalade. On the one hand he was a thug and a menace, but I was certain he would have had an easier run of things if he hadn't had to spend his life in his dishonest father's shadow. No matter what he went on to achieve, talk of his family's criminal connections would never leave him.

Perhaps inevitably after our one-sided brawl, I had my mind on other things. What I wanted, more than anything, was to be back by the hearth in Cranley's cosy kitchen, with lovely Alice and Cook being nice to me. I wanted to see how the work was progressing and discover whether Grandfather had made any wild new resolutions.

Instead, I had a week at school to get through. A week spent learning algebra equations, quotations from Chaucer and Latin ablative constructions, which I would never need again once the class was over. A week being taught by large men with proportionally massive sideburns whose love of teaching came from the corporal punishment they could inflict upon the younger boys.

If my tone isn't clear enough, I think it's fair to say that I've never been a fan of my school's educational methods. Though my father always insisted that Oakton Academy was where he learnt to be a man, I've yet to discover what he would have otherwise turned into.

My three best friends were all called William. They were shy, bookish types who looked and talked just like me, but weren't the sort you call for help when someone wants to knock your block off. As we sneaked about the school each day, with our eyes peeled for Marmaduke Adelaide's attack force, William, Will and Billy were good company. It was a little like having my own personal guard, except, instead of a trained squad of career soldiers, I had three podgy boys who liked nothing more than a spot of afternoon tea.

I managed to escape any more physical punishment that week, both from my sadistic teachers and my sadistic peers. When Friday finally arrived, and I found Todd waiting for me at the school gates to drive me to Cranley, I forgot all about Oakton with its red bricks and screeching blackboards and dived back into my grandfather's world.

He was even more animated than the last time I'd seen him, and things were changing faster than I could have imagined. Work on the front façade of the hall was nearly completed, the ballroom had been refreshed and modern equipment had been installed in the kitchen – including Captain William Howard Livens' hand-powered dishwasher, which I had to try myself as I simply couldn't believe that such a convenient device could exist.

I didn't see as much of Lord Edgington that weekend. He had purchased a new gramophone and a library's worth of records and spent most of his time catching up on modern music. He did pop down to the kitchen on Friday night to compliment Cook on her canard aux asperges creation though and ended up staying for a hand of cards.

My grandfather had never been a man to stand on ceremony, but even for him this was unusual behaviour. During his career, he had become acquainted with every type of character from Britain's great human tapestry, so it wasn't exactly a surprise that he would treat his staff with the respect they deserved. And yet, since his reawakening, I felt that he was making a concerted effort to show me that the barriers I had viewed my whole life as both rigid and ingrained were nothing of the sort.

The subsequent weeks went by in much the same way and being at school felt like a punishment for some dark crime. I avoided Marmalade, got my friends to teach me rummy, as that seemed to be the game that was played most often below stairs, and read Martin Chuzzlewit for the third time, even though it's far from Dickens's best.

I also did my part for the preparations for the spring ball. Fellowes provided a contact for a dance band that he assured me were top notch. There was no time to audition them sadly but, as rude as he often was, I trusted Grandfather's old faithful to come through. I even created a menu that went beyond cakes, though I did have to overrule some of

Cook's more exotic suggestions out of fear for my family's reputation.

Those weekends passed in seconds while the weeks took years, but then the spring ball was finally upon us. School would be closed for a whole three days for the Whitsun holiday weekend and there was an air of expectancy, even within the gloomy corridors of Oakton Academy. Students who came from further afield would stay behind with Mr Hardcastle and the other teachers but I was finally free!

When Todd came to collect me, my friends peered down from the upper floor of the building like convicts on a ship to the new world. For their sake, I attempted to hide how happy I was as I waved goodbye. For a moment I had an inkling of what my father meant about Oakton making a man of me. It was not the school itself, but the years I had spent there and now, already sixteen and getting taller by the day, I was helping to throw a society ball in one of the grandest houses in England.

This is exactly what I was thinking of as Marmaduke Adelaide came flying towards me. My joie de vivre had set me off guard and he appeared out of nowhere. His immense fist caught me right in the eye and I crumpled to the ground like a house made of straw.

"Whoop!" he yelled in celebration as he lined up his knuckles for a second blow. Like a rabbit who knows its only defence is to play dead, I lay on the ground, as stiff as a mummy.

Luckily, Todd was quick to action and sped from the driver's seat to confront the marauding Marmalade. The chauffeur grabbed the bully by his lapels, and I don't like to think what would have happened if the headmaster hadn't arrived.

"Is that what you teach your students?" Todd spat the words at the teacher who blustered and faffed in reply.

Mr Hardcastle had seized my attacker to cart him back inside and attempted to recover from the insult by shouting a belated retort over his shoulder. "You're a darned chauffeur. You've no right to talk that way to me!"

"Enjoy the ball, Cinderella," Marmalade added for good measure.

Todd crouched down to talk to me. "Are you all right, Master Christopher?"

I opened my one good eye to check that we were alone. "I could be worse but... Well, I suppose I could be better too."

He held out his hand and pulled me up to standing. "You shouldn't let toffs like him push you around."

I didn't know how to reply to that, so I pretended I hadn't heard and got inside Grandfather's Silver Ghost. It was not the most fashionable vehicle in the Cranley collection, or even the most recently acquired, but it made me feel like a king every time I sat in the back seat for Todd to drive us off the school grounds.

"Oh no you don't," he complained. "Sit in the front with me. We need to talk."

In his green livery and cap, Grandfather's driver had a steady, competent manner about him and it was hard to refuse. He was the youngest male member of staff too and the best spoken by far. He could have easily fitted in with my brother's friends in fact, had Albert not viewed all servants as a different class of human being.

I climbed into the passenger seat and he started the engine.

"You need to stand up to people like that chap." He kept his eyes on the road but prodded at me with the words.

"That's easier said than done. I don't think I'm really cut out for… fisticuffs." I had managed to land on the most juvenile word available.

"Then I'll give you a few pointers." He smiled and we drove through the Oakton Academy gates. "I did a bit of boxing when I was your age and I can't tell you the confidence it gave me."

I made an appreciative sound but inside I was wondering what could be worse than the sight of chubby little me in shorts and boxing gloves, coming up against Todd the stocky stallion.

He laughed briefly and we spent the rest of the journey in silence. Well, not total silence. My eye was throbbing in time with the second hand on my wristwatch and I let out the odd whimper. I'd never experienced such acute and absolute agony before and couldn't wait to run to the ice house at Cranley to fetch a cold piece of meat to relieve the pain.

CHAPTER SEVEN

"It is not a question of to whom the money belongs, Father. It's a matter of principle." Dressed as ever in his hunting jacket and cap, Uncle Maitland had returned with his sister to make one final attempt to derail the celebrations.

"This is your absolute last chance," Belinda announced, as Todd brought the car to a halt at the front of the property. "Call off the ball or we'll contact every last guest ourselves."

Surveying the completed work as labourers packed their horse and cart with the last remnants of the scaffolding, Grandfather was not intimidated by the threats.

"How many times do we have to go over the same ridiculous arguments?" Severely unimpressed, he turned his concrete gaze on his two eldest children. "No one is trying to do you out of your inheritance, nor have my actions besmirched the family's good name. I just want to entertain our friends and let my hair down."

Aunt Belinda, who had lived her life with her hair particularly high on her head, looked horrified by the very idea. "Let your hair down?" She made a low, guttural noise in her throat to express her distaste. "A man your age shouldn't even know such a term, let alone put it into practice."

I got out of the car and tried to head inside without being noticed.

"That's not the issue." Maitland immediately extended his index finger in my direction. "I need you to tell me what you intend to do with that boy and why he has won favour here at Cranley!"

My grandfather looked exhausted, and I disappeared inside before they could blame me for all their worldly woes. The last thing I heard was Belinda demanding that her caddish son George came to live with Grandfather as tribute. I'd always known she was old-fashioned but it turned out that some of her ideas were positively mediaeval.

Away from their squabbling, I was free to take in the transformation that had occurred in three short weeks. Cranley Hall had been cleaned, buffed and polished from top to bottom. The smell of dust and ageing furniture, which I expected to encounter on entering the building, had been replaced by the scent of beeswax and lavender. The normally unwelcoming entrance hall, with its stuffed animals and framed horrors, suddenly seemed brighter. Its portraits of bloody biblical scenes now took on a heroic quality which I'd never appreciated before.

Though the builders had left the property as promised, they'd been replaced by a host of new faces. The ball was only a day away and my team of party-planning assistants were already hard at work. Pretty young ladies in smart, white outfits, who looked like the secretaries at father's work, were rushing down corridors with chairs and decorations to distribute. Strapping gentlemen in smart overalls were shifting furniture in the grand salon and I decided against entering the ballroom just then. I wanted to wait until the day itself to witness the improvements that had been made there.

For the first time I could remember, Cranley Hall had come to life. It felt like a patient who had been saved from their fate at the very last moment and would go on to enjoy a full and happy existence. The buzz and bustle of the place, which would only be amplified the following night, had an incredible positivity to it. I seriously doubted that the house had been so busy in decades.

Rather uncannily, everyone seemed to know who I was and smiled at me as I explored this unfamiliar environment that I had known since I was a child. The young ladies soon set upon me with questions of floral arrangements and refreshments.

"Oh... well I think that whatever you decide will be just perfect," was my standard response. Normally, when I plumped for such vague answers with my family or teachers I got told off for dithering, but these sunny individuals nodded and got to work. It was most refreshing.

Fellowes was at the heart of everything, and looked relieved that I had arrived to take on some of his burden.

"Chrissy!" he shouted, once I had completed the initial part of my duties. "I think there's something you'd better see."

The curt retainer offered up a grin and led me to the billiards room, which was being used as the centre of operations for our mission. Well, that was the plan, but you could no longer enter the room as it was filled with flowers.

"One field of delphinium, half a field of peony and a copse of lilac," he dryly repeated. "The florist was very apologetic about the whole thing. She felt sure there'd been a mistake, but I hear you insisted."

I sneezed in reply. All that pollen was going straight up my nose. "I… Oh, dear." No great explanation sprung to mind. "Now that I see them all together like this, it does look rather a lot, doesn't it? Do we have enough vases?"

"Did you order any vases?" I could see he was enjoying this.

"No, I…"

"And did Lord Edgington not give you a budget for the party? Or did you think that a small fortune for flowers seemed like a reasonable price?"

I had a moment of sheer panic at the thought of my grandfather's temper being directed upon me. Eventually, Fellowes took pity and helped calm my nerves.

"Don't worry about it, lad." A smile curled across the butler's face. "I told the old man already and he didn't seem too worried. I believe the words that he used were, 'They will add some colour to the place.'"

I took in the endless harvest which had been stuffed into the room before us. The white delphiniums were as bright as any star and their luminescence reflected back off the walls. They'd transformed the usually drab billiard room into a spring meadow. I realised that there were no peonies just as Fellowes pointed to the smoking room.

"This is just the beginning, there are more across the hall."

It was fairly clear now that I should have taken the florist's advice.

Despite this minor setback, all other preparations were progressing well. Our regular staff were in on the act and the work didn't let up for a moment. Todd would be doubling as a footman for the next couple of days, when not ferrying guests about. Fellowes had more opportunities than ever to bark orders at everyone and the maids were hard at work getting the house ready for an influx of tipsy overnighters. Alice spotted me soon after I arrived and fussed herself over my black eye.

"What were ya thinking, getting into a fight, Master Christopher?" she asked in her perfectly melodious Tipperary accent.

Luckily, she didn't give me time to reply but ran off to fetch a chunk of ice to get the swelling down. It stung a little as she pressed it against the bruise but this gave me the perfect opportunity to gaze upon her ice-white skin and nigella-blue eyes. Marmaduke Adelaide, dull, dusty classrooms and even warring relatives seemed very far away just then. For a moment, I could imagine that we lived in a world where the grandson of a lord was free to confess his adoration to an émigré housemaid.

I imagine I'd been gawping, as Alice looked rather out of sorts. I pulled back from her and pretended that I hadn't been imagining us walking hand in hand on a sunlit beach.

"I… Well, I should probably find out whether the operator has a telephone number for vase rental." I took the ice from her soft, soft hand and held it to my eye. "Do you know if that's a service which exists?"

"And sure how would I know?" she replied, in rather short fashion and went off to attend to her duties.

Through an incredible stroke of luck, a call to Selfridges put me in touch with the right people. At ten o'clock that night, a lorry turned up from London full to the brim with porcelain vases. Sadly, all the temporary staff had finished work for the day which meant that, as it was essentially all my fault, I had to stay up until four in the morning putting the flowers in water to make sure they didn't wilt and die.

By twelve o'clock I was barely able to keep my eyes open, but then an unexpected assistant arrived.

"Two fields of flowers, eh?" My grandfather stood in the doorway to the billiard room enjoying my misfortune.

"Not quite two." I yawned and snipped open my hundredth bundle of lilac. "Less than one and three quarters in fact."

"Come along, Chrissy." He surprised me by pulling a chair over to the bridge table where I'd been working. "I'll give you a hand."

He moved with a swiftness and determination which belied his advanced years. In one flowing movement he scooped up a bundle of flowers from the floor, deposited them between us, then pulled a crate of vases up next to him.

"Do you know anything about flower arrangement, Grandfather?"

"I know that you shouldn't handle delphiniums with your bare hands. They can be quite toxic in fact. We'll have to ring for some gloves. Except for that… no, not very much." He surveyed the ranks of vases I had already filled. "Though, clearly, neither do you."

I smiled and we worked out who would do what in our newly

formed production line. I enjoyed the precision with which he did everything. Even this mundane task was invested with great care and concentration. Perhaps it was my fatigue, but I felt oddly close to him then and, before I knew it, the words had fallen from my mouth.

"Grandfather, why exactly do you talk to your staff the way you do?"

He kept his eyes on the peony stems which he was dealing with. "How do you mean?"

I realised the weight of the question I'd just asked him, but there was no going back now. "Even Mother keeps her distance from our staff at home, and she's quite modern compared to most people. But you…" It was hard to express my thoughts without sounding terribly judgemental. "Well, you're rather unique, aren't you?"

He allowed himself the briefest of glances in my direction before responding. "Yes, I suppose you're right." I thought that this was all he would provide in way of an answer but then he finished one of the arrangements and sat back in his chair. "It's not just the staff here at Cranley, I try to treat everyone as equals, no matter their standing or station in life."

Now that the gate was open, I found that the questions came flooding out of me. "Yes, but, have you always been like that? And why do you let Fellowes act the way he does? And why go to the kitchen when-"

He interrupted before I could get anything more out. "No. I haven't always been so enlightened on the matter but, after I saw the sacrifice of so many ordinary citizens during the war, I realised that class is not the great divider that so many believe."

He paused again and looked at me as if trying to decide whether I was old enough to understand such concepts. "You know, during the time I sat in my tower, like Rapunzel waiting to be saved, the world changed so much. I followed what happened in newspapers and novels to try to understand how humans could bring such misery upon ourselves."

I could see that this question was still running through his mind as he spoke. "Perhaps I'm too much of an optimist, but I'd like to believe that the tragedy that we've lived through could give us a greater appreciation of just how precious a resource our fellow humans are. It doesn't matter where a person comes from or what they're trained to do, we are all born equal and we all have the potential to do good."

I'm not the best at pretending to understand what people are talking about. I imagine I had my usual distant look in my eyes as I nudged him back to my original questions. "And Fellowes? Mother says he acts like he's the master of Cranley and that you don't notice."

My lordly grandfather laughed at this. It was a big, booming sound that shook the table we were sitting at. He reminded me of a Father Christmas I'd once seen at a children's party. In fact, with his white whiskers and impressive height he'd fit right in at the North Pole (though he should probably gain a few stone first).

"I notice. Of course I notice. Fellowes is as much a pain to me as anyone. You don't think I've suffered having no one but him for company for the last ten years?"

The deeper we got into the conversation, the less I understood for certain. Instead of hanging on his every word, I went back to filling the vases as though I was really very blasé about the whole discussion. "Then why not fire him?"

The answer that I'd been pondering for so long came straight back to me. "Because I trust him." The old man was watching me as I made a terrible job of splashing the overfilled bucket of water about the carpet. I pretended I hadn't noticed and let him keep talking. "The last thing I need is a yes man, and Fellowes is far from it. We've known one another for a long time and, without him, I'd probably still be up in my room lamenting my misfortune."

"So how did you meet?" All that practised nonchalance was gone from my voice. I'd only just got the question out when he changed the subject.

"Do you know what I'd like to talk about?" He came to a halt and I was worried for a moment that it might not be a rhetorical question. "I'd like to know about the black eye you've acquired. Did you get any punches in yourself?"

I attempted a laugh. "Of course, I did. I was a positive mauler, just like Jack Dempsey. They had to put the fragments of my opponent in an envelope to send them home to his mother."

Grandfather's moustaches pulled wide in a smile and we continued with our work. I was coming to realise that, no matter how many mysteries I might unpick in my family, there would always be more to discover.

CHAPTER EIGHT

It was almost too good to believe when the evening of the ball finally arrived and our guests appeared. My aunt and uncle's attempt at sabotage had not materialised, we'd got everything ready in time and I even looked rather dashing in my top hat and tails, or at least, that's what Alice told me in a whisper as she served canapés.

"You look fat," was my paternal grandmother's contrasting perspective.

"Oh, do leave him alone, mother." For once, my father came to my defence. "He's not fat, he's got Daddy's big bones."

My grandmother was a rake of a woman with a grip like a metal clamp and a voice as loud as a radio transmitter. She was not one for changing her mind.

"Your father was fat! His bones were big, but so was all of the flesh on top of them." She addressed me directly then. "Boy, what have they been feeding you? A strict diet of lard and butter no doubt."

"Don't listen to your grandmother, Christopher," Father intervened once more. "She tells Albert that he's too skinny. Nothing is ever good enough for Mummy."

The old lady looked scandalised. "What is the world coming to when my own son would say such a thing? A young boy should always listen to his elders."

"I should check on the other guests," I said, before the two of them could get into one of their favourite arguments. I didn't specifically know which guests I should be looking after but I'd been trapped in the grand salon by a gang of my elderly relatives for half an hour already and was beginning to feel a little aged myself.

Peeking into the petit salon, there was nothing much going on there except for my prehistoric great-aunt Clementine snoring away behind the door with her feet up on an ottoman. I was a little disappointed that so few people had taken advantage of my culinary selection, so I helped myself to a slice of fruit cake and headed back to the party.

It was a whole different situation in the ballroom where things were starting to swing. With its long mirrors, which caught the beams from the crystal chandeliers above the dancers' heads, and all those pretty beaded dresses on the young ladies, the whole place was ablaze with light. While it was true that the vases of flowers which circled the room caused a bit of a crush in the middle of the floor, everyone appeared to be having a wonderful time.

The band had started playing and they were a little racier than I had expected. Most of their musical choices appeared to be of American influence, not that my brother and his friends seemed to mind. They shimmied about the place with arms and legs whipping through the air. Albert had clearly got over his broken heart and only had eyes for the young lovely he was dancing with. He presumably hadn't realised that she was our cousin, Margaret Hillington-Smythe, whose family had recently returned from South Africa.

A few senior guests were standing at the side of the room looking appalled by the display of such frivolity. As far as I was concerned, they could think what they liked. I was on top of the world and no stuffy, old dinosaurs could change that.

Marmaduke Adelaide, however, very much could.

"Hello there, Chrissy!" Oakton Academy's fiercest bully always spoke at a level that ensured everyone could hear him, no matter how large the room. "How's the eye?"

"My mother had to put makeup on it, thanks to you." Why did I tell him this? "If you think you can come crashing in here uninvited, well… you can think again."

He grew even smugger. "Really, Christopher. What do you take me for? I have an invitation just like everyone else."

I seriously considered losing my temper then, but couldn't forget the stomach-churning click I'd heard when his fist had made contact with my eye.

"Oh, yes? And who invited you?"

Marmalade's huge, ginger head displayed a Cheshire Cat's smile right then and I wished I'd had the courage to wipe it off his face.

"He did!" He pointed to the entrance just as a handsome gent in a white suit and silk scarf wandered through with a pack of outrageously dressed girls in tow.

George Trevelyan was Aunt Belinda's only son and an out-and-out bounder. At only twenty-four he'd been engaged three times and run up bills in every club in London which, if the rumours were to be believed, his mother had finally refused to cover. After finishing a degree in moral sciences at Cambridge, he'd shown no great flair for science or morality and spent the years since then as a most notorious gadabout. He was the rogue of our family and I thought he was wonderful.

He held his arms out towards me as he approached. "Chrissy, how marvellous to see you. I play golf with Marmaduke's father and heard he was just desperate to come, so I brought him along. Be a good boy and get our guest a Hanky-Panky, won't you?"

I was clearly confused by the request as he quickly followed it up with, "Don't look so scandalised, Chrissy. It's just a cocktail."

George spoke incredibly fast and had a habit of bowling everyone over with the intensity of whatever he was saying so that we'd end up doing his bidding without fully understanding why. Despite the fact there were paid employees to perform this very task, I zipped to the bar in the corner where Todd was cutting a fine figure in his footman's waistcoat and breeches.

"I could slip something nasty in his drink, if you like?" he (I assume) joked as he poured various bottles into a shaker.

I smiled at him soberly. "Thank you for your support. Who knows, I might even agree before the night is over."

He winked at me and I carried the drink back across the room, by which time the whole gang of new arrivals had melted into the pulsating crowd of dancers.

"Oh, Chrissy?" Aunt Belinda called with a high-pitched giggle. "Chrissy darling, is that for me?"

She was already sozzled but I handed her the mellow brown cocktail. Marmalade was long gone and I couldn't see how one more glass on top of the ten she'd already consumed would make much difference.

"I thought that you and Uncle Maitland had decided not to come?"

Her grey hair was pinned higher and tighter than ever and I had to wonder if there was any blood reaching her brain. She was the only one of her generation dressed in a modern style, but I can't say it suited her. The hemline of her skirt crashed about above her ankles as she attempted to keep herself upright.

"Who am I to turn down an invitation to a party?" She put one finger on my lip as if she was afraid I might answer. "My dear sweet nephew, there comes a time when the invitations disappear altogether. So seize these moments. Enjoy them and seize them."

She was beginning to repeat herself, and I wondered what I could do to escape when my mother caught sight of her sister draped over me.

She marched straight up to us. "Why on Earth are you bothering poor Christopher?"

Belinda managed to support her own weight and her befuddled eyes blinked away the brightness of the room. "How lovely to see you, Violet! It's been far too long. When was the last time we saw one another?"

"Sunday." My mother had a talent for sharp answers and this one was delivered with a surgeon's blade.

"Yes, that's right, well… lovely nonetheless." Sensing her little sister's hostility, Belinda waved goodbye and tottered out onto the floor to display her complete ignorance of how to dance a foxtrot.

"The place looks incredible, Christopher. It genuinely does." My mother was a good sort really and always knew how to cheer me up. "I hope you're having a nice time."

She took a moment to marvel at our surroundings as the slick dance band, dressed in tightly fitted black suits, started in on a new piece of music. A buzz of horror and delight travelled about the room as it quickly became apparent that what they were playing was a good deal 'hotter' than their previous efforts. What they were playing was full-on American jazz.

My brother let out a squeal of absolute glee as he spun Margaret around him. Scandalising the family with immoral, corrupting music – which the national newspapers regularly railed against – was one of our butler's more anarchic efforts. Conveniently absent, Fellowes must have known what sort of band he'd recommended, but I didn't mind. I thought the melody rather catchy and might have gone for a dance myself if the man of the hour hadn't appeared at that moment.

Lord Edgington timed his entrance to build suspense and made his appearance when the party was already roaring. It was another sign of the theatrical side to my grandfather's personality that I had only glimpsed before. He stood in his dove-grey dress suit, with a silver cane in one hand and his top hat in the other, surveying his domain. Any fears I had that he wouldn't approve of the hedonistic entertainment on display were soon quashed.

"This is just how I imagined it," he projected for everyone to hear.

As he walked across the room, he shook hands with friends and waved at others like a film star. I almost expected him to spin his hat through the air, tap his cane on the floor and break into song. Instead, and far more wisely considering his age, he made his way to the small stage where the band were playing and waited for them to finish a speedy one-step.

The dancers came to a rest, the noise of chatter and laughter died down and he cleared his throat to speak.

"Ladies and gentlemen, friends and family, I cannot express how moving it truly is to see you all here."

My father and grandmother, along with a large crowd from the neighbouring salon, had gravitated towards the respectful hush, but there were still a few guests missing. On cue, my second cousin Cora noisily tumbled into the room. Cora was a few years older than my brother and had been the golden child of the family (well mannered, perfect marks at school and a champion archer to boot) until she got to university and… well, things changed. She was dressed that night in what looked like a man's suit, with her hair cut short and a monocle of all things in one eye. A gaggle of old ladies at the back of the room turned their ire upon her, but she laughed it off as Lord Edgington continued with his address.

"I consider this gathering to be a rebirth. A chance to make amends for the time I have wasted and, though I may be in the twilight of my life, I will expend no more of my energy on fear and regrets." He paused and took in the gallery of faces looking up at him. "I'd like my three children and their families to come to the front."

Mother, Father and Aunt Belinda moved through the crowd. Albert and I followed after and I spotted two of our cousins cutting a similar path. Fellowes now appeared with a small silver trolley with a magnum of champagne and eleven pre-filled glasses on.

"What about my son?" Grandfather continued. "Does anyone know where Maitland has got to?"

There was some polite laughter then, but the truth of the matter was that I hadn't seen my uncle all night. The main Cranley clan had gathered in front of the stage by this point and Belinda was quick to snag the first glass of tipple.

"Well, I'm sure he'll be here in a moment." Grandfather carefully climbed down from the stage, took the empty bottle and held it up to his audience. "This champagne was given to me on the day that I married my beloved wife Katherine over fifty years ago. We promised that we'd drink it when the time was right. Somehow, though we attended the weddings of our three children and the christenings of all five of our phenomenal grandchildren, that moment never arrived."

Uncle Maitland still hadn't turned up and I could see that Grandfather was dragging out the proceedings. My cousin George finally strolled over from wherever he had been hiding and, in the crush for everyone in the family to get a glass of the historic libation, got bashed into by Maitland's son.

"Honestly, Francis!" he immediately bellowed. "You're clumsier than a clown."

His flute had smashed into a hundred pieces on the glossy floor and, with the champagne all served, he had to settle for an unhistoric replacement from Todd. Aunt Belinda had long got tired of waiting and was already knocking back her drink. Finally, my uncle appeared from the hall and, once he had collected his champagne from grumpy Aunt Winifred and shouted at his children about nothing in particular, the toast could commence.

With great empathy in his eyes, Grandfather raised his glass towards his loved ones. "That's what I wanted to bring you here to express. Please, don't wait your whole lives for something you could already be enjoying today. Learn from my mistakes. Embrace this beautiful world we share and-"

It was at this moment that Belinda collapsed into a chair with a painful moan. She was clearly suffering and put her hands to her head like someone had drilled a hole through it.

"That's the spirit, sis!" Uncle Maitland raised his drink to her. "Cheers."

The glass was at his lips when my grandfather let out a deafening shout. "Stop! Don't drink that."

He tore the glass from his son's hand, then ran to attend to his elder daughter. Aunt Belinda had not passed out in a drunken slump, her body was convulsing and her eyes were open. Tidal waves of agony passed through her body and despairing cries went up from the people around her as she fell to the floor.

George Trevelyan had lost his smug grin and ran over to see his mother. "She's dying," he screamed, his eyes searching the room for help.

He would find no solace and it was down to our grandfather to confirm the inevitable.

"She's dead."

CHAPTER NINE

I've read plenty of mystery stories. I devoured every Sherlock Holmes tale when I was first at boarding school and, were I more intelligent, insightful and brave, I'd like to think I'd make a first-rate detective. Dickens himself sets up many of his stories as puzzles to be solved, but nothing had prepared me for the moments after Aunt Belinda's death.

Silence.

That was the first stage. Ten seconds of silence in a crowd of sixty people. No one moved, no one said a word, but it lasted an eternity and was only broken when George fell to his knees in front of his mother's lifeless body.

I made the mistake of looking straight at the dead woman. It was a sight too ghastly to bear but I couldn't turn away. Her eyes were wide open and I could see the fear she must have experienced in her last moments of consciousness. Her skin had turned an unnatural shade of blotchy red so that she looked like a ripening plum. I'd never loved my aunt, but still wished there was something I could do to save her from such a fate.

As most of the room remained in a state of shock, my grandfather burst into action. "Fellowes, remove every last drop of the champagne and place it under lock and key. Band leader, play something light but not too fast."

Despite the unimpressed murmuring from the crowd, the band began to play a gentle lullaby and I could feel the soothing impact of the music wash over us.

"Everyone else, I'd recommend you also stop drinking, just to be on the safe side." He raised his own flute to his nose then and sniffed the contents but did not reveal what he had discovered. "I have to assume that whatever killed Belinda was in the champagne alone, but we shouldn't take any risks."

He issued more orders, first for Todd to call the police and then to the rest of us to stay where we were in order to preserve any evidence. All of a sudden, as if aware of his own limitations, he froze in his tracks. For one sickening moment, I was worried that he would meet the same end as his daughter, but his hesitation passed and he climbed onto the stage.

He looked one last time over the faces of every guest, as if memorising their reactions. The crowd had become more agitated by now. Several elderly relatives had retreated to the chairs at the side of the room, which, unhappily, brought them closer to the body. My brother was the only person there who seemed less than distraught, as his beloved for the night was crying on his shoulder.

"The police will be here before long." Grandfather's voice had taken on an official tone and I could see the different forces at battle within him.

On the surface, he was calm and focussed, as he attempted to record the full range of evidence that the scene held. But there were moments when his distress broke free. A small jerk of the head in his daughter's direction told me that he was struggling to process what had happened. A glance down at the floor suggested that there was sorrow welling up inside him, but he wouldn't let it show.

He descended from the stage to speak to his footman and the band played on. "Halfpenny, when Todd and Fellowes return, the three of you will ensure that nobody leaves. Christopher, come with me."

He'd marched halfway across the room before I came to life and followed him. The previously jubilant revellers parted as if he were Moses and they were the Red Sea. I noticed that Marmalade was missing, I hadn't seen him since he'd arrived in fact and it would be the first thing I'd tell the police when they got there. If any savage soul was capable of killing a party or a person, it was him.

My grandfather was waiting for me in the corridor, his face harrowed and drawn. The public mask he had been wearing had slipped clean away.

"I'm going to be honest, Christopher," he said once we were far enough from the ballroom not to be overheard. "I don't know whether I have it in me to cope tonight. For all the differences there were between us, I loved Belinda and I can't tell you whether I'll be able to keep going for much longer."

I realised then that any fear I had felt towards him had disappeared. I reached up to put my hand on his shoulder and, in a strange reversal of our normal roles, attempted to comfort him. "I can see that,

Grandfather. But I know how strong you are."

I thought he might need to nip into one of the salons for a minute alone or call on Fellowes to provide a dram of whisky. I doubt he knew himself what he really required but he showed no more signs of anguish. He nodded, pulled his shoulders back and continued down the corridor towards the drinks room.

I've never counted all the rooms in Cranley Hall but I can tell you that there is one for every occasion. The drinks room was a little way along from the grand salon and was primarily used by the staff for storing and preparing refreshments on occasions such as this one. As a result, it hadn't been used in a very long time and I had never set foot in it, outside of the odd game of hide and seek.

"Wait." Grandfather held his hand out to bar the door before I could step inside and trample any evidence. He removed a pair of white cotton gloves from his pocket and slipped them on. I had to wonder if he was carrying them to complement his outfit or because his detective's instincts had never left him.

We scanned the room from the doorway, though I failed to spot anything out of the ordinary. Beside the window was a small table with a plain white cloth draped over it. The walls on either side held locked cabinets which contained various tools, glasses and paraphernalia for serving. Fellowes would have poured the champagne here, but there were no traces of white powder, unusual objects, or hidden trapdoors. In the mystery novels I'd read, these were guaranteed signs of foul play.

Happy with his initial sortie, Lord Edgington stepped over the threshold and began a closer examination. Far faster than I could manage, he sought out a popped cork which was lying at the bottom of the thick velvet curtains. He crouched to inspect the floor around it, then raised it to his eyes.

As he'd invited me along on the mission, I felt I could at least ask a question. "Sorry, Grandfather, what are you looking for?"

He didn't answer at first, but, rotating the cork steadily between his gloved finger and thumb, he held it to the light. "What do you notice?"

I didn't like to be put on the spot and felt quite nervous. "Well... um. Nothing?"

"Exactly." He let this word sit between us, as if it revealed a great deal. I wondered whether I had time to pop to the petit salon for a chocolate éclair whilst he was thinking. "There are no holes or unusual indents. It is in every way a typical cork from a bottle of Veuve Clicquot champagne, which tells me far more than I was expecting to find out at this point."

I tried to keep up with him. "Do you mean that no one tampered with the bottle?"

I could already sense a shift in the old police officer. The emotion he'd shown just moments earlier had been shut away in some dark chamber of his heart and he was focussed on the task at hand.

"That's right. Assuming that the champagne was poisoned, we're left with far fewer options for how it came about." He paused and looked up at me. "Either the bottle was already contaminated fifty years ago – the probability of which seems low – or the poison was added this evening, after the cork was popped."

I'd been carrying a dark thought with me ever since I'd seen Belinda collapse, and felt compelled to let it out. "It couldn't be the delphiniums, could it?"

Grandfather looked at me like I had the wits of a stickleback. "No of course not. Where would you get such an idea?"

My thoughts came out in a jumble. "You said yourself that delphiniums can be toxic. Wasn't that why we wore gloves to handle them?"

"Yes, but-"

Now that I'd started, I had to get all my fears out in one go. "I thought perhaps that, with so many together, the scent or pollen or what have you could turn to poison."

Pocketing the cork in his waistcoat, Grandfather stood up to explain how far from the truth I'd already led us. "Delphiniums contain high levels of alkaloids. They're toxic, but not poisonous enough to kill so quickly or violently. Depending on the amount you ingested, you're more likely to get an upset stomach than keel over dead."

I felt awfully silly, but that didn't stop me talking. "So what did kill Aunt Belinda?"

I could see him consulting the book of poisons he kept neatly filed in the library in his head. "There are very few substances which would act so swiftly and many of them are only available in far-flung places.

Indigenous South Americans use arrows tipped with poison extracted from Chondrodendron plants to incapacitate their prey. There are also a number of venomous sea creatures which could provide you with a suitable weapon, but I think it was something far simpler and more readily available."

I assumed that he was considering one of the famous poisons that crime novelists love to make use of. Arsenic, strychnine or...

"Cyanide, I'd say." He rid his mouth of the words as though they had a bitter taste to them. "A short intense death. I've heard people say that it's painless, but it doesn't look that way to me. And this is not the first time I've seen what it can do."

He took the cork from his pocket and held it to his nose.

I fell for it and instantly had to ask, "What can you smell, grandfather?"

"Champagne, of course, boy." He looked displeased with me once more. "We've already established that the poison was added after the cork was popped. To discover how that was possible, we must talk to our first witness."

CHAPTER TEN

We left the drinks room and crossed paths with Todd on his way back to the ballroom.

"The police say they'll be here within the hour," he told us. "The local lot might make it earlier but they're sending someone from Scotland Yard. Some inspector who lives nearby."

"Jolly good," Grandfather said as he strode along with the gait and motivation of a much younger man. "Help Halfpenny keep the guests in order. I'll send Fellowes once I've spoken to him. Oh, and lock the drinks room door until the police arrive, we don't want any stray gawkers to interfere with the evidence."

"Evidence, Milord?" Todd had a rather innocent expression on his face just then. "So you do think it's murder?" There was a quickness to the man that told me he'd make a far better assistant than I could.

"It looks that way. Though you should try to play it down if our guests are getting agitated."

The two men swapped places and carried on along the corridor in different directions.

We found Fellowes in the kitchen. I did not consider it the obvious choice of location to store a lethal substance, but I'm sure he had his reasons. Chief among them, no doubt, was the chance to break the bad news to his colleagues.

I was surprised to discover that Cook and two of the maids were in tears.

"But none of you liked her." It was rather clever of my grandfather to have noticed this fact.

Shamefaced, Cook attempted to explain. "Yes, but... Well, no one should have to die like that, should they?"

Grandfather extended one hand to comfort her. "My daughter and I butted heads like mountain goats. She was not an easy person to like, but I've never stopped loving her. Which is why I'm determined to get to the bottom of what happened here tonight."

Fellowes was oddly shy during this exchange. He was leaning against the sink looking like a deflated balloon and was yet to let out a squeak. He displayed none of his usual poise or arrogance and I had to wonder what was going on in that strange head of his.

"Where have you stowed the champagne?" my grandfather addressed him and, with one finger, the butler pointed towards the staff dining room.

Grandfather tightened his grip on his amethyst-topped cane. "We'll talk in there if you don't mind."

Fellowes bowed mutely and the old policeman spun on his heel for us to follow. Delilah must have heard her master as she came scurrying out of her basket to accompany us. The room was locked and Fellowes produced the key to reveal the dim chamber with the drinks trolley just inside.

Grandfather got straight to work, putting his nose into the bottle and examining any sediment at the bottom of each glass before calling me over. "What can you smell?"

I thought this might be another of his tricks but gave one of the glasses a good sniff. "Well…" I hesitated over my answer. "It smells like… Yes, it smells just like champagne."

He actually rolled his eyes at me then. "Apart from the champagne, man!"

"Oh!" I chuckled at my evidently silly reply and tried again. "Well… apart from the champagne… Not much."

He crossed his arms in front of his chest and reflected upon this. "Hmmm, just as I assumed. In actual fact, only certain people can smell cyanide. I spent some time as a young officer familiarising myself with various poisons and so it jumps straight out at me."

"What does it smell like, Milord?" Fellowes, who had been standing discreetly in the corner, was quick to enquire. "If you don't mind me asking."

Lord Edgington raised one brow a little. "Cyanide smells like cyanide, though the fact that it is prevalent in bitter almonds makes many people think of them." He bent low for one last look at the deadly, bubbly delight. "Even if poor Belinda had been capable of smelling it herself, she'd been drinking since before the party began and was in no frame of mind to worry about it. The speed with which she died might also suggest that she had a large concentration of the substance in her glass or simply that the killer used a lot of cyanide to begin with."

He straightened up again and Fellowes and I watched as waves of thoughts, theories and observations passed through him. After some moments like this, he clicked his fingers and pulled a chair up at the table.

The staff rarely used their dining room, as the kitchen was so much warmer. It was a drab, dark space with no decoration or comfort. Grandfather's golden retriever seemed happy to be there with her master and settled on the floor by his feet.

"Sit down, please, Fellowes." The cold singularity of thought which was evidently controlling my grandfather at this time was impressive. He was focussed solely on his task and I could see how such a skill was vital to his detective work.

The butler hovered beside the table for a moment and then did as instructed. I decided to remain standing and leaned against the wall beside a cupboard filled with plain white crockery.

"I need you to tell me what happened between the time you opened the champagne and the time you served it."

Now that the question had been asked, Fellowes appeared to rediscover some of his confidence.

"Yes, Milord. Of course." He needed a moment to assemble his thoughts. "I took the bottle from the cellar to warm a little after the guests arrived, but didn't open it until shortly before the toast."

"You opened it in the drinks room, is that correct?"

Fellowes darted his eyes away from his interrogator who sat, as is only right for the lord of the manor, at the head of the table. "That's correct. I thought it best to do so, given the lively display of dancing taking place in the ballroom. Such precious wine doesn't want wasting."

"But you left the bottle after you opened it, isn't that right?"

Panic tore through the man once more and he glanced at me at the side of his vision, perhaps hoping I would be able to soften my grandfather's resolute tone.

"No, that's…"

"Tell me the truth, man." Lord Edgington's temper flared like a spitting bonfire. "You opened the champagne then left the room, why?"

I'd never seen Fellowes look anything but cocky and self-assured but I swear that he was shaking right then from the pressure. I was not the detective of course and couldn't tell you one way or another whether this was a sign of guilt or merely his fear of landing in the soup.

"I heard a voice."

Those spectacularly expressive white bushes on grandfather's brow twitched higher. "A voice?"

"Well, a sound at first. A tapping on the window and then I thought I heard my name being called so I…"

A tapping on the window of the drinks room which is twenty feet off the ground? Something about his story didn't add up. I felt sure our superlative investigator would jump on such an inconsistency, but he remained calm.

"You went out to see who it was." Grandfather's eyes fixed themselves on a point in the middle distance and I had to assume he was taking mental case notes to pass on to the police when they arrived.

Fellowes was quick to drum up an explanation. "I had plenty of time still, Milord. You see, I'd opened the bottle a little earlier than necessary. It was still five to nine when I popped the cork so I figured I had time to see what was going on."

Lord Edgington attempted to reassure the man with a gentle look, even as he asked another key question. "And who did you expect to find, out in the gardens?"

The butler breathed out heavily. "Well, the gardeners of course. I thought it was Driscoll and Danny. They're always playing jokes and I reckoned I'd be able to get my own back on them if I sneaked out through the petit salon and caught 'em in the dark."

"Once you got outside, what did you find?"

The trusted butler of Cranley Hall tensed his muscles and pursed his lips. Despite his reputation amongst the other staff for being a slippery customer, he was not a skilled liar. His forehead glistened with sweat, though the air in the sombre dining room was tinged with ice.

"Nothing."

"Nothing?"

"I mean, no one." He shrugged his shoulders like a boxer gearing up for a fight and I was reminded of my black eye, which stung with the memory. It also forced me to question where Marmaduke Adelaide had gone before the toast.

My grandfather maintained an impressively unimpressed tone.

"You mean to say there was no one outside when you got there?"

"Yeah. I mean… yes, Milord, that's right. After I'd spent a good five minutes checking the gardens, I returned to the drinks room, poured enough champagne for the eleven members of the immediate Cranley family and wheeled them into the ballroom for the toast."

"Did you see anyone on your way?" Both men turned to look at me. To be honest, I hadn't planned to say anything, I'd been perfectly happy with my mouth locked shut, watching the expert at work. For whatever reason, though, my own thoughts had become manifest.

Grandfather narrowed his eyes a fraction but repeated my question back to our witness. "Yes, did you see anyone on your way?"

Fellowes glanced up at the ceiling, reliving that fateful moment from a mere fifteen minutes prior. "No, no I didn't."

Lord Edgington tilted his head from side to side in a curious fashion. It was hard to say what he was thinking, but he offered no further remark and seemed content to contemplate Fellowes in this silent manner.

"Very well, you can go about your duties."

Fellowes looked even more surprised than I was. "That's it?" He almost smiled, then remembered himself and sat prouder in his chair.

"Unless you have anything more to tell us?"

He shook his head. "No, Milord, nothing else. I swear, I didn't see anything out of the ordinary." Pulling his chair back noisily, he rose to standing. "Thank you, Milord." With an uncharacteristically low bow, he stepped away from the table and left us.

On the great panel of bells just outside the room we were in, the largest and loudest rang profusely – presumably signifying the arrival of the police at the front door. Grandfather made no sign of having heard, but peered out of the window and allowed the stillness to seize the dim space we were in.

"What a sad, strange case." Was all he had to say at first, but I didn't want to hurry him so I bent down to stroke Delilah and waited for him to elaborate. "I have so many questions and so few people I trust to answer them."

I dared a comment then, and immediately felt stupid for pointing out the obvious. "You do realise that there are very few suspects who could have put the poison in the champagne?"

"Oh yes? So you have some names in mind?" The sentence rose to a high interrogative point before fading out.

I needed time to make the list. There were too many people in the ballroom to be sure of course but, through a process of elimination, I could rule out a good number who were not involved.

"Cora for one, she was the last to arrive for your toast. Well, Uncle Maitland was last and then her actually, but he wouldn't have killed his own sister."

"Wouldn't he?"

These two words cut deep within me. Not only was it difficult for me to imagine anyone doing such a thing, coming from the man's own father, the accusation was yet harder to swallow. I stumbled over my answer and failed to make anything more than a moan which Delilah joined in with.

"And why would you assume that he was only trying to kill his sister?" He paused for me to answer, but I had nothing more to say. "From what I can tell, the whole bottle of champagne was poisoned. Perhaps you're right and someone wanted to kill Belinda, or maybe they were after me, but one thing is for certain; they were willing to murder the whole lot of us to achieve their ambition."

A bitter smile crossed his lips then, and I was forced to reflect on the true savagery of the crime.

"You see, Christopher." He leaned in closer to speak in a whisper. "If the killer had his way, we wouldn't be here to search for evidence and uncover the truth. You and I would be keeled over on the floor of the ballroom, with our last breaths long since expired."

CHAPTER ELEVEN

As we trailed back through the house to the front of the property, I ran through the names of those I was confident had not been present in the ballroom at five minutes to the hour, when Fellowes had opened the champagne.

- No.1 - My school bully: Marmaduke Adelaide.
- No.2 - My second cousin: Cora Villiers.
- No.3 - Her grandmother (my great-aunt): Clementine Cranley.
- No.4 - My uncle: Maitland Cranley, the Earl of Croydon.
- No.5 - Our butler: Mr Reginald Fellowes himself.

Walking alongside me, with Delilah at his heels, my grandfather interrupted my thoughts.

"No, no, Christopher. It's really not that simple." He looked down at me with great judgement in his eyes. "You've already decided on the suspects, but there are things I witnessed which you can't have seen. Don't go jumping to conclusions."

He'd really knocked me for six then and I struggled to respond. "How the devil did you know what I was thinking?"

Delilah let out an equally impressed bark as if demanding an explanation herself.

Grandfather replied with nonchalant breeziness to his voice. "I saw your eyes skimming across the portraits of our ancestors on the walls. You paused over certain paintings – the old lady beside the kitchen, of course, the hunter with his gun and brace of rabbits. I can only imagine you've reduced your suspect list to a mere five names, but I'm afraid you're getting ahead of yourself."

I could not hold back my admiration for this impressive feat, and it poured out of me. "Did you learn how to do that in your time at Scotland Yard?"

We'd been practically running along the endless corridor. It was easy to forget that my grandfather was halfway through his eighth decade on the planet, and he paused for a moment to catch his breath and regain his strength.

"Not at all. I learnt it from Edgar Allan Poe's 'The Murders in the

Rue Morgue'. It's no exact science; nothing more than a parlour trick, really. It seldom leads to solid evidence, but it's handy for impressing people." He didn't smile or change his expression, but I could tell he was happy that the technique had worked on me.

When we got outside, the only car to have arrived was the local bobbies' and they seemed content to wait for the head man to appear before getting mixed up in something they couldn't handle.

"Are you going to tell me the names of the other suspects?" I wrapped my arms around myself, as springtime in England isn't all sunshine and flowers. It can get quite nippy at night.

I got the impression that, for all his surface calm, my grandfather was struggling to maintain his composure. He'd fallen back into familiar behaviour from his days in the Metropolitan Police. He was investigating now and the light-hearted back and forth we'd engaged in was all part of that. And yet, I felt sure he was reliving the scene in the ballroom; his own daughter coughing through her last breaths and the fear-stricken faces of every onlooker.

He winced and had to pause before continuing. "You may have seen me," he said when this shudder had passed. "As I came into the room, I scanned those around me. I made a note of each person there, not because I suspected foul play, but as that's what I have done for most of my life. It helps in a number of ways, both professionally and socially. This evening though, it enabled me to keep a record of who was present at that key moment. When I took to the stage for my toast and again after Belinda had died, I performed a similar task."

"You know exactly who was in the room and when? That's remarkable."

He once more attempted to play down his achievements. "No, not at all. It is just another trick. Like the game children play at parties with a tray and a selection of objects. I keep an image in my mind of before and after, then compare the differences. I assure you that anyone can do it."

"So who did you notice was missing when you entered the ballroom?"

"I would have expected you to work it out." His eyes were fixed on the gate at the far end of the drive. "It was a man so many love to hate."

The only name that came to mind was Fellowes, but then we

already knew where he was. I waited for Grandfather to elucidate.

"Why, George, of course."

My playboy cousin, who had made such an entrance to the ball, had apparently slipped back out without me noticing.

"He was there for the toast, though," I pointed out. "He came up to the stage with everyone else. He was there when his mother died."

"That's true, but, when I mounted the stage, I can assure you there was no sign of him. He slipped in from the corridor after Fellowes arrived with his trolley. He could quite easily have gone to the drinks room and spiked the champagne. The police will be all over him, considering what he stands to gain if I were to go the way of his mother."

George Trevelyan was the second in line to the Cranley family inheritance, this much I already knew. It was an open secret that Grandfather had ripped up tradition and planned for his elder daughter Belinda to inherit the bulk of his wealth. This meant that the estate would go to George now that his mother was out of the way.

Perhaps I was too innocent, but all this talk of murder in the family had set me on edge. A pair of headlights shone through the gate and the guard on duty opened it to admit a black Triumph two-seater. I was glad of the distraction and Grandfather walked across the drive to welcome our new arrival.

I was rather disappointed when the man who stepped out of the vehicle looked just about as far from my image of a crack detective as you could get. He was short, shabbily dressed and had stains down his blue, woollen pullover.

"Edgington," he said in a grunt, and I didn't need to hear anything more to know that the two men did not get along.

"Blunt!" It took me a moment to realise that this was not an observation my grandfather was making, but the policeman's name,. "It's been a long time."

They did not shake hands but stood glaring at one another. The sight of a subordinate showing such open hostility to the legendary superintendent surprised me. My mother had only ever told me tales of her father's bravery and prowess. I had never imagined that he'd have enemies within the police.

"Christopher, this is Sergeant Isambard Blunt of Scotland Yard. Blunt, this is my grandson who will be assisting me with the investigation."

The officer made a loud snort to clear whatever muck was in his nose. "It's Inspector Blunt now, as I'm sure even an old fella like you must have heard. And furthermore, this is not your investigation. You are not a serving member of the police and I'd recommend you keep your nose out of it."

Lord Edgington did not appear to be intimidated. "We'll see about that, old chap. You do what you have to and we will tread our own path."

The little man marched towards us then, his sausagey finger pointed like a pistol. "No doubt you can call up your mates in the top brass and get it all smoothed over, but I'm telling you now, I'm going to treat you like any other suspect."

I surprised myself then by answering the fiery inspector back. "My grandfather had nothing to do with the murder and I think it shows an awful lot of cheek to talk to him in such a disrespectful manner."

"Oh yeah? I thought I'd been unusually polite." Barely looking at me, he curled his lip and thundered past us to shout orders at his underling constables.

The owner of the estate that the vile little man had just invaded watched him go with a mix of annoyance and amusement shaping his face.

"He can't talk to you that way, Grandfather."

"Yes, he can." He hesitated, as if he needed time to accept the truth of this himself. "And he's right, I am a suspect, like anyone else. I've been at locked horns with Belinda and her brother for weeks and Fellowes wasn't in the drinks room when I wandered past. It only makes sense to consider my guilt."

"Oh, please!" I'm normally a rather placid individual. I don't know whether it was my grandfather's temper rubbing off on me, or my innate reaction to Inspector Blunt, but I was suddenly fuming with rage. "That would mean you were willing to kill your whole family and leave Cranley to some distant relative for the sake of a petty argument? The very idea is absurd."

"The question of absurdity rarely comes up in a criminal investigation, Christopher." He gripped my arm and led me back towards the house in the footsteps of the officers. "I am a suspect until I can prove that I had neither the inclination nor opportunity to carry out the crime."

"I can accept that, but why was the inspector so rude to you?"

As we crunched down the gravel path, he did not immediately answer but stroked the long white hair on his chin.

"I can't say for certain, my boy. I suppose he just doesn't like our sort. Most people I worked with accepted me as one of their own, but Blunt only ever sees rank and class. He started in the force when I was an inspector and assumed that I got to where I had because of my family's wealth. He could be commissioner of the Metropolitan Police and he'd still be angry that I was a lord."

"I always thought that it was wealthy folk like us who were supposed to be the snobs."

He laughed a little and waited by the entrance for me to walk past him into the house. "Oh, no, Christopher. In this world, anyone can be anything."

CHAPTER TWELVE

More officers arrived from the villages around the traditional Hundred of Edgington, but it was Inspector Blunt's operation to run. He launched himself down the corridor and into the ballroom, determined to stamp his mark on the proceedings.

"Has anyone left this room since the body was found?" the Inspector demanded of Todd, who was on duty at the entrance to the room.

"Only those who have returned, Sir."

"Did anyone try to resuscitate the deceased?" His eyes swung about the group of guests whose grand gowns and formal attire now looked frivolous and self-indulgent.

No one spoke, so my grandfather sighed and delivered his answer. "I checked her pulse; she was already dead. It happened extremely quickly and there was nothing we could do for her."

Blunt didn't reply, but his eyes traced a path across the room to where my aunt had slumped over.

The new heir to Cranley Hall was sitting on the floor beside his mother's stiffening corpse. All the fizz and bravado George Trevelyan had brought with him had disappeared. From the red streaks in his eyes it was clear he'd been crying. I didn't blame him. I was glad that I'd been allowed to walk around the house instead of being trapped in the ballroom.

"Who are you?" Blunt spat as he approached my cousin.

When he spoke, George was a faint, spectral version of the young man I knew. "She was my mother."

I found his phrasing rather unusual. The fact he'd already put her into the past tense seemed too soon, too sudden. And instead of answering the inspector's question directly, he'd reframed the information.

"All right." Blunt signalled to his subordinates. "Put him in another room and cover up the body. We'll need statements from anyone with anything worth hearing. It's going to be a long night."

George was pulled up to standing by one of the uniformed officers and then he stumbled towards the corridor with a futile glance over his shoulder. Though I'd assumed he was now resigned to the inspector's authority, my grandfather rushed forward to stake his claim to the case once more.

"You can lead the interview, Blunt, but Christopher and I will be in that room when you speak to my nephew. This is my house and I won't have it any other way."

I expected a loud rebuttal but, instead, the middle-aged officer simply huffed, turned his back to us and got on with his work. While he spoke to our still nervous butler, I went to see my family. They were huddled together, far from where Aunt Belinda had collapsed.

It was hard to tell what my mother was thinking. Rigid and barely moving, she sat in a chair between two gigantic vases of delphinium. Albert was the one who seemed most distressed, though not for the reasons one might have expected.

"I don't care if she's my cousin! I just want a girlfriend."

Our father had apparently broken the news of exactly who Albert had been dancing with and my brother retreated into the corner to be alone.

"How are you doing, old chap?" Father asked. He was awfully good at hiding his feelings and there's nothing like tossing an 'old chap' into a greeting to make everything seem normal.

"I've been working on the investigation with Grandfather. We've narrowed down the list of suspects." I still wasn't privy to the names of everyone on that list, but my family didn't need to know that.

My mother, who was staring into space and had not even blinked until now, heard what I said and came to life. "Well done, darling. I'm sure you're a wonderful help to your grandfather. How do you think he's coping?"

Though she was putting a brave face on things, I could see in her eyes just how much sadness she was battling through. Those deep brown orbs glistened under the light of the chandeliers, as the reality of her sister's death permeated her every thought.

"I'm doing what I can." Boys at Oakton Academy are taught from an early age that it's essential not to discuss, show or, in fact, possess any emotions in public. "Grandfather is on the trail of the killer. There's no doubt about it."

My father frowned, before declaring in a solemn voice, "It doesn't bear thinking about what would have happened if Belinda hadn't drunk before everyone else."

My mother did not like the way he'd expressed himself and directed a disapproving look in his direction. "Oh, so everything's fine then? It's only Belinda who died. As long as we're all right, nothing else matters."

He swiftly crouched down to comfort her, though the gesture was born more of appeasement than apology. I thought about going back to see Grandfather, or up to my bed for that matter, but before I could decide what the best course of action was, I'd been cornered by the very last person I wanted to talk to.

"Christopher, you've got to help me." With his hair tussled and his tie askew, Marmalade had made it through the party and out the other side, but it was his face that had borne the brunt of the damage. His cheek was bleeding and there was a bruise beneath his right eye that mirrored my own. It was hard not to think that some justice had been served.

"What happened to you? You look like you've been mugged by a gorilla."

His voice was deeper than normal, as if he had a point to prove. "I went into the garden and fell down in the dark. Never mind that, I need you to talk to your grandfather for me. I need you to tell him I was with you when that woman was murdered."

"Why should I do anything to help you? I didn't even want you here tonight." It probably wasn't the moment to bring up such petty issues, but forgive me for still being upset about the black eye he'd given me.

"Please, Chrissy. I know we're not friends, but this is serious. They'll think I'm the killer, I know they will. Did you hear that policeman? He's a savage. As soon as he finds out who my father is and that I don't have an alibi, I'll be for it." The plummy tone he normally spoke in had worn off and more popular expressions broke through.

"Why would they think that, Adelaide? Where were you before she died?"

He had no interest in explaining himself and checked that no one was listening before stepping in closer. "Just do what I told you." His usual malevolence rung out once more. "Your grandfather can get me off the hook, I know he can. One word to the police and he'll smooth it all over. Do it, or I'll-"

I wasn't in the mood for another threat from him. "It's too late for that. He already knows you weren't in here before the toast. In fact, you're one of the very few people who was absent at the time that the champagne was poisoned."

"Poison? I didn't have anything to do with that."

I paused to watch his reaction. I'm not one to take pleasure in the suffering of others, but, I have to say, he had it coming. "I'd run if I were you, Adelaide, before the police get wind of what you've done."

I could see that he wanted to even up my face with his fist, but there was no time for that. Taking a quick glance around the room, he looked to see which of the exits were unguarded, then casually strolled over to the French windows.

With my typical Christopher-ish weakness, I felt a little sorry for him. The desire to help him almost overcame me, so I forced myself to shout, "Watch out, he's making a break for it!" and Blunt caught sight of him just in time.

All the police officers and even my Uncle Maitland ran to intercept him, but that just meant he was free to double back and run out to the corridor. Lithe and lanky Marmalade had been sprint champion at every school sports day since we'd started at Oakton and the comparatively round bobbies didn't stand a chance.

The last thing he shouted as he disappeared from the room was, "Thanks, Chrissy," and Inspector Blunt looked mortified that he'd already lost a suspect.

"Well, go after him then, you bunch of idlers," he admonished the nearest officers before his words faded to silence.

Still struggling to work out whether I'd intentionally helped Marmalade escape, I spotted the wry expression on my grandfather's face as his own nemesis suffered his first defeat.

CHAPTER THIRTEEN

The natives – by which I mean the great and good of Surrey – were becoming restless. There was only so long that the police could keep everyone there before one of the distinguished guests threatened to write a highly critical letter to The Times or call up Inspector Blunt's superiors for a serious discussion.

Though he didn't seem too worried about such an occurrence, it was becoming clear that dealing with the large group of still tipsy revellers was only making his task more difficult. As voices grew louder across the hall, the inspector decided he'd have to address the crowd.

"From what I've ascertained-" he began, in his typically flat manner.

"We can't hear you, man!" a hidden heckler exclaimed. To be honest, it was probably my grandfather throwing his voice. "Get up on the stage, why don't you?"

With a tired groan, Blunt did as instructed and began his speech once more. "From what my officers have been able to ascertain, there were only a few people who were not present during the time at which the bottle of champagne could have been poisoned." The noise from the audience rose again and he had to shout to be heard. "If your name isn't called, you can provide your details to one of my officers and you will be free to go."

The chatter took on a more optimistic tone and Blunt looked at the notepad he was holding to read out the list.

"Lord Edgington…" He announced this first name with great joy. "Maitland Cranley, George Trevelyan, Reginald Fellowes, Cora Villiers and Clementine Cranley. And if anyone knows of the whereabouts of one Marmaduke Adelaide, we'd be interested in talking to him and all."

"What about my son!" My belligerent grandmother bellowed from the back of the room. She sounded quite indignant that anyone would overlook a member of her family, even in such a salacious matter. "He left the room where we'd been talking and I didn't see him again until the toast was made. You would be remiss in your duties not to include him."

"Well, thank you for noticing!" Not for the first time in his life, my father was unhappy to be in his mother's thoughts.

Replying with one of her classic eye rolls, she would not be swayed by her son's disapproval. "I'm only telling the truth, Walter. We wouldn't want you to be cleared of a murder without sufficient evidence. That would be like winning a race without breaking into a run."

The fact that this conversation had been conducted extremely loudly and in public led several members of the family to have a good chortle at my father's expense. This was followed by a burst of muttered disapproval as sober heads reminded us that a woman was dead.

Blunt sensed yet another opportunity to make a toff's life difficult and pounced on the new revelation. "Is this true, Mr Prentiss?"

My father replied with an embarrassed shrug. "Well… yes. But I only popped outside for a breath of fresh air. I can't have been gone more than five minutes."

"Make sure he doesn't leave, boys." A wicked grin shaped Blunt's face before he addressed the room one last time. "If you have no further information for me, then I will thank you for your assistance and say goodnight."

Ten or fifteen people requested their shawls, coats and purses from Alice, who was already on hand, but the vast majority stayed exactly where they were.

Blunt looked confused and it would fall to my grandfather to explain the problem. "Most of them are spending the night here. If you wish to speak to your suspects alone, I recommend we retire to the smoking room while my staff see the other guests to their quarters."

Looking increasingly infuriated, Blunt stamped off the stage without another word and motioned to a few of his men to round up the persons of interest.

"The smoking room is to the left!" my father shouted after him as the inspector turned right along the corridor and instantly had to double back. It was a small victory on Daddy's part, but I could see he enjoyed it.

Feeling a little guilty for leaving them at that moment, I waved sombrely to my mother and Albert, then scurried after my grandfather who was waiting for me by the door.

"Quite revealing, don't you think?" he said as I reached him. "The police appear to have eliminated any of the staff but Fellowes. Maybe

Blunt is more useful than I'd given him credit."

"You knew about my father, didn't you?" I hadn't intended to sound so hostile, but his previous reticence to reveal the names on his list now made sense. "Why didn't you tell me?"

Instead of giving me a straight answer, he said, "Come along, Chrissy. There's no time for sentimentality in this job," and turned to leave.

It had been a while since I'd caught sight of my great-aunt Clementine but I needn't have worried about her. She had been roused from her nap and was already in the smoking room, singing an old song to her accompanying officer. Her voice was almost as bad as her memory and I was expecting Blunt to shut her up at any moment.

> **"Come, holy night!**
> **Long is the day and ceaseless is the fight;**
> **Around us bid thy quiet shadows creep,**
> **And rock us in thy sombre arms to sleep!"**

She moved her arms gently through the air as she sang, her wide eyes fixed on nothing as was usually the case. She was dressed in a purple ball gown, which had been accessorised with a large pink polka-dot hat, several sparkly brooches and, at some point in the course of the evening, a delphinium corsage. When she had concluded Elgar's tragic lament, she froze, apparently waiting for our applause.

"Thank you, madam." As it happened, Blunt was quite moved by the performance. "My mother used to sing that song, God rest her soul."

Clementine nodded humbly and took her place in one of the armchairs scattered around the heavily carpeted space. A fire roared in the grate, yet the scent of tobacco was overwhelming and infused every inch of the room.

Except for Marmaduke Adelaide, the complete list of suspects was there. At the front of the room, Cora and my father were puffing on two gigantic cigars in a cloud of their own making. Daddy always hated being far back in the theatre and no doubt wanted a good view. Uncle Maitland was pacing up and down in front of the fireplace and poor, orphaned George inevitably looked distraught. He had draped himself across a bookshelf and chewed his nails nervously as we waited.

Fellowes poured whisky from a decanter and, when he served

Clementine, she thought it would be rather funny to return the favour. Still in the over-the-top, theatrical style of her previous performance, the old lady made a big show of splashing out the single malt into a tumbler for the butler.

"You know," she began, in her high, quivering voice, "when I was a girl, we ladies were never allowed in smoking rooms and now here I am serving the gentlemen drinks! What thrills!"

She launched into another song as she poured her granddaughter Cora a drink of her own. Fellowes looked unsure how to react, but decided to humour the mad old thing and stood back against the bookshelf with the discretion required of his position. Once Clementine had finished her task, and her song, the inspector began.

"There's a killer in this room." His opening line was appropriately direct. "Someone you all know planned and carried out a murder. I want you to think about this simple fact and remember that keeping secrets won't do you nothing but harm."

I was one of the few people present who could not actually have killed my aunt. This felt jolly good to know, but Inspector Blunt's demand still had its desired effect. I looked about at the figures who'd been a fixture in my life for so long and processed the fact that one of them had not only murdered Belinda, they'd almost wiped out my whole family.

Blunt continued to address us in a truly bizarre manner. Presumably attempting to sound like a member of the upper classes, he added extra Hs to the beginning of words. "If *hany* of you know *hanything*, you must tell me now. Whatever you were up to between eight fifty and nine *ho'clock* this evening, give *hor* take a few minutes, I need to know about it. Whatever you're keeping to yourself, don't."

I took in the reactions of those around me as he spoke. Chic, modern Cora peered through her monocle at the inspector. She was obviously nervous and hugged her glass close to her body, but barely took a sip. Clementine was peering out of the window and humming once more, Uncle Maitland's round, ruddy face looked as vexed as it ever did and I couldn't bring myself to look at Father just then as I was still trying to ignore the reality that he was a suspect.

The inspector swept his searchlight eyes from one side of the room to the other. "This is not my first time investigating a case like this. And it doesn't matter if it's a car stolen in Hounslow or a man stabbed to death on the steps of Westminster Cathedral, people like you always make the same mistakes. So, whatever you think you've got to lose by telling me the truth, it can't be worse than being arrested for murder."

Standing beside me at the back of the room, the most experienced officer there nodded his approval at his old rival's message. My grandfather was a fair man, even when faced with unpleasant people.

"So," Blunt continued, "what have you got for me? *Hanyone* want to admit to seeing *hanything* suspicious? *Hanyone* want to cough up to the crime?" He waited for a response and, when nothing came, he abandoned his posh tone altogether and addressed his subordinates. "Nah, didn't think so. Right, separate 'em all up into rooms of their own and don't let any of 'em say a word to one another. It's like I said, boys, it's going to be a very long night."

As the constables dispersed, he pointed to my grandfather then with malicious glee. "And start with that one!"

Lord Edgington was incensed and shot his response across the room. "You can't do this, I told you what will happen if you shut me out of the investigation."

Blunt just ignored him. "And make sure that there's no phone in the room you lock him in."

CHAPTER FOURTEEN

The police carted their suspects off to separate cells along the corridor. I noticed they shut Grandfather up in what amounted to a cupboard used for storing silverware, while I was left out entirely.

It had gone eleven by this time. I could tell that Blunt would make them wait before starting the interviews and, as most people had retired for the evening, I decided to do the same.

My parents have a suite beside my own and so I called in to see my mother before bed. I very much hoped that, wherever the staff had stuck Albert, he was far away from our cousin Margaret Hillington-Smythe.

"Aren't you worried about Father?" I asked as I watched my mother's pearl-handled brush fall through her long, brown hair for the fifth, tenth, one hundredth time. I've always found watching her at such tasks to be most soothing, but even this was no balm after that night's cavalcade of disasters.

She stopped the movement to answer me. "No, Christopher. Of course I'm not worried about him. There is no way on this green and pleasant Earth that your father could be mixed up in my sister's murder." Her soft voice peaked then. "And besides, do we even know it was intentional? Could it not simply be that the champagne was fifty years old and had turned to acid?"

I considered this for a moment, but it didn't seem possible. "Grandfather doesn't think so. He said there are very few poisons that could have killed her like that and cyanide is the most likely."

My mother shivered a little then. Cyanide was a poison you heard about in penny dreadfuls and ghastly newspaper stories. It was not the kind of thing we dealt with at Cranley Hall.

She looked at my reflection in the mirror on her dressing table. "Your father had nothing to do with it and nor did mine." I felt she was saying this for her own reassurance. "I really can't imagine that anyone from the family would want to hurt poor Belinda."

I was running through the suspects again in my head and probably didn't tread as carefully as I should have. "But that means it could only have been Fellowes or Marmaduke Adelaide."

She turned around in her chair to look straight at me. "Well, there you go then; it must be that horrible boy. He should never have been at the ball after what he did to you, and I've heard frightful stories about his family."

I thought about this for a moment. Adelaide was a savage at school, but could he really have murdered someone in cold blood? "I'm not so sure, Mother. The way he was acting before he escaped this evening didn't suggest that-"

In a single moment her whole demeanour changed. "Christopher, that's enough!" She threw the brush down so that it skidded across the carpet and came to a rest under the window. "You're not a detective and I'm sure this will all be resolved by the morning anyway."

Her hollow voice shot over to where I sat at the end of the curtained bed. We looked at one another, neither of us quite sure what to say next. I thought of apologising and, knowing mother, I'm sure she did the same. In the end, we couldn't break the deadlock, so I mumbled, "I should probably leave now," and did just that.

The problem was that I didn't want to go to bed and couldn't fall asleep when I tried. I just lay there, going over the events of that night and trying to understand who could be behind my aunt's horrendous fate. I was somehow colder under the scratchy woollen quilt than I had been outside, but I must have drifted off at some point as, several hours later, I woke up to find a figure sitting in the armchair by the door.

A patch of moonlight cast a silver halo around my grandfather and made his white whiskers shine. He didn't say anything at first, and I could tell he was lost in his thoughts. I sat up in bed, but even then he didn't react.

"Are you all right, Grandfather?"

He made a questioning *hmmm* sound as if he'd just noticed me there and then voiced aloud the notions that had been playing in his mind. "Blunt got the better of me this evening. I'm not too big a man to admit it. But this was just the opening gambit and tomorrow the real investigation will begin."

Still groggy, with a heavy head and half-closed eyes, there wasn't much I could say to this. Luckily, he stood up from his chair and pulled his shoulders back like a soldier being inspected by his commanding officer.

"I'll need you up nice and early. We've work to do if we want to catch the killer before he strikes again."

This woke me up. "Do you think that's likely?"

"Oh, almost certainly. With so many people around at the time of the murder, there are bound to be loose ends that the culprit will need to tie up. Killing once is a test of character, but the second time comes more easily." He put his hand on the door and, with an incongruous smile, said, "Sweet dreams, Christopher."

And with that, he was gone.

CHAPTER FIFTEEN

After that unwelcome interruption, I had a restless night. My dreams were filled with giant ginger bullies and dying aunts. I imagined each one of the suspects confessing to their part in the crime, but, when I woke up, the details of each explanation were gone from my head.

I was feeling more positive than the night before though, if for no other reason than the thought of all the cakes left over for breakfast. When I got down to the dining room, the staff had laid out a truly sumptuous feast. There were custard tarts, fondant rings, Eccles cakes, Danish pastries and a huge assortment of petit fours which Cook had prepared especially and no one had touched. Sadly, there was a scrum of old family friends and distant relatives already helping themselves, so I joined the back of the queue and waited.

Fellowes was hard at work being rude to the family but the only other official suspect I caught sight of was Great-Aunt Clementine. She was singing Noel Coward's 'There's Life in the Old Girl Yet' to her captive audience. As a result, once the food had been taken, very few people stayed in the room to eat. On the bright side, I hoped that her caterwauling might make the scroungers and loiterers head home sooner.

Just when it was my turn to take my fill of the sweet selection, Grandfather appeared.

"No time for that, boy," he informed me. "There's work to be done."

I almost cried, but put my plate down and hurried after him. Five seconds later, I changed my mind and pushed back through the crowd to claim a cream horn. Aunt Belinda was dead and she wasn't going to get any deader because I'd had a spot of breakfast.

"Where are we going?" I asked as I licked granules of sugar from my fingers.

"We'll interview Blunt's prime suspect first, see what he knows. With a smooth fellow like George Trevelyan, it's best to catch him when he hasn't had time to prepare his answers."

He was full of energy that morning and strode up the stairs to the wing of Cranley Hall where guests normally slept.

"I was up before the dawn." He breathed in noisily, like he was recalling the fresh morning air. "I've spoken to the servants already.

Every one of them has an alibi and the extra staff we'd hired to help with the preparations had all left before the ball began."

Halfway along the upper corridor, he came to a stop and banged on the door. He didn't wait for an answer but marched straight in.

"Morning, George!" he sang, on his way over to the window to throw back the curtains and let the pale sunshine into the room. "Sorry to wake you, old boy. I thought we had better have a chat before things get out of hand."

"What the hell are you doing?" Our first suspect stayed hidden beneath his sheets, but it wasn't hard to tell why. George was not alone.

Grandfather was a step ahead as usual. "Awfully sorry to interrupt, Margaret. But I think you had better get back to your own room, don't you?"

Margaret Hillington-Smythe, my cousin on my father's side – so thankfully no relation of George's – scrambled to pull on a dressing gown and bundled up her clothes. Barefoot, the poor girl picked her way across the room, then paused by the door. She looked like she had something to say, but changed her mind and ran out.

George himself was unrepentant. "Good morning, dear Grandfather. And what a beautiful morning it is." He pushed himself up to sitting then leaned across to his bedside table to extract a long, thin cigarette from a golden case. "I didn't get much sleep thanks to your friends from the force, but I'm always up for a chinwag."

"I was thinking more along the lines of an interrogation, but your choice of word sounds a little friendlier." Our grandfather pulled a chair to the end of the bed and so I copied him and we both sat down. "Perhaps you could start by telling us where you were last night before your mother died."

My cousin took a long drag on the cigarette. He held the smoke down while staring at Grandfather, then released it in small puffs like a train. "I don't see that there's a great deal of sense in me answering your questions. You've surely all decided that I'm the one to blame."

I'd been relishing the thought of seeing the famous Superintendent Edgington in action and he didn't disappoint. His voice immediately soared and he struck a self-righteous note. "Do you really think so little of me that I would condemn a man with no evidence?"

George fired back an answer without fear. "That's what you do in this family. Guilty until proven innocent will be the inscription on my tombstone."

Grandfather crossed his legs and softened his tone. "You know, I've never thought badly of you, George. As far as I'm concerned, you can drink what you like and spend time with whomever you wish to. As long as you remain on the right side of the law, you won't hear me say a word against you. But your mother is dead and I need to find out why."

He took another puff. "And what's little Chrissy doing here?"

"He's my assistant."

George sneered. "How adorable."

It was funny to hear grandfather say this out loud. Technically, I was his assistant for the ball. My role in the investigation had never been discussed. It made me a little nervous as I found myself pondering the fates of the partners he'd had when he was in the police.

Grandfather returned to his original question. "So, where were you?"

"Oh, all right then." He whistled through his teeth before continuing. "I'll tell you exactly where I was. I was with Marmaduke Adelaide and he was with me. Ask him and he'll confirm it."

"You know full well we can't. He ran away last night and no one's found any trace of him. Besides, you didn't answer my question. Where exactly were you?" Grandfather had perfected a sharp yet focussed tone of voice and I could tell he was happy to fall back into his old role.

"We were out on the terrace, getting some air."

"Did you see my father?" I asked, as this was still the factor I was most concerned about.

A look of confusion crossed my cousin's face. "No, I didn't. Perhaps he's the one you should be talking to."

The old detective would not be dissuaded from his mission. "Tell me about your mother."

George smiled. "Well, she wasn't on the terrace. She was busy drinking herself to death." A sad, cold laugh came out of him. It made me wonder how he could be so cruel and casual at such a moment.

"That's not what I meant and you know it." Grandfather was losing his patience. "Can you think of any reason why someone wanted her dead?"

"Hmmm... money, I imagine. But surely it wasn't just her they were trying to get rid of. And that's another reason I couldn't have had anything to do with the murder. The whole Cranley line would be extinct if Mother hadn't been our canary down the mine."

"Except you." A childlike joy danced across my grandfather's face right then.

"I'm sorry?"

I'd like to have stood up and given my grandfather the round of applause he deserved. Instead, I stayed silent and waited for him to tear George's argument to pieces.

"You spilt your drink and went to get another before your mother collapsed. You made quite the fuss about it in fact, as though you wanted everyone to see exactly how you ended up without any champagne."

George pulled a pair of glasses on to get a better perspective on the old man who was putting him through the mill. They had thick lenses which made him look rather a swot. It was no surprise, therefore, that I'd never seen him wear them before.

"So let me get this clear. You're suggesting I attempted to kill our whole family so that I would be the heir to Cranley Hall?" He came to a stop and did a careful impersonation of someone deep in thought. "Wouldn't it be rather obvious that I was behind the poisoning if I was the only one to survive?"

"I'm sure you'd have come up with some clever explanation, but the plan didn't work, so we'll never know." Grandfather gave an absentminded shrug of his shoulders and looked down at his hands. "Is that why you invited young Adelaide to the ball? To provide you with an alibi? Only he got panicked and ran off, and now you're in a spot of bother of your own."

Our grandfather had gone from defending George's innocence to laying the case out for his guilt and it was very difficult to know which he believed the more likely scenario.

My cousin could see that his unflustered response was not having its desired effect, so he tried a different tack. "Really? I'm your eldest grandson; I would hope you could think better of me than that."

"It's not personal. I'm just doing my job. And if you look at it from my position, it is rather suspicious. We know you didn't get on with your mother and that you run up debts everywhere you go. I hear it won't be long before the bailiffs come calling. It would hardly be a surprise if you resorted to drastic measures in order to climb out of the hole you've found yourself in."

His voice broke as he appealed to our sympathy. "But we're family. Even if you think I'm guilty, doesn't some part of you want to protect me?"

The Most Honourable Marquess of Edgington (to give my grandfather his full title) answered straight back. "I don't know if you're guilty, but I do know you're a fool. You've jumped into bed with the wrong people and I'm not talking about Margaret Hillington-Smythe. If you owe Horatio Adelaide money, there's not much I can do for you. Of course, if you don't tell me the truth, there's nothing I can do for you at all."

The mere mention of Marmalade's father was enough to strike fear into my cousin. Though there were countless rumours at school about where Mr Adelaide got his money I had no idea which of them were true.

Perhaps afraid of what the old man might turn up next, George swung his legs out of bed and pulled his white dinner jacket on. "You don't know anything about me."

I've no idea why I tend to feel sympathy for the wrong people, but for all his faults, I'd always liked my eldest cousin and couldn't stand seeing him reduced to such a state.

"Listen to Grandfather, George," I attempted. "He's good with this sort of thing."

His startled eyes fixed upon me. "Don't get involved in matters which you haven't the first clue about, Chrissy. If you know what's good for you, you'll stay out of this whole sordid business."

He was fully dressed by now and halfway to the door. I thought that the interview was over but Grandfather shot to his feet to block our suspect's path. "You may not see it, George, but I'm trying to help you." His words were one long plea. "I could be the difference between you living a long, happy life on the estate you deserve to inherit and swinging from the neck at Pentonville Prison. So what's it to be?"

George's only response was a disgruntled snarl as he stepped around the old policeman and out of the room.

CHAPTER SIXTEEN

"He was lying," I said once we were alone.

Grandfather was still staring at the door, but there was no chance George was coming back.

"They all lie, it's what people do. What I don't know is exactly what he was lying about."

Not for the first time, I felt like everyone in Cranley knew more of what was going on than I did. "Grandfather, how exactly did the Adelaides become so rich?"

He looked around the bedroom then. It was white and nondescript, just like ten other guest rooms in Cranley. With this inspection complete, he turned to me and said, "Come along, Christopher, there's something I need to confirm. I'll tell you all about Horatio Adelaide on the way."

Not feeling I had much say in the decision, I got up to accompany him and he started his tale. "When I first knew Marmaduke's father, he was a lackey for the Foley gang. Back then, the Foleys were one of London's most vicious crime families and Horatio did whatever he could for them. I arrested him myself a number of times, but he'd always find a way to wriggle free. He's that kind of person, an opportunist who lands on his feet. But a few years later, when the Foleys were eliminated by their rivals, Horatio Adelaide was in the right place to inherit their empire."

We'd made it back downstairs and turned towards the ballroom.

"So he's a criminal?" I prompted.

Grandfather's moustache wriggled a little before he replied. "Yes and no. You see, there were three things which Horatio wanted. He wanted to stay alive – so he knew it wasn't a good idea to remain in the business which had got the Foleys killed. He wanted to maintain his newly found wealth – easier said than done in that world – and, perhaps more than anything, he craved respectability. He had no interest in being Harry Adelaide of Hackney so he changed his name, changed his business and cut ties with some of the more colourful characters he'd previously worked with."

My Grandfather often spoke as though the message of what he

was saying was incredibly simple. Maybe I was a dunce, but I couldn't always grasp it.

"So… he's not a criminal?"

That drew a laugh from the old boy. "Just listen and I'll get there. Nothing Adelaide has ever been involved in is strictly legitimate, but he runs a fine line between legal and otherwise. He made his money in black market goods and counterfeiting but soon moved on to bigger things. He had a network already in place and simply changed the merchandise. With wealth came the opportunity to make a name for himself – or rather buy one. He purchased an estate in Hampshire, became the Baron of somewhere or other and sent his children to good schools.

"But, most importantly, this success led to more opportunities. He had plenty of money at a time when a lot of old English families were running out. So he'd give them loans at exorbitant rates and, when they couldn't pay him back, he'd take their houses instead."

"What does he want with a load of crumbling piles?" I asked, not fully comprehending the point at hand once more.

"He doesn't care about the houses, he wants to sell the land on for a profit."

I'd been doing a very simple jigsaw in my head and the pieces finally fitted together. "So you think that George has borrowed money from Horatio Adelaide and, if he doesn't pay it back, they'll repossess the Trevelyan estate?"

"There you go, I knew you were smarter than everyone says." It was hard not to take this as an insult.

"So does that make it more or less likely that George is the one who put poison in the champagne? And if it wasn't him, what was he really doing before the toast?"

He came to a stop outside the petit salon. "Christopher, you have just succinctly summed up the two doubts I am currently most eager to resolve. You are shaping up to be a most capable assistant."

This compensated a touch for his previous comment, and a grin stretched out across my lips.

"Now, let's forget about George for the time being and focus on what happened here last night."

I clicked my heels together and saluted. "Yes, sir."

He looked at me like I was missing part of my brain, so I put my hand down.

"Fellowes says that he heard a tapping at the window, which is impossible of course because we're high above the level of the gardens. As I generally trust the man, let's see what we can find outside."

The salon was occupied by Uncle Maitland's family. His wife Winifred and their children Francis and Eleanor were lucky enough to have had a free run at the breakfast table and were clearly enjoying the cakes I had ordered.

"Good morning, all." Grandfather shot an absentminded glance in their direction, as we walked past them and out through the French windows.

We descended the steps down to the Italian gardens with their peaceful fountains and neatly laid-out flowerbeds. The air was warm and there were irises and violas flowering wherever I looked. It was the perfect day to investigate a murder, if one had to do such a thing.

In the distance, I could see my uncle bounding towards us on his morning walk. He waved and shouted, but was too far away for us to hear what he said. We went to take a look at the ground beneath the drinks room window. Grandfather stopped still and became rather mysterious for a moment.

"What do you think of that?" he asked, pointing at a small, smooth stone which matched the gravel path that circled the house.

"I think it's a stone."

"Oh, come along, Christopher, you can do better than that. What do you make of the fact that such a stone is some five yards away from the path where it normally resides, bearing in mind that a team of gardeners has worked tirelessly to ensure that not a leaf was out of place in preparation for last night's celebration?" This was a very long sentence, but I managed to follow it.

I looked at the stone, then at the path and then at the window and felt quite proud of myself. "Someone took a stone from the path and threw it at the window to get Fellowes's attention."

"Bravo." He did not inject much enthusiasm into this response and I had to wonder whether he regretted not choosing Big Francis or Eleanor to be his assistant after all.

"Maybe whoever threw it was working with the killer and knew that Fellowes would leave the champagne unattended."

"Maybe." He sounded even less convinced now, so I decided to stop offering any more theories of my own. "But if you're right, and we're looking for two culprits rather than one, it will make solving Belinda's murder a great deal more complicated."

"Can't we dust the stone for fingerprints and find out who threw it."

He crouched down to look at it more closely. "Well, we could, but I don't think that will be necessary."

"Why not?"

"Well, for one thing, it was a white tie ball and most of our guests were wearing gloves. But, even more significantly, I believe I know who is responsible."

He'd really impressed me this time and my voice rocketed towards the clouds. "Just by looking?"

He answered with a furrowed brow and a shake of the head. "No, Christopher. I may be an experienced detective, but I can't see invisible fingerprints."

"So how do you know who-?"

He didn't wait for me to finish. "Think about what Fellowes told us. He went outside and there was no one there, yet he was gone for at least five minutes." He sounded quite amazed by my ability to ignore important evidence. "I felt sure you'd notice that."

"You mean he met someone down here and it wasn't one of the gardeners?"

"Correct."

"But it *was* one of our suspects."

"That's right."

I did some working out in my head. That didn't get me far, so I tried it out loud instead. "Uncle Maitland and my father can't stand Fellowes. Marmalade and George were supposedly together on the terrace. Great-Aunt Clementine was asleep upstairs... which only leaves Cora."

Standing back up again, he twirled one end of his moustache and regarded me appraisingly. "Well, your reasoning is pretty shoddy, but, you got to the right outcome. Unless of course-"

I was looking forward to discovering his theory, and perhaps getting a little more praise for, in my opinion, my most commendable detective work, when Maitland caught up with us. His face was puffed up from the no doubt arduous stroll he'd undertaken. He looked like a tomato that had been left in the sun for too long. I couldn't imagine how he'd cope with the walk back upstairs.

"Father, I need to talk to you." He looked deadbeat and sounded paranoid. I could only assume that he had been kept up half the night by Inspector Blunt. He was dressed, as always, in his tweed hunting jacket, though, to paraphrase my mother, Maitland was a terrible marksman and couldn't hit a horse with a hammer from half a yard away.

"Can't it wait, my boy? We're really very busy."

My uncle became rather miffed and eyed me angrily. "No, it cannot. You've got all the time in the world for this little moneygrubber, but none for your own son. Do you know what I suffered through with that obnoxious policeman last night?"

Grandfather had picked up the stone with his sleeve, so as not to get fingerprints on it, before slipping it into his pocket. "Well, yes. I can imagine."

"This is a nightmare for me. Imagine how shocked people will be when they find out that Maitland Cranley, the son of Lord Edgington, is a suspect in the murder of his own sister!"

His father was unmoved. "Not nearly so shocked as when they find out that Lord Edgington is a suspect in the murder of his own daughter."

Getting angrier by the word, Maitland paced up and down on a small patch of path but came no closer. "Oh yes, brush me off with your witty observations. That's typical of you, Father. You're too clever for your own good." He stretched his arms out in an attempt to make himself more noticeable. "But here I am, your flesh and blood, asking you for help and you won't lift a finger."

Grandfather sighed and stepped out of the flowerbed. "I'm sorry, Maitland. You're absolutely right. I don't make enough time for you and I should." He sounded quite sincere. "Tell me what the matter is and I will do whatever I can to help."

The tubby hunter wasn't expecting this and didn't appear to know what to say next. "Oh… Well, I have to concede that is awfully good of you and I accept your apology." He whistled a falling note as he tried to process this development.

"If it makes you feel any better, dear boy, I never imagined for one second that you would have killed Belinda. The two of you were in cahoots from the day you were born. If you were planning to kill anyone, it would surely have been me."

The two men laughed then, and it appeared as though Maitland had forgotten what he'd come to say. "Thank you, Daddy. I really mean it."

"Is there anything else you'd like to get off your chest?" Grandfather's eyebrows climbed higher up his forehead.

"Well, there was one thing and I didn't think much of it at first but it's been niggling in my mind all morning and I realised I should probably say something. You see, the reason I wasn't there just before the toast last night was because…" He paused and looked around, and I felt sure he was about to reveal some vital fact of the case. "… because I'd gone to use the commode. But, on my way back, I saw something rather puzzling."

Grandfather did not display any of his usual impatience, but listened intently to what his son had to say. "Do go on."

Maitland looked around once more. "Well, you see, as I was walking along the corridor, I spotted Fellowes leaving the petit salon, and-"

His sentence was interrupted by a resolute BANG! Well, it wasn't quite a bang actually, it was more of a THWACK! Or perhaps a TWANG! Yes, let's stick with that.

TWANG! went the noise, and Maitland had just enough time to glance down at the crossbow bolt that had pierced his chest before he collapsed to the ground with a shriek.

CHAPTER SEVENTEEN

It was Grandfather's instinct to grab his son and pull him back towards the cover of the house. Whoever had shot my uncle must have been firing from one of the upstairs windows and wouldn't be able to hit us from there. Maitland was too heavy for his ageing father to shift, though, so I had to help. Luckily, the ancient crossbows we have at Cranley aren't the quickest weapons to reload and no more shots were fired.

I got the two men to safety, then ran back up the steps, shouting, "The armoury!" as Grandfather attended to Uncle Maitland. When I got to the top, my cousins Francis and Eleanor were both staring down, trying to work out what had happened to their father. Inside, my aunt Winifred evidently didn't think anything of the rumpus and was tucking in to a currant bun with her feet up.

I ran through the petit salon to the corridor, just in time to see Cora Villiers nip into the smoking room. By the time I got to her, she was sitting reading a book beside the fireplace, with her grandmother Clementine snoring away nearby.

"What happened?" She asked with a look of pure innocence on her face. "I heard a scream. Who was it?"

There was no time to deal with her. I pressed on along the corridor and grabbed a silver candlestick, from the bureau in front of the armoury, before seizing the door handle. I'm fully conscious of the fact that tableware can't really compete with an arsenal of swords, knives and guns but, unsure what else to do, I said a little prayer and opened the door.

The armoury was empty.

"Oh, thank goodness for that!" I said out loud. I felt like I might pass out from all that stress (and running). In fact my lungs were carrying out a full rebellion on the rest of my body.

Once I'd recovered my breath enough to stand and walk again, I searched the room for evidence. There were several wooden bolts strewn about the place and a space on the wall where the weapon had been taken from. I noticed that there was a matching crossbow pinned to the opposite wall which looked as though someone had tried to remove it. It was at a slight angle and it made me wonder whether our killer was short and had failed in his task before spotting the other crossbow. Where the murder weapon had ended up, of course, was anyone's guess.

On the carpet underneath the empty bracket, I noticed traces of tobacco ash. I gave it a sniff and decided it was almost certainly from a cigar as it smelt just like the ones my father smoked. This could only mean that we were looking for a short, cigar-smoking murderer. I had just seen someone who fitted that description running from the scene of the crime and, as far as I was concerned, the case was closed.

The window was also closed, but I assumed the police would be along soon to dust for fingerprints. It's a shame that fingerprints are so hard to spot. It would make detective work a darned sight easier if they stuck out like poppies in a meadow.

I went back out to the hall where a crowd had formed. The last lingering guests had come to discover what the commotion was about and I noticed that several of our suspects were close at hand. In fact, assuming he wasn't hiding in one of the adjacent rooms, it was really only Marmalade we could now rule out for certain.

"They say Maitland's been shot," George informed the crowd, as I caught sight of my father at the end of the hall. "What did you find in there, Chrissy?" He was either a very good actor or he really didn't know what had happened.

I studied him for a moment before answering. "Nothing."

"Nothing?" my mother replied, a note of panic in her voice.

"Well, no one."

"And what about Maitland?" as she said this, her tears came. "Is he...?"

In my hurry to catch the killer, I hadn't considered what state my uncle was in. I hadn't even thought to telephone for a doctor, though I was sure one of his children would have seen to that by now. I peered back along the hall, just as my grandfather emerged from the petit salon. His grey morning coat was covered in rusty red stains and his face told us all we needed to know.

My mother ran to him, with great sobs already escaping her slender lips. She buried her head in her father's chest and he wrapped his arms around her. Nobody said a word as we stood watching the tragic scene.

I had never witnessed my grandfather crying before; the sight made me want to lie down on the floor and never get up again. Lord Edgington was a legend, a great detective and a great man. To see that titan reduced to tears was almost paradoxical in my mind and it took my brother Albert putting his arm around my shoulder to steady my nerves.

Two murders. Two dead Cranleys in twenty-four hours and, just as my grandfather had predicted, there was no reason to assume the killer would stop there. His first attempt at murdering my family had failed, and now it looked as though he was keen to knock us off one by one instead.

Through an open window in the billiard room, we could hear the distant cry of my Aunt Winifred as the reality of her widowhood sank in. Right at that moment, Cora tiptoed out of the smoking room to witness the destruction for herself.

My anger burst out from within me. "She did this," I screamed, marching towards her. "I saw her running away from the armoury just after the shot was fired."

Looking unflustered by the accusation, she replied in her usual nonchalant tone. "What a ridiculous insinuation. The boy's a fool."

"So where were you coming from when I saw you?"

My father had arrived and stepped between the two of us to calm us both down. "There's no need for raised voices," he told me, as if this was the real danger we were facing. "Cora, answer Christopher's question."

All eyes fell on my second cousin. "I…" Peering back into the room where she'd taken shelter, she searched for a convincing answer. "I went to get my grandmother some tea." She flicked her short fringe from her face with one darting hand. "Isn't that right, Grandmother?"

Great-Aunt Clementine had presumably been woken by the argument, or perhaps just the mention of refreshments. She sat upright in the armchair she was cradled within and said, "Tea, oh yes, lovely," before reaching for the heavy pot on the table beside her and immediately splashing the amber liquid all over the tray, her black lace gloves and a large part of her dress, so that I had to run over to help her. Rather impressively, she'd managed to miss the cup entirely, and I noticed that the tea was already cold.

My Grandfather arrived then and addressed us in a slow, careful manner. "As you have heard, my son is dead." The words were hard for him to muster and he had to pause to process this fact before continuing. "The police have been called and Inspector Blunt is on his way."

He scanned the faces of everyone there. It was hard to say whether he was searching for comfort in their flabbergasted expressions or looking for signs of guilt. "I have already lost two of my children. The last thing I want is for anyone else to get hurt. So, as soon as the police have interviewed you, I believe it would be best for you to return to your homes."

"I didn't do anything." Cora was finally feeling the pressure of suspicion. "I swear, that I had nothing to do with these terrible crimes. You know me, I wouldn't..."

She never finished that sentence as she could tell from the cold, silent response she received that we would not let her off so lightly. The Villiers and the Cranleys were not close, had not been close for several decades in fact and, given the chance to get rid of us, they would be at the front of the queue.

Possessing a far more charitable soul than the rest of us, my grandfather pulled away from his daughter to comfort Cora and lead her down the hall to wait for the police.

CHAPTER EIGHTEEN

My uncle's death had a curious effect on Cranley Hall. It's not that he was much more popular than my aunt. He was a dull, pernickety man with little of his father's charm but… well, to paraphrase Oscar Wilde, 'To lose one Cranley may be regarded as a misfortune; to lose two looks like a concerted plan of elimination.'

Whereas, the night before, there was a buzz to the house, as curious guests stayed on scene to discover any lurid gossip, those who remained after Maitland's demise were suddenly drained of energy.

My grandfather seemed to be regressing to his formerly distant self. Though he attended to the necessities when the police arrived, he had no vim about him and suddenly looked his age. They say that losing a child is the hardest thing for a parent to contend with and Lord Edgington had gone one step further.

My parents both looked shell shocked, so my brother took them back to their suite and I stayed behind to help Grandfather. When the police arrived, Inspector Blunt had lost some of his vitriol from the previous evening. He spoke to us in front of my uncle's body, which was now covered over with a heavy blanket, as if to stop him from floating away.

"And there are witnesses to attest to your presence with the deceased before he was shot?"

My grandfather gave only the faintest monosyllabic answers. "Yes."

This was something I could help with at last. "Grandfather and I have been together for most of the morning."

The crumpled little man was almost hesitant. He must have decided that the suffering his former colleague was enduring trumped their longstanding rivalry.

"We'll keep you informed if we discover anything." He addressed his comment to the stony path and was yet to look either of us in the eye.

Shrugging his shoulders like he was terribly cold, Blunt wandered inside to interview the staff. My grandfather showed no sign of knowing what to do next. He remained rooted to the spot for several minutes before drifting back towards the house and up the steps. I was afraid to ask what his plan was, but felt myself magnetically pulled along behind him.

I followed him all the way to his suite of rooms, where he took up his old spot in the armchair beside the window. I could see his transformation reversing before my eyes. When he sat back in that chair, his stature reduced down and I watched his confidence fade. He was folding himself away for easy storage and, if I hadn't done something about it, he might have given up altogether.

"Please don't do this, Grandfather," I pleaded with him. "You can't stop now. Blunt isn't going to work out what's going on here, but you will."

His gaze possessed that singularly distant quality that I'd seen in him every time my family had visited since I was six. He looked off across the grounds, over the lake and out towards the woods.

When his reply came, he sounded only vaguely aware that there was anyone around to hear him. "He might get lucky. Maybe there'll be another murder and it will make it easier to catch the killer."

My voice was broken through with tears and I shouted at the great Lord Edgington for the very first time. "That's our family you're talking about! What if this lunatic goes after my mother next?"

At school we were taught from a young age that such open displays of emotion are a sign of weakness and only women and feeble men would ever allow themselves such hysteria. I don't like my school and think this is a stupid attitude to have, so I felt no great shame.

With my face all red and my nose running, I moved closer to him. "There are hardly any suspects and you know them all well. This should be easy for you."

He shook his head and looked straight through me, but said nothing. It made me want to storm about the place breaking old vases and pulling one of his precious Turners from the wall.

"Don't you have some sort of oath to seek out the truth? Why did you join the police in the first place if you won't search for your own children's killer?" Gripping hold of the arms of his chair, with my face right next to his, I was screaming with absolute rage.

For a few moments, the only sound was the rattling of plates on the dresser as my words rebounded about the room. I took another step closer, and he looked at me at last.

"I joined the police because I never wanted any of this." He looked around the room at his fine possessions, then cast his gaze off through the window. "It was never supposed to be mine in the first place. My brother was set to inherit Cranley. He'd been prepared for it from birth. Like your cousin George, I was wild and carefree back then and my parents despaired of me. I told them I didn't want to live the way they did. I wanted a life of my own."

I would have asked more about this time in his life but, in that same weary manner, he had already continued with his story.

"I joined the police because I thought I could make a difference, instead of simply living off this estate and the people who work for us. You have to understand that the last century was a time of grand ideas. I read Voltaire and Engels and saw the world through a very different lens from that of my family. As a young man, I couldn't bear the idea of getting rich from another man's labour or having servants wait on me. In the police, I was nobody and I liked it that way. I rose through the ranks, not because of who my father was or my family's wealth, but because I was good at the job."

I found myself caught up in his story and, when he came to an abrupt halt, I was hungry to know more. "So, what changed?"

He shook his head and I had to assume I'd failed to understand the point of his tale. "My fool of a brother was killed in the Transvaal Rebellion. He'd been in the army for years, but always safely away from the action until Westminster decided that a future lord should have a company of men. He got himself and half of those under him slaughtered, left poor old Clementine without a husband and their sole daughter fatherless. In time, my parents passed Cranley on to me."

His words dried up once more and I could tell that, despite his criticism, he still mourned his older brother. "My parents demanded I leave the police but I wouldn't give in. If you're ever in such a position, you must know that you don't always have to do what is expected of you. I'm a lord and a copper. I worked my way up to become a superintendent of the Metropolitan Police, but I also took on the duties required of me here.

"My parents were wrong to think that I couldn't do both and I was wrong to think that being the Marquess of Edgington was an indignity. I have tried to run this house and protect the wards of our estate with compassion. And I pray, with every fibre of my being, that whoever finally succeeds me will do the same."

He had become more confident as his speech went on, but his voice still sounded as though it could give way at any moment. I wanted to shout and scream at him to make him see sense. I wanted to pull him up by the lapels and make him listen to me but I knew it would do no good.

So instead, I leaned down to his level and spoke in the softest tone I possessed. "You said it yourself; you're a copper; present tense. You never stopped, and I'm not going to let you rot away in that ugly old chair. You've got a job to do and a killer to catch."

He looked down at the armchair with its fraying fabric and lumpy seat. "I suppose it might have seen its best days." He spoke as if this was the most convincing part of my argument.

I smiled. "But you haven't, so stand back up and let's get to work."

CHAPTER NINETEEN

Grandfather got changed into another of his grey morning suits and we set off towards the armoury. He wanted to have a professional inspection of the room – after my entirely amateurish poke around – but Alice accosted us in the hall.

"I'm so sorry to disturb you, Lord Edgington," she said, all flustered. "I wouldn't want to bother you at a time like this, only-"

"Spit it out, girl." Some of his quick anger had returned to him, but he saw how upset she was and lowered his voice. "Tell me what the problem is."

Alice looked at me then and, from the expression she wore, I was worried that I'd been a bit too obvious with my longing looks at her at the ball. I was sure she was about to denounce me to her employer as a blackguard and a bounder.

"It's Mr Fellowes, Milord. There's something wrong with him. He's been in bed half the morning. He barely had the strength to lay out the dining room for breakfast and Cook's made him lie down. He says it's nothing, but I really think we should send for a doctor. He looks awfully sick."

I noticed that she smoothed out the stronger notes of her Irish accent, and I could tell how nervous she was. Even in an unconventional house like Cranley, it wasn't typical for a maid to address a lord. With Fellowes incapacitated, the usual order of things was at risk of falling apart.

Grandfather's moustache curled in. "Take me to his room, this instant."

My lovely Alice turned on the spot and scuttled away down the corridor, like a mouse escaping from an elderly cat. Grandfather had found his strength of will once more, but could not maintain the pace and she soon had to slow down. She gave me a shy smile and, despite the two corpses and our ailing butler, I couldn't help feeling a little cheered that I was not in her bad books after all.

As we cut back through the hall, I saw no sign of Blunt, but his minions were hard at work. There were even more officers there than the night before. In every room we passed, they were picking through drawers and taking books from their shelves, in search of some elusive piece of evidence.

We took the servants' stairs to the hidden away corner of the house where Fellowes and the other household staff had their rooms. It was a dark, gloomy spot, little more than a basement really with one small window permitting a meagre allowance of light to shine through. Alice knocked on the door at the end of the corridor and entered.

"No!" Fellowes instantly wailed. "What did you bring him down here for?"

With no windows open and the curtains drawn, the room smelled like death itself. Cook was sitting at the bedside with a bowl of cold water and a flannel. Her patient was writhing in agony even as we entered.

"I've told him we need a doctor," the gaunt-cheeked chef explained. "He won't listen to me though so I sent Alice to fetch you. I hope it's not an imposition, Milord."

"Never mind that now." My Grandfather went straight over to his retainer, unafraid of what terrible infectious disease might be ripping through him. "Tell me exactly how you're feeling."

Fellowes was as white as a cloud and just as clammy. The sweat was dripping off him as he clutched his bedclothes between two clenched fists. "It's my stomach. It feels like I've been swallowing glass in my sleep."

"When did it come on?" I wasn't sure what medical knowledge my grandfather possessed but his brusque and aggressive bedside manner was still a lot milder than that of the terrifying matron at school.

Fellowes swallowed before answering and Cook took this as a sign that more fluids were needed. She plied him with some steaming-hot elixir from a chipped china mug.

"In the night, I suppose." He moaned out again. "Didn't think too much of it until this morning when I could hardly stand."

Grandfather stooped over the sick butler and produced a small, electric torch from his pocket to examine his pupils, before moving on to check his pulse. "Give me your hand." When Fellowes was slow to respond, he barked at him once more. "Come along, man. Quickly."

With great effort, Fellowes raised his right hand a few inches off the bed and Grandfather seized it. He held the flaccid wrist in silence for a few moments before delivering judgement. "Well, I imagine you've got a fair bit of vomiting to get through. The good news is that, if it was going to kill you, it would have done so by now."

He smiled then, as though this made everything better. "I'll call my doctor, but, from the look of things, you'll recover before long."

"Doesn't feel that way now," Fellowes peered around the room for a moment before clutching his stomach and closing his eyes.

"One last question," Grandfather said. "How long ago did you come down here?"

Fellowes looked rather nervous then. He studied the old man's face and I thought he was trying to work out how much trouble he would get into by telling the truth. "Less than an hour. I'm sorry I can't attend to my duties, Sir, but I'm sure that Halfpenny can cover for me and Todd at a push."

My grandfather looked pensive for a moment before replying. "You needn't worry about that, old friend. We'll manage without you for a couple of days."

It was quite touching to see the affection which the two men had for one another and I wondered yet again about the history they shared, which I was not privy to.

"Alice, fetch some bicarbonate and keep the infusions coming. Ginger tea, garlic juice, anything that you think will ease his pain." He nodded, satisfied with his plan, then rose to leave. "Come along, Christopher."

I was beginning to see that my main task as Lord Edgington's assistant was to fulfil the role Delilah usually occupied. As his lazy old golden retriever spent most of her time asleep by the hearth in the kitchen, it was my job to scamp along happily after Grandfather.

"Very interesting, don't you think?" he asked once we'd left the staff quarters behind.

"Yes, very interesting," I agreed, though I hadn't a clue what he was referring to.

"Perhaps it was just an accident of course, or he helped himself to a few more cakes last night than he should have. But if the killer wanted Fellowes out of the picture, why not use the cyanide again?"

I hadn't considered until this moment that our butler had been poisoned. "Well…" I began, hoping that something clever might come to me. "Perhaps he ran out. Perhaps the fiend used all his cyanide up last night and there was none left for anyone else."

Ducking into the empty smoking room, he froze on the spot. His face was clouded over with a fog of questions. It was something of a thrill to see his mind running with ideas.

"I suppose it's possible, but that seems rather foolish, considering…" He never finished that sentence as, just then, a new idea occurred to him. "More importantly, of course, we have to find out what it was that Fellowes saw that would have made him a threat to the killer."

He took a seat near the unlit fire, where Cora had sat the night before. The smoking room still smelt like the inside of a pipe as no one had cleared the ashtrays. The vases of our flower arrangements were almost as pungent and I couldn't help but feel proud of the colour they still provided to the musty old room.

Salacious ideas from boy's own adventure magazines filled my head. "You said yourself that Fellowes was hiding something. He went out of the room after the champagne was opened for far longer than made any sense. How do we know he wasn't working with the killer and the blighter double-crossed him?"

My grandfather waved the idea away with one hand. "Don't be ridiculous, Christopher. If you can't make a sensible suggestion, don't say anything at all."

This was the kind of thing my father always said to me. I didn't like it from him and I couldn't stand it from Grandfather either.

"Well, you're supposed to be the master detective!" I raised my voice to quite a level. "Why didn't you grill Fellowes a little harder yesterday? Come to think of it, why were you so kind to Cora this morning? And George for that matter?"

His steely eyes shot towards me then and I was petrified. For a softly spoken, modern-thinking man, he had an awful lot of anger boiling beneath the surface and I was worried he would shoot it straight at me.

Instead, he took a deep breath and replied at half his usual volume. "You don't catch flies with vinegar, dear boy. And, besides, some questions don't need asking. Some things are clear and it's better not to upset the applecart if it can be avoided."

I found myself shouting a line back to him that my English literature master had scrawled across the last essay I'd submitted.

110

"'You're mixing your metaphors!'" It wasn't the strongest of ripostes. "Is that a crime?"

"No, but failing to investigate a suspect because you can't imagine them being involved in a murder is tantamount to one." I don't know why I was getting so angry. Perhaps it was because we'd been investigating all morning and I'd only eaten one measly cream horn.

He let out a sigh and, remaining calm, asked for my opinion. "Go on then, tell me what you think happened and how Fellowes could have been part of this terrible plot you're so convinced of."

I was a little shocked to be honest as I didn't have a clear idea of what I wanted to say.

"Well, it's obvious, isn't it?" I waited to see whether he would explain what was obvious so that I didn't have to. "The killer can't be anyone in the immediate family. It would have looked very odd if he was the only one not drinking just before we all died. Even George spilling his champagne couldn't have covered his guilt."

"So that reduces our suspect list nicely." Grandfather made it sound like I was really onto something.

"Exactly. It means we're only left with Fellowes, Clementine, Marmaduke and Cora."

He slumped down in a chair then and I could tell he was thinking over the enigma that lay before us. "Go on, who's your money on?"

Everything had been happening so quickly that I'd lost track of the possibilities. I took a moment to remind myself why I was angry.

"It has to be Cora."

"I see," he replied, with all the calm in the world. "Why?"

"For the reasons you laid out already. Her grandfather was supposed to inherit Cranley and, as there was no male heir, you took his place. All of this should have gone to her father and, eventually, she would have been a very wealthy woman. She was nowhere to be seen when the champagne was being served and very much in the vicinity of the armoury when Maitland was murdered. I hardly think Clementine can offer her a reliable alibi and you can't deny that Cora completely failed to explain any of that when I asked her."

He rolled his shoulders and raised his chin before responding. "I can't, but I don't have to. Cora has other reasons for keeping her counsel and we'll interview her in good time."

There was no point in pursuing my theory with him if he wasn't going to listen. I clearly hadn't learnt my lesson though, as I instantly offered up another suspect.

"Fine, then if it wasn't her, it must have been Marmaduke Adelaide."

He actually laughed at me then. He tipped his head back and had a good chortle at my expense. "Why on Earth do you say that?"

"Because the boy's a savage, he has criminal connections, he hates me and I doubt that you're his father's favourite person after you arrested him so many times. Add all that to the disappearing trick that Marmalade performed last night and it spells guilty."

I thought that the terrier of Scotland Yard might at least be interested in this theory, but he barely even considered it.

"Why do you call him Marmalade?"

I sat down in the chair in front of him and leaned forward to reply. "Well, his name is Marmaduke Adelaide and he's got ginger hair."

"A little obvious, though, isn't it? Surely you could have come up with something more creative."

Not knowing how to respond to this, as I'd always thought it a particularly witty piece of word play, I went on the offensive once more. "You're totally missing the point. Marmaduke physically assaulted me two days ago. There's no blacker soul than his and I think he's the killer."

He raised one eyebrow. "Along with Fellowes?"

That stumped me again. "No... Or actually, yes." New ideas were forming by the moment and I decided to see where they would take me. "Last night, Adelaide threw the stone at the drinks room window to give Fellowes the sign to make himself scarce, then ran upstairs to poison the champagne. He wasn't in the house today when Uncle Maitland was killed, so someone else must have been involved and Fellowes is the only person I know here with a shady past that you make a point of never talking about."

I realised there was a piece of the puzzle that I'd left out and raced to correct myself. "And George... Well, George gave the boy an alibi because he's in debt to Marmaduke's dad." I clicked my fingers with glee, feeling really rather proud of myself. All loose ends tied up; case closed once more!

He did something then that I really wasn't expecting. Tossing the long flanks of his coat from his lap, he started to clap. "Bravo, my boy. I take it all back, you are the pinnacle of creativity. I don't know if we'll make a detective out of you, but you've certainly got a future writing for theatre. Bernard Shaw himself would struggle to come up with quite such an engaging plot."

My initial excitement at his enthusiasm soon wore away. "So you don't think I'm close to the truth then?"

He leaned forward to confide in me. "I'm not saying it's impossible, Chrissy, but I'm afraid it is rather unlikely."

I had lost my combative edge and wanted to understand what his superior mind had gleaned. "Why?"

He did not hesitate to tear my idea from its roots. "Your whole argument is based on the concept of Marmaduke Adelaide's innate degeneracy. Such lazy misconceptions are the first resort of the frightened and ignorant. When a murder is committed, we like to imagine that some random, savage beast has come in off the streets to satiate his bloodlust. I can honestly tell you that, in all my years on the force, I heard of few such cases."

He paused and turned his head slightly, as if reappraising me. "It is a comfort to think that these dark incidents can be explained away so easily. In actuality, the evil we search for lies far closer to home. My parents' generation were obsessed with such ideas. Look back through the fantastical inventions of the last century – to Frankenstein, Dracula, Jekyll and Hyde. People long to understand the savagery they encounter and so they create monsters to hide the fact that it is ordinary humans we should be frightened of."

"But you don't know Marmaduke. He takes such pleasure in hurting the boys at school. He gave me this!" I pointed to the bruise around my eye that had now turned purple.

Grandfather smiled a little then. "I know, my boy. I do. But I think that is better explained by the fact that he is a sixteen-year-old boy, rather than there being any inherent wickedness within him."

Against my better judgement, I forced myself to ask, "So he's not guilty?"

"I see no reason to believe he would be."

"Then if it's not Marmaduke, who's the killer?"

He hesitated and I really thought he might have an answer for me.

"I can't say that yet, but I can tell you that you've been asking the wrong questions. You have to consider why Maitland was murdered. Why did the killer only poison the butler, not kill him? Where did Fellowes go when he left the champagne? And who knew what we'd be drinking last night?"

I obviously didn't have the answers to any of these questions, so I was rather relieved when Inspector Blunt blustered into the room to interrupt.

"I thought I'd extend the courtesy, gentlemen," he said, in quite the least courteous manner imaginable. "You might like to know that, as soon as Reginald Fellowes is capable of walking, we'll be arresting him for murder."

CHAPTER TWENTY

"This is preposterous." Grandfather's voice roared across at the grubby little man. "On what possible grounds have you arrested my butler?"

Blunt possessed a look of pure smugness. "He's a criminal. Got a record longer than my wife's nightie. Assault, battery, theft of every variety. It's hardly a stretch of the imagination to conclude that the convicted felon in our midst is involved in all these murders that have been going on."

"And what possible motive have you come up with for his crimes? The man's been with me for years." Grandfather stood up to confront the allegations.

A good foot shorter than his old enemy, Blunt drew himself up to his full height to answer. "You knew, didn't you?" He let out a vicious laugh. "You knew that Fellowes was a criminal and you didn't tell us."

My grandfather did not like the insinuation and glanced past the offending officer and out towards the hall. "People change."

In a rare moment of confidence, Blunt looked his former superintendent straight in the eye. "Well, you haven't."

"Careful what you say, Blunt, or I'll be on the telephone to your superiors faster than you can say *miscarriage of justice*." The threat was made more real by the fact there was a telephone in the room for him to point at.

The inspector wasn't scared and took a step closer. "Oh, I'm always careful what I say. You were a rotter back when you were in the force and you're no better now."

It was an odd sight to see a man of seventy-five facing off against a rival. Blunt himself couldn't have been far from his sixtieth year and, had it come to blows, my money would have been on Grandfather.

In the end, like any number of the brief confrontations I'd witnessed in Oakton Academy's yard, the confrontation resulted in little more than flared nostrils and a staring match that Blunt was only ever going to lose.

"I've got a man stationed downstairs until Fellowes recovers." He said by way of revenge. "If there's a trace of poison on his clothes from last night, we'll find it. We have all sorts of modern techniques an old codger like you wouldn't know anything about."

I think this insult was almost more upsetting to my grandfather than the idea of the wrong man being arrested. He was about to bite back, but held the words in at the last moment. Blunt tipped his hat to us and breezed from the room.

Once we were alone, Grandfather let out a frustrated cry. "Why do I let that supercilious prig get to me? It was the same when we worked together. He took every opportunity he could to undermine me." He hit his hand against the side of his head three times in fury. "Why did I threaten to call his superiors? I was playing up to every assumption he's ever had about me."

I thought it wise to bring him back to the topic at hand. "Perhaps there are more pressing matters, Grandfather?"

"Yes, of course." He stopped his nervous movement and put a hand on both my shoulders, as if he had some wise words to impart. "I expect that Cora will already have left, so seek out Todd and get him to prepare one of the cars. I'll make sure the doctor is coming to see Fellowes and meet you at the main entrance."

"Wait, why Cora? Why now?"

"All in good time, Chrissy."

Blunt's announcement had given my grandfather the impetus that he required. He was a tornado of pent up energy as he blew from the room. Once he had gone, I had to pause just to catch my breath.

I went to look for the chauffeur in the kitchen. He was nowhere in sight, but Delilah latched onto me, as I set off to my next port of call. I found Todd in his usual retreat, the barn where Grandfather kept his car collection. He was polishing the MG 14/28, which looked like it had never been driven. In fact, some of the cars in there were so new that the only journey they'd been on was from the manufacturer's factory to their new home. It was one link to the wider world which the old man had maintained. His car collection had grown substantially over the years of his seclusion, even if he'd never gone to visit them.

I launched my question at the under-worked chauffeur as soon as I was through the double doors. "I don't suppose you've seen Cora, have you?"

Todd didn't look up but continued with his careful attention to the front of the sports car's bonnet. "She left a little while ago. The police interviewed her first and then she took Clementine home so I didn't have to." His knowledge of the comings and goings at Cranley Hall were rivalled only by Fellowes's own. "Have you ever noticed how that old woman smells of pine cones all year round?"

"Yes, I have. I think it's rather sweet really. Like she got lost in a forest somewhere and had to spend the night."

Todd looked at me like I was a knife, fork and spoon short of a place setting. His quietly judgemental manner reminded me why I'd come.

"Grandfather says you're to get the car ready."

The elegant young chap could hardly believe what I was saying. "I'm taking Lord Edgington out?"

I frowned, no longer quite sure if this made sense. "Well, I think that's what he meant."

He looked down the barn at the small fortune in automobiles which Delilah was happily running between. I spotted a Lagonda, two Alfa Romeos, several Rolls and even a couple of American cars Grandfather had imported over.

"Which car does he want?"

"Oh," I was once more bamboozled by a truly simple question. "He didn't actually say. What about the…" I pictured some of the more stylish young detectives I'd read about in novels and considered which car they would choose. "Yes, I think the Aston Martin should do the trick."

It certainly did the trick for Todd, who jumped in the air like Chaplin in 'The Kid'. "Master Chrissy, you're a star!"

I don't know when it was that everyone decided I should be called Chrissy, but I still didn't like it. Of course, I was not about to tell Todd that. He had a suave worldliness about him which made me rather envious. I'd seen the way that Alice and even Cook looked at him and had my fingers crossed that I'd lose my puppy fat, – which my mother insisted was adorable – find a hairstyle that suited me, and turn into the leading-man type that women go wild for.

I should probably have crossed my fingers a little harder.

It was fun to see him run off between the two rows of automobiles, like my happily wagging companion. While several other cars were no doubt more expensive, the pale grey Aston Martin Cloverleaf was a thing of true beauty and, most importantly for Todd, had been built for speed.

Its unblemished interior sparkled. It was all leather, steel and chrome, with the very latest in modern gadgetry set into the dashboard. Our chauffeur didn't even need to crank the engine to get it started. He merely turned the ignition and it hummed into life, like a spell had been cast over it. Delilah bounded up into the passenger seat and barked for me to join them.

Clearly elated at the prospect of the journey before us, Todd eased the car out of the barn, with all the tenderness of a father encouraging his child's first steps.

"I reckon she could hit eighty miles an hour on a straight," he informed me, but I don't know anything about cars, or velocity for that matter, so I smiled and nodded. I climbed into the hollowed-out rear seat and Todd roared along the gravel lane to the main drive.

CHAPTER TWENTY-ONE

Grandfather was already waiting for us at the front of the house and a look of wonder crossed his face, which was only rivalled by his chauffeur's.

"That's more like it!" he said, practically running over to board the stunning vessel. "Good choice, Todd. Away we go."

Our driver turned to wink at me, and I didn't mind him taking the credit. I was slightly less happy that big, fluffy Delilah decided to jump on top of me in the back seat to spend the journey whipping me with her tail.

But, oh what joy it was to speed down those English lanes in the unexpected heat of early June! With the cover drawn back and the wind in our hair, we felt like the gods of Olympus taking flight from the Earth. It was enough to make me forget the terrible things we'd witnessed over the last twenty-four hours and trust once more that everything was right with the world. Sadly, there were rather a lot of flies about that day and the ones that didn't end up in my eyes, went straight down my throat. Delilah did not seem troubled by them and let out yelps of glee the whole way there.

Though protected by his driving goggles, Grandfather had lost his initial buzz of excitement and seemed perturbed by our situation once more. His visage was not the easiest to read. It was hard to tell whether he was reliving Maitland and Belinda's deaths, working through his hypotheses on the case, or preparing for the interview he was about to embark on.

"We'll go to Langford House first, Milord," Todd explained. "If Cora isn't there, we can always drive on to Holly Tree Cottage."

He was distracted for a moment before finding his reply. "Very good, Todd. I need to have a word with my sister-in-law anyway. Whether the old thing will make a jot of sense is another matter."

Langford House was one of the minor residences in the Cranley family's possession. It had been occupied throughout its history by spinsters and dowagers. When her husband died in the First Boer War, Clementine was shipped out of Cranley Hall to make her home there. I have no doubt it was once a grand building, but it had fallen into decline under her stewardship.

The façade of the grey stone property was patchy and crumbling. The garden, which my great-aunt had once kept immaculate, was now overgrown. There were leaves and fruit still rotting on the ground since last autumn and the whole place looked like it needed a good clean. Yet, there was something charming about the scene that made me miss my own family home. It suited the nice old lady who lived there and, no matter what anyone might think of her mental state, I could imagine enjoying the life she had.

There was a Crossley 19.6 parked beside the house and, racing ahead of us, Delilah soon found Cora taking tea with her grandmother in the wild back garden.

"Beautiful weather for ducks," Clementine called across to us as we made our way to a once-white table under the shade of a greengage tree.

My grandfather looked up at the blue sky above us with an exaggerated twist of his neck. "What on Earth are you talking about, Clemmie? The day couldn't be finer."

As if the sound needed time to travel over to her, Great-Aunt Clementine didn't reply for a moment and then, in a most indignant tone said, "And who says ducks can't enjoy a bit of sunshine?"

He offered up a mocking smile. "As much as I always love our conversations, my dear, we're mainly here to see your granddaughter."

Cora hadn't moved a muscle since we'd arrived. With her hands gripping the armrests, she looked as though she were bracing herself for a car crash. She still wore the long, narrow trousers and cream jacket she'd had on at the ball, but her normally smooth hair was unkempt.

"Perhaps you'd prefer to talk to us alone, eh, Cora?" Grandfather suggested and she pushed her boyish fringe from her eye before replying.

"No, Christopher can stay." She glanced across the garden, as if she had no interest in looking at my grandfather directly. When he didn't reply, she realised his implication and added, "Oh, you mean Grandmother? There's nothing I can't say in front of her."

Cora reached one slender hand across the table to the woman who had largely raised her. As her parents had died when Cora was still young, the two women had always been close. My cousin had only left the bucolic surrounds of Langford House for a place of her own a few years earlier, though this may have precipitated the small estate's decline.

Nestled in beneath a thick Welsh quilt, the old lady smiled affectionately at me just as Todd appeared from the conservatory with two more chairs. He nodded silently and returned to his far comfier seat back in the Aston Martin.

"If you've come all this way to accuse me of murder, then it was a wasted trip." Cora reached into the small, sequined purse on the table in front of her and extracted a cigarette and some matches. I took careful note of what was written on them, as, so often in detective novels, matchbooks provide a vital clue to the identity of the killer. I couldn't see how the fact she preferred Swan Vestas over Bryant and May's own brand particularly helped me though.

"And what makes you believe that we had entertained such a possibility?" Grandfather stroked the bristles on one side of his face as if considering his own question.

Cora studied him for a moment and in a brisk, workmanlike manner replied, "Oh, it makes sense, doesn't it? Who would benefit more from your family being brushed out of existence in one fell swoop than I would?"

"It's true that, had the killer's plan been executed, the Cranley estate would have transferred to your grandmother and ultimately you." Cora scoffed but the old man hadn't finished speaking. "But, please remember, I held you as a tiny baby, Cora. I watched you growing up and I like to think that I took on the role your own grandfather would have occupied. So, you're wrong, I don't believe you could be guilty of such a horrific crime."

I was once again confused as to why a man who had built his reputation as a ruthless, hard-nosed police officer could go so lightly on a suspect. If Cora was responsible for the murders, she had him wrapped around her finger.

"I imagine that the rest of the family are simply desperate to see me behind bars." There were cracks beginning to show in her steely persona. Her voice sounded as though it might break altogether and I was trying to judge whether it was all just an act. "I've never really fitted in with the Cranleys, have I? When I was little, Maitland called me wild and Belinda treated me like some kind of savage because I once visited my parents in Africa and came back nut brown."

A thread of pure anger suddenly emerged in her. "It isn't much better now that I'm an adult either." She adopted a voice then that sounded just like my stuffy aunt Winifred. "*A woman with short hair and trousers! Whatever next? Women soldiers? A lady prime minister? The very idea doesn't bear thinking about.*" She had to catch her breath after these theatrics. "Dear George runs up gambling debts wherever he goes, seduces half the debutantes in England and you all think he's marvellous, and yet I'm the black sheep?"

Grandfather's eyes flicked across to his sister-in-law who was feeding Delilah bits of jam-covered scone and showed no interest in our conversation.

He kept his voice steady as he replied. "You know that's not what I think of you."

Cora's stare hardened. "So then why are you here? What do you want from me?"

"I need you to tell me where you were just before I gave my toast last night and again this morning when Maitland was killed."

Like a gunslinger from the American west, she fired straight back at him. "Just asking that question proves you don't believe me."

The ferocity of Cora's words had startled her grandmother. Peering around the other faces at the table, as if she couldn't work out where she knew us from, Clementine distracted herself by pouring some more tea from the pot.

It was Grandfather's turn to raise his voice. "That's not why I'm asking. I may not consider you a suspect, but I still need to know where you were and what you were doing at the time that the murders were committed."

She looked down at her hands, as though considering what they were capable of. When she eventually spoke, her voice was a distant breeze, barely audible over the hum of the natural world which surrounded us. "You already know, don't you?"

The unmown grass swishing in the air, a pair of bumblebees inspecting a patch of cranesbill geraniums, the brook which ran behind the house and a blackbird tossing leaves about in the middle of the orchard; they were all far louder than her whispered question.

My grandfather looked back at her without hesitation. "I believe I do. But until I hear you say the words, I can't be sure."

Her head drooped. The determination faded away and she pulled a breath deep down inside her before replying. "I was with Fellowes on both occasions."

"Thank you, dear child. Thank you for your honesty." Grandfather clearly found some shred of relief in her answer. Despite dismissing my theory, perhaps the possibility of Cora being the killer had been weighing on his mind all along.

He held his hand out for her to hold, but dear, batty Clementine took it instead. To contrast with the sad moment we'd just experienced, Grandfather couldn't hold back his laughter as the old woman looked affectionately at him.

"Oh, Clemmie." His mirth soon infected the rest of us. "For all your quirks, I can't deny that you've always had a sense of humour."

His face curled up in a broad smile but his words didn't connect with the old lady. She pulled her jam-stained hand back, as if afraid he was mocking her. To compensate, Cora leaned over to hug her grandmother and Clementine's usual cheerful expression reshaped her face.

Grandfather wasn't to be distracted and returned to the matter at hand. "I'll need you to tell me the exact circumstances of what happened last night. Did you throw a stone to get Fellowes's attention? Were you waiting for him in the garden? Did any of that actually occur?"

Cora glanced down at the table, clearly still reluctant to go into details. "Yes, it did. I was acting like a spoilt child and couldn't wait to have Reginald to myself, so I interrupted his duties for a few minutes. He came outside and we hid beneath the steps to the petit salon to… well, I think that's a part of the story I can keep to myself."

She giggled like a little girl and Grandfather asked his next question.

"Did you see anyone else when you were out there?"

She took a moment to prepare her answer. "No, though we did hear someone running up the steps immediately after we arrived. He was positively sprinting. I think it must have been a man from the sound of his footsteps. I can't imagine any of the women running like that in their ball gowns."

"And afterwards?"

"I went in through the offices on the lower floor so that no one would see the two of us together. I stopped at the first mirror I could find, to make sure I didn't look a total mess and then went back upstairs." She let out a lascivious laugh and something finally clicked in my brain. "By the time I got to the ballroom, Reginald was serving drinks and the toast had begun."

Forgive my naivete, but it had taken me until now to understand what my chic, pretty cousin and our uncouth butler had been doing together. The revelation of a romantic entanglement between a servant and a member of my own family sparked a feeling of shock. The snobbery that had been hammered into me during the decade of my elite education rushed to the surface and, in the voice of my vitriolic headmaster, I thought, *How dare they do such a thing!*

Of course, this unease was quickly kicked from my head to make way for the realisation that, if Cousin Cora could fall in love with Fellowes without my Grandfather instantly disowning her, perhaps there was hope for Alice and myself. And as joyful as this made me, I couldn't help wondering where Cora's explanation fitted in with what we already knew of Belinda's murder.

We now had the confirmation that she had thrown the stone against the drinks room window. It followed, therefore, that Fellowes had opened the champagne, then gone outside to meet Cora and do... whatever men and women do when they're alone together (I have to admit, this is not something I'm entirely clear on. I did once ask my father, but his cheeks turned scarlet and he said, "It's awfully complicated, old chap. My advice would be to get a book from the library.")

So they were kissing, etc. when the killer slipped into the drinks room to put the cyanide in the champagne. The two of them finished up outside with the hugging and whatnot, Fellowes brought the champagne into the ballroom and Cora stumbled in, shortly after. Which was all well and good but it didn't get us any closer to identifying our culprit.

No doubt going through a similar thought process to my own, Grandfather allowed her story to stew in his mind before formulating a response.

"Now, my dear, I'm sorry to tell you that Fellowes is in trouble. The police found out about his past and they're going to pin the blame on him. It's not because they have evidence, or he has any motive for murder, but because he's the easiest fit."

Cora bridled at the accusation. "They can't do that."

"They can and they will. They'll say that he's a disgruntled servant who couldn't stand being ordered around anymore. They'll find out from our relatives how rude he can be and the police will use whatever they come across to paint him as a violent, confrontational man. Blunt won't listen to me, and there's little I can do to control him. If you don't tell the police about your relationship, I suspect that Reginald will at best spend his life in prison and worst book a trip to the gallows."

Seizing hold of her belongings, Cora shot up to standing. "I must go, I should never have left the house this morning, not with the state that Reginald was in. I'd gone to check on him, you see, but when we heard people screaming outside, he feared that someone would notice I was missing and he begged me to leave."

"Wait one moment. Did you see anyone else?" my grandfather followed up with. "Last night when you returned to the house or earlier this morning? Any of the other suspects perhaps?"

She thought for a second, her brow becoming furrowed. "Well, yes actually, I did. As I was leaving the servants' quarters this morning, that boy was there."

"You mean, Todd?" My grandfather asked, jerking his head back in the direction of the house.

"No, the tall boy with red hair who was at the ball. The one the police were after."

"Marmal-" I began and then felt a bit silly and corrected myself. "Marmaduke Adelaide."

"If you say so," Cora replied, but I could see her mind was seven miles away with her stricken lover. She was already drifting towards her car. "He was lurking around and it was odd because we rather caught one another. He knew I wasn't supposed to be there and I knew the police were looking for him. It was a stalemate and so he smiled, shook his head cheerily and got out of my way."

"Thank you, Cora," my grandfather had to shout across the garden for the words to reach her. "I hope you can explain away any queries the police might have."

Once she had gone, the old man fell into a silent fog of thought. He put his hands together and stared at a point beyond the end of his nose for some time. There wasn't much I could do but wait. As there was no food left, Delilah took the opportunity to stretch her legs and went bounding across the messy garden after a wood pigeon.

"You haven't drunk your tea, dear boy," Great-Aunt Clementine kindly pointed out, so then I felt obliged to sip at the cold, milky brew. It tasted like bathwater but I showed my appreciation all the same.

I wondered how anyone thought it was a good idea to allow a person of her age and impairment to live all on her own with a staff of just five full-time servants. She was not exactly *compos mentis*. Her long white hair was fixed on the top of her head in a fashion which was far too young for her. Though she'd shed her eccentric ensemble from the previous evening, the outfit she now wore was tatty, creased and in a dull, floral fabric which looked older than she was.

In fact, everything about her was noticeably dishevelled, I doubt she'd brushed her teeth in a week, her fingers were black and grubby, as if she'd been foraging for food in Cranley Woods, and I couldn't help worrying about the old girl. Drinking her disgusting tea was the least I could do.

She patted me on the hand once my cup was empty and said in her high, almost choral tone, "What a good boy you are. I'll pour you some more."

Luckily, this was the moment that Grandfather came back to us. "I don't suppose you've got a clue what went on this morning at the house, have you, Clemmie?"

She looked a little concerned, perhaps fearing that she'd done something wrong and was about to be told off. "There was a ball, wasn't there?"

"No, that was yesterday." My grandfather attempted to hide his impatience.

"What was yesterday?"

"The ball!" My grandfather failed to hide his impatience.

"So then why were you asking about this morning?"

He groaned and appeared ready to give up when she spoke again.

"It was a lovely evening, I danced and sang and talked to so many wonderful people. Someone complimented me on my singing you know?"

"Yes, thank you. We were there. Though I wouldn't put much stock in a compliment from Inspector Blunt."

She rolled her eyes. "Not that scruffy little policeman, this was a man in a smart dinner suit, with a chiselled jaw and pure black hair like

Rudolph Valentino's. He popped up in the petit salon and startled me."

I couldn't say the words right then, so my grandfather said them for me. "Christopher's father? Was it Walter you saw?"

In much the same carefree manner with which she'd entertained us in the smoking room the night before, she waved one hand through the air and said, "Well you know that I'm not good with names. He came rushing up the steps from the garden and it was quite a shock, as I'd dozed off for a moment. That's why I sang to him; to calm us both down."

CHAPTER TWENTY-TWO

I can't say I'd seriously entertained the possibility of my father's involvement in the crime until that moment. And, obviously, the fact that he was in the garden did not make him a murderer. What was troubling was that he hadn't told us anything about it. He said he'd been on the terrace to get some air, not to traverse the house. So what was he doing out there?

"Todd, climb into the back seat please," Lord Edgington told his chauffeur when we returned to the car.

The adventurous young fellow didn't look too happy about this and I could see the excitement fade from his eyes.

"Oh, come along, man," Grandfather yelled. "You can take the car out another day, but I need to talk to my grandson."

He did as instructed, leaving me free to occupy the luxurious passenger seat – which Delilah immediately made more cramped by landing with a thump on my lap. A look of elation on his face, Grandfather pulled a pair of his own leather driving gloves on and started the engine.

"I want you to stay calm, boy." He told me as we pulled out of Langford House and onto a country lane. "Just because your father has been hiding something from us, it doesn't mean that he was plotting to kill you, me and our entire family."

I nearly swallowed my tongue just then. "Thank you, Grandfather. But such a thought hadn't entered my mind."

"Jolly good." The words came out as both apologetic and judgemental. As if he was sorry to promote such a dark hypothesis, but a little disappointed that I hadn't struck upon it myself.

Though I may have been slow, my grandfather had certainly set the ball rolling. My brain was storming with the evidence of my father's wickedness. I saw him running around the house to put the cyanide in the champagne in order to inherit Grandfather's estate for himself, before slipping back into the ballroom. I imagined how he could have accessed the armoury in order to murder his brother-in-law and continue with his plan. I thought about his dark moods over the last few months as investment after investment in the City tumbled.

Could my distant but gentle father really be capable of murder?

Accepting that he was willing to kill his wife, sons and wider family was not an easy thing to do and so I distracted myself by focussing on my grandfather's words.

"It's that Adelaide boy loitering in my house that concerns me."

This came as a surprise and so I told him just that. "When I said that Marmaduke was involved, you told me I was being foolish."

He made a short hmmm before replying. "No, I told you that we couldn't jump to conclusions and condemn a man based on the idea he was a born monster. If your school chum is involved, it's because he thought he could get something out of it or someone forced him to do it. I can tell you for certain that savage bloodlust played no part in these murders. The killer may have taken advantage of the circumstances, but he had a calculated plan. I still don't think that a boy like Marmaduke Adelaide could be the person we're looking for."

As he spoke, my grandfather was paying more attention to this discussion than the speed we were travelling at. I could see from the steel dashboard that we were shooting along at way over sixty miles per hour. My father had never broken forty in our Bentley and was so protective of his favourite toy that he got nervous taking it out of the drive.

As the wind attacked my hair, I experienced a mix of fear, excitement and nausea. To be perfectly honest I'm not sure that humans are designed to travel at such a clip and it's probably not too healthy for the brain. I clung onto Delilah for dear life.

"Perhaps that's it!" I was beginning to think that detective work came to me naturally after all. "Perhaps someone forced Marmaduke to come to the ball and poison us. His father is the obvious suspect, but George brought him; maybe he's involved."

My grandfather didn't respond so I continued. "What if George owes Mr Adelaide a chunk of dough-"

"Must you really use slang, Christopher?" he interrupted. "There's a perfectly good word for money, it's *money*. I do find such linguistic barbarity offensive."

I tried to board my train of thought once more. "Oh... Sorry, Grandfather. But suppose that George is in debt to Horatio Adelaide – a man you arrested more than once – who sent his son to the ball to get even? Marmaduke could have acted as a lookout while George did the deed. We know he spilt his champagne. If it weren't for Belinda's impatience, he'd have been the only one not to drink."

Grandfather bit his lip and pushed the Aston Martin faster along the smooth tarmacadam road. The sunlight cut through the trees we were passing under and the warm breeze seemed to will us back home to Cranley.

"Weren't you the one who pointed out how obvious his guilt would be if George was the only man left standing as we dropped about him like flies?" He had to shout to be heard by this point and I thought his choice of simile rather insensitive considering the bombardment Todd was enduring in the back seat. "And besides, if it was money George was after, he could have killed me and been done with it. I'm not going to suggest that his mother was an easy person to get along with, but I refuse to believe he would have murdered her and our whole family without necessity."

Todd leaned forward from the back seat. He looked oddly green. "Milord, are you sure you want to be driving like that? There's a bend ahead and you're pushing seventy."

Unruffled, Grandfather looked back over his shoulder with an enigmatic smile. "Oh, have some faith, man. It's not the first time I've driven an automobile, you know!"

He put his head down like a racing driver as we approached a twisting chicane. I felt like closing my eyes, but it was impossible to look away. Sadly, my grandfather didn't have any such qualms and turned to address me.

"I should never have locked myself away from the world for all those years. There is so much to do and I've so many wonders still to experience. My dear Katherine wouldn't have wanted me to surrender like that."

"Grandfather, the road!"

He winked at me and we flew through the bend with barely a tap of the brake.

"This is the stuff!" he said, before emitting a joyful whistle.

When we pulled up at the house, Todd and I remained in our seats in traumatised silence. Grandfather did not seem concerned.

"Todd," he muttered, climbing from the vehicle to gaze at it with appreciation. "If you happened to hear anything that the boy and I were discussing, I'm sure you'll keep it to yourself. There's a good chap."

He dusted down his cuffs and turned towards the house with Delilah at his heel. "Come along, Christopher. There's a fugitive on the premises and the matter of some murders to solve. We've no time to waste."

I've never ridden a camel, but imagine that it's a less than comfortable experience. On arriving at my ancestral home, I felt as though I'd crossed the Sahara on one of the wretched beasts. I climbed carefully out of the car and had to check my legs were still functioning. After a few cautious steps, I followed the old man inside.

We might just as well have taken the tradesman's entrance, as Grandfather headed straight towards the kitchen where the staff were convened for their early lunch.

"No, no, don't get up," he commanded, but every last person put their cutlery down and sat up straight out of courtesy. "Somewhere on the property is a young man with curly red hair and a nasty demeanour. The police are after him, but I'd rather that one of you found him first."

Driscoll, the gardener, cleared his throat. "Excuse me, Milord." Without looking up from the table – as if he were addressing a communion wafer rather than another human – he said his piece. "I think I might'a seen the fella in the gamekeeper's hut this mornin. He were bedded down there overnight but I chased him off."

His employer folded his lips into his mouth before replying. "Oh, well, it's a sighting at least. I should have realised last night that the boy wouldn't have been able to get far without a car of his own. Please keep an eye peeled and bring him straight to me if he appears."

As the unofficial head of the household staff in Fellowes's absence, it was down to Cook to respond. "We were all terribly sorry to hear the news, Milord. And I just wanted to say…" The bold woman, who had bossed me about and kept me in line ever since I was tiny, was suddenly unsure of herself. "Well, whatever we can do to help, you know that we will."

My grandfather placed his hands on the back of Fellowes's empty chair. "Thank you, Henrietta." He gazed at his staff with thanks and affection. I was surprised he even knew her name. I'd never heard her addressed as anything but Cook before. "I can't tell you how much I appreciate you saying that."

He bowed his head respectfully and left the room. I didn't follow him. I just stood there with my tummy rumbling, staring at the food. The meal Cook had prepared looked comparatively edible and I would have loved to sit down for a bowl of leek and cabbage soup with thick crunchy bread and salty butter. Sadly, my grandfather had other ideas and poked his head back into the kitchen to admonish me.

"Don't dawdle, Christopher. You're as bad as Delilah sometimes."

To be honest, I was jealous of the dog who had already returned to her basket with a healthy chunk of lamb between her teeth. But it was Alice's sympathetic expression that my eyes lingered over as I reluctantly trundled from the room. It was almost as if she could sense how hungry I was.

CHAPTER TWENTY-THREE

"Next stop: Reginald Fellowes," Grandfather explained as he shot along the corridor away from me.

The doctor had been and gone, but whatever he had administered at least meant that the poor man could sleep. When we got to the butler's room, Cora was sitting in a chair at his bedside and he appeared to have regained a little of his natural colour, though the scent of sickness hadn't left the dark, featureless space.

"I spoke to the police," she told us without prompting. "That Blunt fellow is… well a little odd, but I got the impression that he's not the type to gossip. He took my statement without the other officers being present and he seemed satisfied that Reginald wasn't involved."

Her great-uncle came to place a hand on her shoulder. "That's good news. And, for all his faults, Inspector Blunt is nothing if not professional. I'll have a word with his superiors to see if he's moved the investigation on. He's a real hound, that one. Doesn't like to give up on his theories until there's incontrovertible proof otherwise."

Cora looked down at the man who most people in the family couldn't stand but she was apparently in love with. "Thank you." She stopped speaking and I thought that was all she would manage but then she flicked her gaze back to us. "Thank you for accepting what I told you and not being horrified. I don't think there are many other people who would have."

Grandfather nodded and squeezed her shoulder a little tighter.

Once we were back outside, I had a question for him and it might not have been entirely selfless. "Do you think they'll be all right?"

He was already striding off down the corridor, his long coat flapping in his wake. He didn't answer until we were back upstairs in the main wing of the house. "I think it will be difficult for them. It's difficult for any two people from different backgrounds. Cora is a woman of some wealth and Fellowes has a far darker past than many of the men I've locked up for life."

I hadn't had the opportunity to ask about this until now. "So why did you give him a job in your house? Why do you trust him so deeply?"

He stopped beside the door to the armoury. "That's not something which he would want me talking about. But I'll tell you this, the man saved my life once and anything I can do to pay him back is worth it."

I tried to make sense of this revelation. Fellowes couldn't be more than thirty-five years old and my Grandfather retired in his sixties which means that Fellowes must have been around my age when he was convicted of whatever offences Blunt had dug up on him. As I processed this new information, I realised that I wouldn't want anyone to judge me for the rest of my life on the actions I had undertaken up to now. I couldn't say what sort of criminal activity he had engaged in, but it only seemed right that Fellowes had been given a second chance.

"Come along, boy." He turned the amber glass handle of the thick oaken door. "I have a question for you."

Inside the armoury, little had changed but there were signs of police activity. Iron filings had been spilt on the floor and, though I'd seen no footprints when I'd inspected the room, a number of large, dusty treads were now visible on the carpet.

Grandfather looked around the scene meticulously. His quick, inquisitive eyes carried out a topographical study of every chest and fixing. The armoury had never been designed for storing weapons, it was simply that my family had acquired such an extensive collection over the years that they needed a room of their own. There were two suits of armour by the door which gave the place its name. I walked back to have a closer inspection, as I'd barely looked at them on my first visit that day.

"Grandfather?" I didn't like to interrupt him but the most extraordinary thought had entered my mind. "What if whoever shot Uncle Maitland was hiding inside one of these when I came in and then slipped out when we were distracted?"

He said nothing for a moment and I felt a little pride to know that he was giving my theory the weighty consideration it deserved.

"You know, Christopher, that is one of the most ridiculous ideas I've ever heard. There's a rather large hole in the visor. You'd have spotted the killer instantly. Besides, he'd have had plenty of time to get away before you arrived, what good would hanging around here have done him?"

"Oh… Um." I didn't really have an answer to that. "Well, it was just a thought."

He continued his examination, bending low to sniff the cigar ash, just as I had. With a twitch of the nose and a sidelong glance, he soon moved on. Pausing to examine the empty space where the crossbow had been, and then its twin on the opposite wall, he made a contemplative clicking sound in his cheeks. Finally, he walked over to the window and angled his head to look out. "Tell me something, boy. Did you actually see this window open when Maitland was killed?"

I thought for a moment. "Well, no, I didn't. I mean, the shot must have come from this general direction but… well, I suppose I saw the crossbow bolt and assumed the killer was in the armoury."

He hummed in reply and moved to the side of the window to assess the angle required to fire at Maitland, before turning his eyes up to the ceiling. "Yes, a logical conclusion, I have to admit. And obviously our culprit would have come in here to fetch the weapon, but we can't be sure that this is where he fired from. The window wasn't open when you got here, for one thing. Who would have gone to the trouble of closing it, knowing that the whole house would be up in arms as soon as Maitland's cry rang out?"

I had to hope this was a rhetorical question as I hadn't the foggiest idea. I was once more inclined to think that my role in the investigation could have been filled by a shop mannequin or perhaps a ventriloquist's dummy. It seemed that my main function was to make it appear as though my grandfather wasn't talking to himself.

He took another look around the room and distractedly twisted his long white beard around one finger. Apparently satisfied with his examination, he nodded his head and said, "On we go, Chrissy. Time and tide wait for no man."

I was desperately low on energy by this point and struggling to stand. "Where are we off to next?"

He spun back around to me. "I think you'll like this." He let the words run through my head for a heartbeat or two before putting me out of my misery. "It's lunchtime!"

Did Dickens himself ever transcribe any two words more beautiful than those? Did England's immortal Bard strike upon any such moving a couplet? I could have jumped into my grandfather's arms and given him the sort of warm embrace that has never been a feature of Cranley family interaction.

"That doesn't mean you can let your guard down," he said, as he marched away. "I expect you to keep your eyes wide open for evidence. You must remember that anyone could be guilty."

I practically sprinted down the hallway to the dining room then immediately prayed that Grandfather's warning would not prove prescient. The only guests who would be joining us for lunch were Mother, Father and my lovesick sibling.

"It's a rum business, no doubt," my father announced once we were all sitting down and Albert had mopily rung the bell for lunch.

"Darling," my mother interrupted, before Father could utter any other such inanity. "Belinda and Maitland are dead. I think it's a little worse than that."

He looked stunned that his normally deferential wife would have felt the need to correct him. "Oh… um, quite!"

As he helped himself to a good measure of whisky from the corner cabinet, I noticed that my grandfather was looking at his son-in-law through the corner of his eye. No one else saw it but I realised then that, for all that he'd tried to reassure me, he hadn't dismissed the possibility that my father was the killer.

This also made me question his attitude towards Cora and George. Had he really been as soft on them as I'd believed or was he lulling them into a false sense of security? And if he had crossed them off our list, who did that leave us with? Fellowes who was already sick at the time of the second murder, a batty old woman who could barely look after herself, a missing bully with few ties to the family and…

It was my turn to look at my father in a different light.

"I just meant to say that it's a thoroughly…" He was ruffled by the stony atmosphere which, in a few clicks of the mantelpiece clock, had occupied the space around us. "Or rather, it's really very-"

"Thank you, Walter," Grandfather interrupted, a half-smile on his face. "I appreciate the sentiment."

The cheeky blighter was at it again. Lord Edgington of Scotland Yard wasn't the softy I'd mistaken him for. His years in the wilderness had done nothing to dull his instincts and his skill for manipulation was as strong as ever. With one simple look, he'd defused the tension in the room. My father, who a moment before had been pulling at his collar and shifting in his seat, was suddenly at ease.

My grandfather was a true magician.

Our first course was wheeled into the room just then by Halfpenny, the head (and only) footman of Cranley Hall. He was a stooped old fellow who I always felt bad for when he had to carry something heavy. I barely noticed how awkwardly he hauled the tureen from the trolley, though, as I was distracted by the idea that my father was a brutal murderer who wished us all dead.

That still wasn't enough to put me off my food and, when my bowl of Vichyssoise was served, I had to stop myself from plunging my face into it and lapping up the contents like a dog with poor table manners. Even though Cook had substituted the potatoes in the recipe for cauliflower and, for some unfathomable reason, added sheep's trotters, it hit the spot nicely.

My mother and brother were engaged in a debate upon how distantly related two people had to be before it was acceptable to consider marriage.

"In the past, cousins used to marry all the time." He emitted one of his most expressive sighs. "I don't see why we shouldn't continue that tradition."

Mother took his hand across the long dining table which was shrouded in a chintzy white cloth. "We've been through this, Albert. People did all sorts of things in the past that today would be frowned upon."

Once I'd drained the contents of my bowl and my hunger was a little less agonising, I was free to examine the man who had sired me. I'd always considered my father a stuffy, old-fashioned sort of fellow. Despite choosing a wife who was interested in the most modern of social causes – suffrage, helping the poor, rights for dogs and the like – his worldview was firmly rooted in the Victorian age.

For Walter Prentiss, it was as if the twentieth century was yet to arrive. He could normally be found in a black double-breasted frock coat that ran down to his knees, though could just about be persuaded to pass it up in favour of a linen lounge suit at the height of summer. He positively despised modern fashions in fact and I distinctly remember him criticising his father-in-law for dressing like a dandy.

I never blamed my father for his aloof manner, of course. As

William Wordsworth said, 'The Child is father of the Man,' and I'd add that the parents of the child are therefore the grandfather of the man (which is not so catchy but hopefully the meaning is clear.) I doubt my paternal grandparents came within arm's length of poor little Walter, so it's hardly surprising that he struggled to communicate much to his sons beyond the importance of punctuality and clean fingernails.

And though he was no different from many fathers, this coldness suddenly spoke volumes to me. Could his upbringing have imparted a viciousness within him that would make slaughtering his family a simple task? Or perhaps he had been driven to despair by his poor investments and, in his detached, rational way, sought out a desperate solution to dire financial straits.

I wasn't the only one quietly examining him either. My grandfather was still at it, even as he engaged in conversation.

"Such a relief when spring arrives in earnest, don't you think, Walter?" There was more weight in the question than he'd have us believe.

My father squirmed under the pressure of the old man's gaze. I could only imagine what he'd be like if this was a serious interview. Before he could answer, one of the police constables marched past the open door and he practically jumped out of his seat.

"Oh yes," he attempted. "A lovely time of year… what with the weather and the little birds singing and… um… flowers and such."

"Flowers?" Grandfather was quick to pounce on this, his voice hardening just a touch.

"Yes, you know, daffodils and crocuses or should that be croci? I'm never sure with that sort of thing. But they're awfully pretty at this time of year, wouldn't you say?"

The old man showed no emotion as he ignored the question and replied, "Daffodils are poisonous for human consumption, Walter. They'll give you the most dreadful digestive problems, though are not generally fatal."

My brother dropped his spoon into his empty bowl and, once the clatter had died out, no one made a sound.

Grandfather's gaze shifted off around the wood-panelled room and he finally took pity on his son-in-law. "But such flowers are long gone by now. It's practically summer already, you can feel it in the air."

"Yes…" My father swallowed noisily. "Practically summer."

"We should go down to Brighton for the weekend soon," my mother intervened, as if the dead bodies of her two siblings hadn't just been taken away in an ambulance. She was awfully good at smoothing things over, but this was a step too far, even for her.

My grandfather let out a frosty laugh as Halfpenny arrived with the second course. The meal continued in silence with only the odd comment on the food and I was glad when it was over and I could beat a hasty retreat.

CHAPTER TWENTY-FOUR

Something approaching normality had returned to Cranley Hall. Though there were still police officers poking about the place, and the ballroom was closed off to everyone, a hush had fallen over the house that I hadn't experienced there for some time.

My mother was eager to get back to our house at Kilston Down, but Grandfather convinced her to stay another day and seemed quite distraught at the idea of her leaving. It was hard to say if this was for her sake or his, but she reluctantly agreed. Albert was in no hurry to go back to university, so sat in the grand salon moping to himself and polishing off Cranley's stock of ginger wine.

With the police trampling about the place and the staff still busy cleaning up after the ball, I was at a loose end. It presented me with the dilemma of having to decide whether to return to my copy of Martin Chuzzlewit or head outside for a stroll. In the end, I grabbed my binoculars, checked in with Cousin Cora to see how Fellowes was doing and took Delilah with me for a trip to the woods.

As much as I adored birdwatching, I can't say I was particularly good at it. Take warblers for instance, there are just so many of them and they all look so darned similar to one another that I could never tell a willow warbler from a garden warbler – and don't get me started on chiffchaffs!

That notwithstanding, just seeing the little blighters hopping about in the bushes filled me with calm. You might think that taking a large, waggy dog with me would not be the best idea, but I swear that Delilah was just as keen on my hobby as I. She was perfectly happy to hide in the undergrowth with me for an hour to spot the family of woodpeckers. In fact, her big, soulful eyes lit up with joy whenever mine did.

We cut through the Italian gardens, around the lake and were in the woods in no time. In fact, we were just gearing up for a nice long sit on the ground, when I noticed something at the foot of one of the ancient oaks. There were papers strewn about the place. Wax wrappings from the butcher's, along with a trail of crumbs that the birds were yet to get to. I followed them a way, hoping that they would lead me to whoever had dropped them, but sadly they went in a circle through the trees and back to where we'd started.

I recognised the wrappings from Cook's larder. There were all sorts of goodies in paper parcels there, from pies to cold meats and… well, that was the bulk of it actually. I'd been known to raid it myself for afternoon snacks. I didn't have to think long to work out who had been hiding in the woods.

I planned to abandon my stint of ornithological observation but then I spotted a nightingale, which turned out to be a sparrow, and that slowed me down a tad. But five minutes later, with one of the wax papers pocketed as evidence, we returned to the house in search of Grandfather.

I found him looking maudlin in the library. He was slumped in an armchair in the corner with books strewn all around him. I had a quick peek at the titles but they weren't the kind of thing I was interested in. There was no fiction at all, in fact, and they appeared to be largely scientific in nature. Most had long Latin sounding titles which I couldn't decipher.

"Chin up, Grandfather," I told him somewhat inappropriately, but he was too distracted to pay me any attention.

The library at Cranley was the real gem of the estate. It was started by… well, one of my ancestors no doubt, and had been expanded over the centuries by each successive generation. Whatever your area of interest, you could find a trove of information there. The uppermost shelves were housed on their own floor, which was accessible by a moveable staircase that spiralled around towards the heavens (appropriately, this was where we kept the religious literature.)

I loved the sight and smell of all those books. The green and red spines recalled memories of the first time I was allowed in there aged five. I'd just mastered the simpler books at school and the thought that there were so many tomes still left for me to enjoy was both joyous and frightening. I'd read my way through the meagre children's section several times over before I turned nine and discovered my love of Charles Dickens.

I had never noticed before, but perhaps the one thing missing from the collection were detective novels. I could only assume that Grandfather preferred real life to fiction, which would explain all the dry books he was surrounded by.

"I thought I had it cracked," he told me, his gaze now off through the window. "I felt sure that, after two murders in a short space of time, the killer would have made a wrong step. With such a short list of suspects, how can I still be so lost?"

It was hard to see him like that. He'd been passing in and out of sorrow all day of course and I was worried this would be the straw that broke the camel's proverbial.

"Please don't be so despondent," I tried again, though I knew that a few empty words couldn't bring his children back. "I'm sure you're close."

He shook his head but did not reply. He was watching the tiny dabs of cloud gliding over his estate and I could only imagine the thoughts coursing through his mind. Perhaps he could have borne the strain of Belinda's death. But to lose two of his children in such a short space of time, was too much even for a man of his resilience.

Unlike my grandfather, I'd run away from the scene of the crime. I didn't have to witness the life draining out of poor Maitland, didn't have to hear my uncle's last words, which were surely still echoing about the antechambers of the old man's mind.

When he spoke again, his change of topic surprised me. "Did I ever tell you about the Bow Boys gang?" he blurted out and I took a seat beside him.

"No, Grandfather. You've never told me about any of your cases."

He looked at me, narrowed his eyes uncertainly and started on his tale. "Tommy Bow was a savage. A real monster of a man, as tall as an elephant and almost as broad, there were rumours he'd once ripped a rival's head clean off its shoulders. And though we knew what he was capable of, and believed him responsible for any number of crimes, we never had enough evidence to convict him."

He took a breath in and held it for a moment before continuing his story. "Back in those days, the police didn't always do things by the strict letter of the law. My colleagues tried everything they could to frame the fellow, but Tommy was too clever. For five years of my career, I thought of little else but sending him to the hangman's noose, when all I needed was to bide my time."

He came to a halt, so I urged him on. "And how did you catch him in the end?"

145

"He made a mistake of course. I'd had a man in his gang for a few months, he managed to get wind of an attack they were planning on another gang and we got there just in time to arrest everyone involved."

I allowed his story to play out in my head but couldn't understand its purpose. "Grandfather, why are you telling me this?"

He looked straight at me, his sombre expression temporarily lightening. "Isn't it obvious?"

This was a ridiculous question to put to me as I rarely find anything obvious, even if it's inches from my face and covered in flashing lightbulbs.

When I failed to reply, he continued regardless. "Maitland was supposed to have died last night, so what happened this morning couldn't have been planned ahead of time. The killer is bound to have slipped up somewhere, but I can't see it. I can't even tell you for certain why he would have murdered Belinda and Maitland but not Fellowes."

This surprised me somewhat. "So you're sure that Fellowes was poisoned?"

"Yes, of course he was. It's too much of a coincidence otherwise, and I do not believe in coincidences. I can't say exactly what he ate, as there are too many toxic plants in the gardens alone, but it wasn't in Cook's dinner last night that, or else the rest of the staff would have come down with it too."

"Couldn't it have been from the champagne? Mightn't he have had a snifter to try for himself?"

Grandfather shook his head witheringly. "I've already told you, boy. Cyanide would have killed him outright. Whatever Fellowes consumed must have been far weaker or he'd be lying in the mortuary with Belinda and Maitland. The question is whether he was ever meant to die in the first place. Had the killer run out of cyanide and made do with whatever substance was at hand? Or did he only wish to keep our faithful butler quiet for a while and not actually hurt him?"

I considered his questions. "We spoke to Fellowes last night and he swore he had nothing of note to report. We know he went outside with Cora but surely, if either of them had seen anything out of the ordinary, they would have told us."

Somewhat petulantly I thought, Grandfather kicked one of the leather-bound books on the floor. "You're probably right. But I know there's something I'm missing in all of this and I should be able to see it."

Delilah walked over to comfort her master by plumping herself down on his feet and I remembered what I'd discovered in the woods. "Grandfather, I went for a walk and found this."

He stared back blankly at the wax paper I'd produced. "Yes, very nice."

"It's from the butcher's," I explained, but he still didn't understand why I was bringing him a piece of litter. "I think that Marmaduke Adelaide has been stealing from the larder and camping out in the woods. If he wasn't here to kill Maitland, it could explain why he was in the house when Cora saw him."

"Or it could be from a poacher's lunch. They're not known for their good habits and we get plenty of them on the estate." He bit his lip and looked once more at my grand discovery. I think he must have relented a little as, when he spoke again, it was in a gentler tone. "You may be on to something though. And if you're right, and young Adelaide is still around, we'll find him before long."

I thought I'd try to make myself useful and went to pile up the abandoned books that Delilah wasn't using as a nest. "Do you think he could be involved after all?"

He brought his hands forward to form a pyramid. "It's possible, Christopher. We still can't rule anyone out."

"Except poor Uncle Maitland," I replied, with the books now stacked beside his chair.

Though my Latin is not the best, I could see that the titles were all related to chemistry. From what I could tell, they were largely on poisons and toxic substances. I had to hope that they'd found their way to our library because of my grandfather's profession, rather than any nefarious motivation my ancestors had possessed.

"That's right." He paused and his face fell once more. "If only we knew what he saw before I made my toast."

I thought for a moment about what my uncle had told us. "He said he saw Fellowes leaving the petit salon, but we know why that was. Fellowes had been to see his secret girlfriend. It's another red herring."

"That was only the beginning. What if Maitland had more to say? I think that my son witnessed something he shouldn't have, which is why the killer took a risk to keep him quiet." Grandfather delivered this last sentence with such gravity that it was clear he considered it to be the linchpin to the whole case.

"So what do we do now?"

He shuffled his feet under Delilah and took his time to reply. "Now, I sit here and think for as long as it takes for the solution to come to me."

CHAPTER TWENTY-FIVE

I had some thinking of my own to do, so I retired to my room without another word to my family. In the seclusion of my chilly quarters, I took out my book of ornithological observations and wrote, "Possible nightingale, definite sparrow." I like to keep a record of my sightings and it's really quite fascinating to go back and read the names all the birds I might have, though probably didn't see. There are wheatears and golden orioles (which I'm more or less certain was a starling catching the light of the sun) firecrests and yellowhammers.

There was no time for my favourite hobby right then though, as I had urgent matters to attend to. I cracked open a fresh page at the back of my notebook and wrote down our list of suspects. Just looking at the names helped me focus on what I knew about each person. I tried to write an account, not just of the things I'd discovered that weekend, but relevant facts I had always known.

Marmaduke Adelaide could be summed up in two simple words: absolute thug. But the others were more complex. To begin with, my second cousin Cora was an odd case. She'd been quite the darling of the family in her teenage years. She'd excelled in school, not just academically but in arts, sports and cookery too. She'd represented Surrey in archery competitions for years, had one of her paintings displayed by a London gallery and been offered a place at Cambridge after she finished boarding school. I never discovered what caused her to cut her hair short, swap her elegant dresses for masculine suits and loiter around London instead of making the most of her talents.

Everyone had an opinion on her transformation, of course. My father put it down to the negative influence of the flapper movement on young women – not that such a movement actually existed outside of the lurid minds of Fleet Street journalists. My mother claimed that Cora had woken up to the possibilities of the fairer sex, though I don't see what this had to do with her hairstyle, and Albert said that Cora was very pretty with long or short hair, and she could do whatever she liked.

I don't suppose my opinion counts for much, but, if you ask me, she was a very sad person. Her parents had lived abroad through her childhood and died of typhoid when she was still young. Most young men her age had gone off to war and either come back scarred by the horrors they'd seen, or failed to return at all. So it's not really surprising that Cora would have struggled through all of that now, is it?

I moved on to my cousin George, who was just young enough to have missed out on the war himself but would have felt the same pressures in different ways. He belonged to a generation which had been hacked through before it could reach its prime. With all that expectation on the remaining few, it only made sense for them to rebel. I was more of a conformist myself, but I sometimes wished I had the courage to stand up to my father and say, *I'm not going to be the person you want me to.* Flappers and war veterans, tomboys and playboys were the ones changing the world. Albert and I just did as our parents told us.

Naturally, there was a dark side to George which I'd have been a fool to ignore. As good as he was at getting his own way, he didn't always seem happy to succeed. Perhaps it just came too easily. For years, his mother had idolised her only son and wouldn't hear a word against him. His father was dead, his friends had followed their illustrious forebears into city jobs or family life and George had opted for a more scandalous existence; spending every night in a different bed, living for the roll of the dice and the spin of the roulette wheel.

He had been the second in line to the family fortune and had by far the most to gain from his mother's death, as Cranley Hall would pass on to him once our elderly grandfather died. Perhaps her patience had run out and she'd finally taken him to task for his aberrant behaviour. Perhaps this wasn't the first time he'd crossed the line of what was strictly legal and his mother had found out. Or perhaps…

My mind ran with vivid imaginings of just what George might have got up to before planning to murder the whole Cranley clan. Arms dealing, opium addiction, gangsters and blackmail – there was no evidence for any of it of course, but it was exciting to consider the possibilities.

I was getting carried away, so I lit an extra candle for warmth and got into bed. The technological advances of our burgeoning century, such as central heating and electric lights, were yet to reach my quarters at Cranley.

I tried to think dispassionately about my cousin, to examine the hard facts. George was friends with a criminal – that much was certain. He'd brought Marmaduke Adelaide to the party as a favour to his father, who had made his fortune from petty crime on a massive scale. Had George helped Horatio Adelaide to exact revenge upon the legendary Lord Edgington? And, if they were to blame for the murders, what part did Marmaduke play?

An image came back to me then, of Marmaduke at the ball after the police had arrived. His clothes were unkempt, just like after any fight at school. There was a bloody bruise on his cheek, which certainly hadn't been there when he'd arrived at the ball, and his flaming red hair was dishevelled.

But, perhaps most significantly, Marmaduke had begged for help. He'd been shaking as he spoke to me, terrified in fact. It was hard to imagine that he could have switched from budding murderer to frightened schoolboy in such a short space of time. Perhaps he'd seen something he shouldn't have, or helped in the killing and regretted it. He wasn't coming to gloat or tease, he'd needed my help and I'd sent him packing. Even the black eye he'd given me didn't warrant that.

With my head growing ever heavier, I moved on to the evidence against Great-Aunt Clementine. She had been set to inherit Cranley before her husband died and had to make do with the modest existence she'd enjoyed. She'd raised Cora as her own daughter, so the two could have been accomplices. She wasn't in the ballroom at any point on the evening of the murder, so maybe she was distancing herself from the crime, and…

I've no doubt I would have done a grand job at coolly examining the evidence against her (and Fellowes and my own father for that matter) but I'd had two sleepless nights in a row and… well, I nodded off.

I'm sure that just such occurrences happen to the best of detectives. Sherlock Holmes meditates and smokes all sorts of wicked drugs and no one thinks badly of him. I merely had a five-minute snooze. And while I confess that the five minutes became ten, and the ten became minutes four and a half hours, perhaps my brain was working on the case all that time and the truth we were searching for would miraculously reveal itself.

Admittedly, that's not how things turned out, but I did wake up to an unexpected discovery.

"Chrissy?" The hissed word made it sound as though there was a snake hidden in the darkness. "Chrissy, are you in here?"

CHAPTER TWENTY-SIX

My candles had extinguished – as they tend to in such draughty confines – and I could make nothing out in the dim moonlight which cut through the gap in my thick brocade curtains.

"Chrissy? It's me, Marmaduke."

Despite my previous speculation on the boy's innocence, his presence there in my quarters made me instantly nervous and I scrambled about on my side table in search of a match. On striking one, I held it like a cross before a vampire. When the light caught him, it positively ignited the shock of red hair atop his head.

"Why are you here, Adelaide? I don't want anything to do with you."

He didn't seem particularly frightened of my talisman as he sat on the chest at the end of my bed.

"I didn't have anywhere else to go." I'd never heard him so weak or hesitant before. His voice was close to breaking. "I couldn't exactly walk to the village from here. It must be at least ten miles and there are police cars everywhere."

"You could always hand yourself in!" I sounded like a young boy squabbling with his brother.

Instead of sniping back at me, Marmaduke looked down at the floor. "I didn't do anything. I swear I didn't. I know what everyone thinks of me, but I would never kill another person. It's just not right."

Coming to accept that he was not there to attack me, I took the moment to light all three arms of my candelabra before the match could burn my fingers. "What do you want?"

He looked up at me and a rather unexpected smile sprang to his lips. "I told you last night. I need you to talk to your grandfather. You have to convince him that I wasn't involved in the murder."

"Murders," I corrected him, with a snarl. "Why don't you convince me that you had nothing to do with them, and then we'll see what Grandfather has to say on the matter?"

He looked shocked then. "Did someone else drink the poison? I swear I didn't have anything to do with it. You have to believe me."

I didn't answer immediately. I thought about the way the great detectives in novels interview their witnesses and decided to keep

153

the news of Maitland's death close to my chest. If Marmaduke was lying, and knew what had happened that morning, he might yet give himself away.

I shimmied back to lean against the headboard and plumped my pillows theatrically before replying. "Why would I believe a word from your mouth? If people have come to the conclusion that you were involved in my aunt's murder, it's because you gave them every reason to. You're not exactly a sympathetic character."

He stifled a sob then. "No, you're wrong about me. I swear."

Pleased with the impact my words had made, and enjoying a little revenge for the broken noses and twisted wrists he'd doled out to so many of my peers at school, I drove home the advantage. "So then why run away? Why not talk to Lord Edgington yourself? You're as guilty as Dr Crippen."

I could see that old anger rise up within him, but then he cut it short.

"I'll tell you." He sat up straighter, as if addressing one of our teachers. "But you have to promise that this won't go any further."

"I'll promise nothing." I have to say that it felt rather wonderful to have so much power over him. For a few moments, I was invincible. "You're lucky I don't march downstairs this moment and tell the police that you're here. At the very least, they could have you up for stealing food from the kitchen." This was a trivial threat to make and I instantly regretted it.

"Just hear what I have to say before you do anything." His voice jumped higher. "That's all I'm asking. If you think I'm lying you can tell the police, but I'll be long gone by the time they get here."

I allowed myself a moment to examine him. He was still dressed in his suit from the ball, but it was stained and crumpled and I could only imagine the discomfort he'd suffered spending the night in the gamekeeper's hut. Even his skin looked grubby and I was amazed at how fast the transformation had occurred.

When I gave no answer, he began his tale. "George owes a lot of money and so I had my father call in a favour and bring me to the ball. But that wasn't the end of it."

It was tempting to interrupt him again; to bellow another accusation of his guilt. I wanted to hear what he had to say though, so I kept my mouth shut and listened.

154

"In return, my father told me to watch George whilst I was here. He said I was to follow him all evening and report back because your cousin had a task to carry out and he couldn't be trusted to go through with it."

"What did he have to do?"

His eyes shifted about the room. He looked scared that there was someone lurking behind the drapes, or hidden away in the wardrobe. "You have to understand, Chrissy, that my father is not someone I answer back to. When he tells me to do something, I say, 'Yes, sir.' I've never seen him become violent, but I have no doubt that he could."

"Answer the question, Marmalade." The power had gone to my head! I don't know how his nickname had emerged from my lips and, for a moment, I was terrified he'd launch himself across the room to blacken my other eye.

"George isn't the only Cranley who owes my father money. He came here to tell your uncle that, if he didn't pay back his debts before the summer, he could expect trouble."

I breathed in theatrically, like an over-the-top hero on a radio drama. It wasn't just the news of Maitland's dilemma that surprised me, Marmaduke had used the present tense. So far at least, it really seemed as though he knew nothing of the second murder.

"But what does that prove?" I asked. "Both men owed your father money. How could that have anything to do with the poison that was planted in the champagne?"

He pondered his answer before continuing, his visage still gripped with fear. "I overheard them, you see. I did as my father asked me and, when I saw George head outside, I followed him out through another door. He spoke to your uncle further along the terrace and I hid in the shadows to hear."

"What did they say?"

"Maitland dismissed the threat outright. Said he wouldn't be scared of some boy, no matter who'd sent him." He took a deep breath before continuing. "George didn't like that, he seized your uncle by the collar and forced him against the wall. He said that things were about to get very nasty for him very soon if he didn't do as instructed." Marmaduke came to a sudden stop, as he relived the scene.

I was gripped by his story and needed to know what came next.

"So, what did Maitland do?"

"That's the thing; when Maitland wouldn't give in, George went wild. He was shouting the place down. They were only twenty yards along the balcony from the entrance to the ballroom, If the band had stopped playing, everyone inside would have heard."

He turned to look through the curtains but continued with the next morsel of the story. "He said that it wouldn't just be Maitland who would suffer, but his whole family. But it wasn't enough. No matter what George said, Maitland laughed right back in his face. I must have leaned out too far from the bay I was hiding in, as that's when George caught sight of me. Five seconds later, he'd stormed over and started pillorying me about the face."

The account of his beating forced him to stop once more and I couldn't help but feel bad for the fellow. If there's one person on the planet who I had never expected to feel sympathy for it was Marmaduke Adelaide. Yet I could see that, for all his brawn and bluster, he was just as scared as any boy our age would have been.

I felt I had to ask the obvious question, nonetheless. "But why did he hit you? Wouldn't your father have taken exception to that?"

"Your cousin hit me because I was insignificant." His voice had fallen even quieter. "He couldn't very well send your uncle back into the party with bruises all over him, but no one would look twice at me. George hit me so hard that my head is still ringing, but his eyes were on your uncle the whole time and, when he was done, he dropped me to the ground and said, 'I have my orders, Maitland, and you've had your chance. Don't blame me for what happens next.' Your uncle cut back into the house then and George gave me one more contemptuous look before following after through a side door."

I let these last details settle in my mind. If what Marmaduke was saying was true, my charming cousin, the heir to our family estate, was a brute and a blackmailer. He was in debt to a dangerous man and had threatened Maitland's family, mere moments before the champagne was laced with poison.

But was it enough to explain the murders? Maitland was the one whose debts had been called. If George was working for Adelaide, surely his own situation was not nearly so precarious. Would he really have poisoned our whole family just to dig himself out of a hole?

"After what I'd heard, I was scared that George would try to kill me too." Marmaduke spoke with great certainty then. He clearly believed that my cousin had murdered his own mother. It was almost too horrible to consider. "I'm not sure of the exact timing, of course, but it seems as though he would have had the opportunity to poison the champagne."

I didn't want to traumatise the chap, but there were still holes in his story that I needed to plug. "Do you know anything about the money the two men owe? Or why your father used George to threaten Maitland?"

He shook his head despondently. "All I know is that your uncle has been in debt for years and my father is tired of waiting. He seemed to regard his sway over George as a real feather in his cap. He called him, 'a charming young gentleman who can get into places where Horatio Adelaide will never be welcome'."

The revelations spun like a tornado, and it took me some time to settle on a response. "I believe you, Marmaduke. Maybe I'm a fool, but I think you're telling the truth. If you repeat to my grandfather exactly what you just told me, he'll know what to do next."

Marmaduke froze for three whole seconds before reacting. He pulled his arms into his chest and rolled his fingers into fists. "No chance. I'll leave this minute and spend the rest of my days in the woods if I have to. I'm not going to go anywhere near George, or the police for that matter. Not until the killer's been found. Your grandfather may have retired, but he still thinks like a bobby. He'd hand me over before I stepped through the door."

"No, he won't. I promise. You've probably heard the stories about him, but Lord Edgington is different from everyone else." I thought about these words and realised how true they were. "Over the last month, I've come to see that Grandfather is nothing like the man I imagined him to be. He doesn't judge the world according to preconceived ideas or other people's expectations. He analyses each new moment based on the evidence before him. I have no doubt in my mind that he'll listen to what you have to say."

He shrugged then and I saw a flash of the Marmaduke Adelaide that I'd known from school. "Fine, take me to him. He's darned ancient, anyway. It's not as if he can keep me here by force."

As my former bully and now apparent ally got to his feet, I thought, *Well, I wouldn't be too sure of that,* but said nothing more.

CHAPTER TWENTY-SEVEN

Grandfather hadn't moved a muscle since I'd left him in the library after lunch. He was sitting in the same chair, his hands joined together in front of him and his elbows at right angles. He made no sign of having heard us as I knocked on the door and entered the room.

"Grandfather?" I was worried for a moment that he was-

"What do you mean by coming in here without permission?" He jerked back to life, his face, distorted with rage until he caught sight of me and relented. "Oh, Christopher, it's you."

"I've brought Marmaduke Adelaide to see you. I thought you'd want to hear what he has to say."

He sat up in his chair but showed no surprise at the presence of our uninvited guest.

"Indeed. Bring him in."

Marmaduke skulked along behind me as I made my way deeper into the sanctuary.

"Good evening, Lord Edgington." He sounded nervous again and I realised that, despite his unparalleled arrogance at school, there were some figures of authority he feared after all.

"Well here we are, boy. What have you got to say for yourself?"

I moved aside and Marmaduke took a step closer to my grandfather. "I'm very sorry to intrude, and for all the trouble I've caused. I know I shouldn't have run away, but my father's not a big fan of the police and-"

"Let me tell you, Adelaide, the police aren't too keen on your father either." Grandfather took a moment to examine the lanky specimen before him. "That being said, I learnt in my career that, sometimes, the apple and the tree are infinitely far apart from one another."

He glanced at me then with a searching look that I didn't know how to respond to. Apparently reassured, he turned back to Marmaduke and, in his stentorian voice, intoned, "If you've a story to tell me, then you had better begin."

Marmaduke clutched his hands together and ran through his version of events almost exactly as before. Grandfather fired off questions throughout but, when the boy's tale was complete, the old

man said nothing. He stared at my schoolmate with a perplexed look, as though figuring out a particularly tricky conundrum. I watched from my armchair as Adelaide stayed right where he was, awaiting his judgement.

"Very good, Marmaduke," was Grandfather's appraisal when it came. "I'll ring for Todd to take you home."

My schoolmate's face fell even further, and I thought he might turn and bolt. Perhaps predicting what the boy was thinking, the old policeman spoke again. "But do not worry. I will explain what happened to the police and your father too if necessary."

He surged to his feet and over to a panel by the door with various buttons on. Normally, Fellowes would have acted as an intermediary between any lower staff members, but there was no other option and so Grandfather rang the garage directly.

A few minutes later, the dashing chauffeur appeared in his usual green livery, with a smudge of grease on one cheek and the smell of beeswax about him. Grandfather issued his commands and Marmaduke turned to leave.

"Wait one minute." The old man held his right hand up like he was swearing on a bible. "I need you to pass on a message to your father; he'll remember me."

"What is it?" Marmaduke replied, with a hint of his usual insolence.

"Tell him that, if he had anything to do with the murders here this weekend, I will find out and there will be nothing he can do to stop me exacting recompense."

Even at seventy-five, my grandfather could strike fear into people and Marmaduke swallowed hard. His face blanching a little, he still had something to say to me before he left.

"I'm sorry about the black eye, Chrissy. You know I only wanted to be invited to your party." Before I could reply, he spun on his heel and hurried out after Todd.

When we were alone once more, Grandfather started pacing the diagonal of the room to have the most space possible. I could tell he didn't want me to interrupt, but if I was to be his assistant, I felt it only fair that I knew what he was thinking.

"Doesn't this prove that you underestimated George?"

He stopped and looked offended. "Not at all, I have never over or underestimated another person in my life." Clearly, this statement needed qualifying. "It merely surprises me that, if what your friend says is true – and we have no reason to believe otherwise – George is not the man I took him to be."

I considered for a moment whether what he and I had said was actually any different. It was too much of an enigma for me to solve, so I accepted that he was cleverer than me and asked another question.

"But this does mean that George is the likely suspect, doesn't it?" I didn't quite achieve the self-assured tone I was aiming for and sounded as though I wanted him to set me straight on the matter.

"Why in heavens would you say that?"

"Because..." I stumbled over my reply. It was hard not to when trapped within my grandfather's cold, grey gaze. "Because George threatened our family and then fifteen minutes later, we almost died."

"Why would he kill his own mother to hurt Maitland? Why would he have had poison with him? Just in case he fancied dabbling in a spot of mass murder?" His voice rose with each question.

"Two birds with one stone," I retorted, feeling unnerved by his lack of faith in my ability to construct even the most basic of motives for our suspects. "He could get Adelaide off his back and inherit Cranley in one go. He was never going to drink the champagne himself; his little stumble made sure of that."

Having raged at me one minute prior, Grandfather was now beaming. "That's my boy, we'll have you thinking like a detective in no time. But there's one thing you overlooked."

"Oh, yes!?" I hadn't calmed down even if he had. "And what's that?"

He walked over to his chair and took a folio of paper and a fountain pen, which he dipped in a bottle of ink before answering.

"Sorry, the brain isn't what it was. I need to write these things down sometimes in case they escape me." I didn't quite believe him, but he finished the task and looked back up. "You forgot about Maitland himself. How do we know that he wasn't the one to poison the champagne? Just because someone killed him after, it does not rule him out as a suspect."

The very concept of this came as a revelation to me. How could I have been so foolish as to ignore Maitland's potential as a killer?

"I'm not saying he did it, but you at least need to consider the possibility. Perhaps he killed Belinda, while hoping to get rid of the lot of us and, when George worked out what was going on, he shot Maitland for revenge."

It was all too much for me. I couldn't keep hold of so many threads at once the way he could and I rather wished he'd let me look at his notes to get a better grasp on the case.

"But…" I attempted once more. "Are you saying that Maitland would have murdered his own children? And Auntie Winifred too?"

He straightened up and pulled the tails of his coat down tight to remove any creases as he considered the question. "Winifred, possibly, but I think you have forgotten something." A pause, a flick of the eyes to the door, and then he continued. "Maitland stopped your cousins from drinking the champagne. It was just before Belinda collapsed. He made a big noise, saying they were too young for alcohol. They're older than he was when I first gave him wine and it struck me as odd."

I was struggling to take in this barrage of new evidence. Whatever the outcome, it seemed increasingly likely that there was a killer in the family. I slumped into my chair and waited for Grandfather to deliver yet more tragic revelations.

"Are we any closer to the truth?" he asked instead.

I let out an exhausted breath. "Aren't you the one to tell me that?"

Back on his feet, he zigzagged about the room as if searching for an elusive clue. "I know what I know, but I want you to tell me why the story Marmaduke just told us doesn't provide us with everything we need to identify the killer."

I admit that I did not possess the swiftest mind in Great Britain. I imagine there was a good hour-long lag for most of the conclusions I formed on the case. My grandfather was the genius and I was the fool who accompanied him, but it was at this moment that I realised what the old man was doing; what he had been doing ever since his birthday. He was trying to teach me. Everything he'd done was designed to lead me to the facts which sprung out at him like a frog from a pond.

"Fellowes!" I replied, once I'd had a good think about it. "If George and Maitland were behind the killings, why would they have poisoned Fellowes?"

Lord Edgington clapped his hands together with unrestrained joy.

"Precisely, my boy! Precisely!"

CHAPTER TWENTY-EIGHT

Grandfather was at his sparkling best and we talked until the early hours of the morning. he was full of stories from his career and opened my eyes to the endless possibilities in a seemingly simple murder. He told me of cut-and-dried cases where the perpetrator was apparent from the very first moment, yet the guilty party turned out to be someone else entirely.

He talked of the criminals he had known. Some were savage, but plenty were smart. Despite the worlds between them, he came to consider them as acquaintances, or even colleagues. They worked in overlapping circles; different departments in the same organisation.

And yet, for all his spark and candour, when I went up to bed that night, I realised that he had held a lot back from me. He wouldn't tell me why he trusted Fellowes so implicitly, or share with me his own theories on Belinda and Maitland's murders. Whether he was training me to be his assistant or not, I found it quite perplexing that every time we found a new piece of evidence on one of our suspects, he would make it sound as though the conclusions I had drawn were preposterous.

Fellowes had lied about who he met when he left the drinks room, and yet Grandfather had made me feel like a fool for believing he was involved. Cora was in the right place at the right time for both murders and her family held a longstanding grudge against us, but he trusted every word she said. George was not the misunderstood innocent that Grandfather had taken him for, but I was rushing to judgement by condemning him as our likely culprit.

If this was my training, I think I needed a little more clarification on some of the lessons.

The next day was dark and grim. After a week of sunshine, it came as a shock to feel the cold air rush at me when I threw my windows open in search of warmth. The clouds over Cranley were dark blue with rain and a light drizzle had already coated the gardens with a layer of gloss.

In my thickest woollen jersey and slacks, I went down to breakfast, still unable to shake the chill of my room. Albert looked even more distraught than normal, but would soon be heading back to university to find a new ex-girlfriend. He sat at the end of the breakfast table, staring at Cook's selection of strangely coloured food and feeling hard done by.

"I suppose you've been palling around with Grandfather again," he said with a huff. "Has he changed his will in your favour yet?"

I have to say, I find my brother's bad moods rather amusing. "Yes, that's right. I'm going to inherit the lot. And I'm under strict instructions not to share a penny with you. Grandfather says you'd only have it fished back off you by a bunch of silly girls."

His outraged face was as fine a composition as any portrait in the National Gallery. His mouth hung at a lopsided angle, his lip was raised and I swear that he stopped breathing altogether for a few seconds.

"Mother!" he finally wailed as my parents appeared in the doorway. "It's simply not fair. Why should Christopher get to inherit everything? I'm far more charming than he is; everyone says so. I know what it takes to be a gentleman while he spends his day picking worms up in the gardens and bothering birds with them. It's simply not fair!"

For a grown man of twenty-one, Albert could sound an awful lot like a child of two.

Though father looked put out by our argument, my mother failed to suppress a smile. "Really, Albert. Chrissy's just pulling your leg. I know for a fact that my father would never do anything so rash or unthinking as changing his will to leave the rest of us penniless."

I felt a tad guilty so reassured my brother that our mother was speaking nothing but sense. "Mater is right, old bean. All Grandfather and I talk about is dead bodies and criminals. I don't think he's particularly concerned about the family fortune and, if I'm honest, neither am I."

This went some way to quelling his jealousy, but he still didn't look happy. "Well, I have to say, I feel left out. How do you know that I'd be no help in solving crimes?"

I was fairly certain that corpses were the last thing my preening, perfumed brother would be interested in.

"Come along then," I told him. "Why don't you tell us who you think the killer is?"

He looked rather shaken then. "Oh... I... Well, I couldn't possibly say without having a good think on things but... Well, I don't see why no one is considering batty old Clementine."

My parents both erupted with delight. I managed to control myself and would have laid out exactly what was wrong with the supposition that our octogenarian great-aunt was guilty of a double killing, when my grandfather arrived to do it for me.

"Are you sure about that, Albert?" He swooped into the room like an elderly vampire. Dressed from collar to soles in his traditional dove-grey morning suit, he came to a stop a mere foot away from my gloomy sibling. "Do you really think that a woman of eighty-something has been zipping about the place like a firework, dispatching our relatives with the ease of the grim reaper?"

Albert emitted an awkward giggle and cleared his throat before speaking. "Um… no, of course not. It was just a silly joke of mine. You know how I love to tease."

Grandfather's beetling brows drew together. "Though, of course, it isn't out of the realm of possibility. And it's certainly true that old Clemmie's apparent decrepitude would be the perfect cover for her crimes. Not to mention the fact that, by wiping out our side of the family, she would have ensured that Cranley Hall would go to her own granddaughter. As it should have anyway, had my brother not died before he could inherit it."

Albert was greatly confused by all of this. He laughed once more, then grew serious, then raised one finger before putting it back down again. With no obvious rejoinder in mind, he went for a nice, nonspecific, "Well, quite!"

Grandfather fixed him with a penetrative stare and Albert positively quaked. The old man finally took pity on him and his thunderous laughter shook the room.

"You love to mock, Daddy," my mother commented as she sat down beside me at the table. "Don't be so cruel."

Grandfather puffed up his chest rather proudly. "If any of you know anything about me, it's that I never rule out a possibility until all evidence suggests otherwise. As long as old Clemmie is capable of putting one foot in front of another, she's a potential murderer in my book and Albert really wasn't being as silly as you might think."

"Very droll," my father added, and then his face fell as two policemen marched into the room. Inspector Blunt pootled along some distance behind.

"Walter Prentiss?" he demanded, as though he didn't know the answer already.

My father could only muster a nod as Mother rushed around the table to place her hand on his shoulder.

A smile spread across Blunt's face, but even as he delivered his big line, it was his old rival who he directed his glare at. "Walter Prentiss, you're under arrest for the murders of Belinda Trevelyan and Maitland Cranley."

My mother was the first to react. "But I was with my husband when Maitland was killed. We were upstairs together."

"How very convenient!" The inspector was sneering by now.

"This is preposterous." I have no doubt that Grandfather could have called upon any number of fine arguments to weaken the officer's case, but he was soon overruled.

Blunt raised one hand to silence him. "Save it for the trial. I'm not interested in what you have to say. We have evidence that your son-in-law shot your son through the heart with a crossbow and nothing you can say will change that."

"Oh yes?" My father replied, his voice coated with all the pomposity that a City gent should be able to call upon on at such a moment. "And what evidence is that?"

Blunt's needling look grew more aggressive as he pointed to a subordinate who reached into the burlap sack he was carrying.

"We found the bleedin' crossbow in your bleedin' bedroom!"

CHAPTER TWENTY-NINE

"Now, no one worry. I swear this is a good thing."

The police had carried my father off in one of their cars like a common criminal. I suppose that, as far as they were concerned, that's exactly what he was. Albert, my mother and I were in a state of pure shock and could barely squeak out a word after they'd gone.

Grandfather, though, was far from silent. "Without meaning to, the police have provided us with a key piece of evidence. They've shown their hand and it will help us find the killer all the sooner."

I don't think any of us had the strength to believe him just then, but I had to try.

"You do mean it, Grandfather? You do believe that he's innocent?"

He strode over to me and bent low so that our eyes were level. "Of course I do, Christopher. I have never considered your father to be a likely culprit. I promise you that."

It was hard to believe him. "But that's what you said about George and Fellowes and Cora too. If we dismiss anyone else, your dog will be the only suspect left."

He didn't answer immediately, but dropped into a chair and chewed his lip to think over my words. "If it looked that way, it was only part of the investigation. Our friend Inspector Blunt marches about the place, barking at every suspect he comes across, but that is not my style."

I knew he was lying. He wouldn't have been a good detective if he hadn't at least considered my father's guilt.

"In the armoury!" I burst out with. "I saw you checking the angle that would have been needed to fire the crossbow at Uncle Maitland. When you were finished, you glanced up at the ceiling for a fraction of a second. You were considering whether he could have shot down from the upper floor."

I could see that he was taken aback by my deduction and didn't try to deny it. "I've told you many times that, until a suspect can be ruled out entirely, they must remain a suspect, even if they're a member of the family. That doesn't mean I believe Walter is capable of murdering two people in cold blood."

His ferocious response faded out and a hush seized the breakfast room once more. My mother poured herself a glass of water, took a long, desperate drink and dried her mouth.

"None of this matters, as I was with Walter when my brother was killed." She sat up straighter in her chair and raised her chin to restore a little of her usual decorum.

Grandfather sat down across the table from his daughter and reached his hand out towards her. "You were together in the same room, your eyes on him the whole time?"

"I..." she began, but there was already doubt in her voice and my heart sank. "I was in the bathroom which adjoins our sitting room. But... there's no way he would have taken the risk of shooting from there, not with me so close by. And, besides, it's far too long a shot for Walter. He's an average hunter but no great marksman."

"The perfect angle to take it from though," my grandfather put in. "The police have got that much right." He whistled absentmindedly before realising that we were staring at him in horror and he rushed to clarify. "I'm sorry, that isn't to say that he's guilty. I'm merely explaining why Blunt would arrest him."

It was at this moment that Albert decided to abandon all hope and crashed his head down onto the table melodramatically. It was lucky he'd finished his breakfast, or he would have landed right in the black pudding.

"What hope have I got of finding a fiancée now?" he asked through the tablecloth. "Son of a criminal isn't the type of chap women look for in a husband."

Grandfather let out an entirely inappropriate laugh. "You'd be surprised, Albert. I can tell you, you'd be surprised." He became aware of my mother's disapproving gaze and looked a little guilty once more.

"You said that, by arresting Walter, the police had shown their hand." She gripped her hands together tightly as if in prayer. "In what way exactly?"

The old man cleared his throat. "The crossbow! If I ever doubted Walter, the police finding the weapon in his bedroom proves that he didn't do it." He looked at me as he said this. "No one would be fool enough to leave such a vital piece of evidence in a place where it could be linked to them."

"But how does that help us clear Father's name?" Albert's question was one long whine. "How can we catch the real killer?"

"Because whoever shot Maitland must have gone upstairs to hide the weapon at some point. There was only a short period between the murder and everyone leaving. We'll ask the staff and find out who was there."

"That's brilliant," my brother proclaimed, finding a jolt of positivity.

"Unless of course Walter wanted us to think that he was too clever to leave the weapon right there and, in actual fact-" Grandfather was thinking out loud again and failed to consider how his words would be received.

My mother let out a downhearted sigh and Albert's head crashed once more against the breakfast table.

"I'm sure that's not the case." He wriggled his moustache from side to side and rose to standing. "Come along, Christopher. We've work to do."

Delilah had been keeping my feet warm under the table and now surged out from behind the long white cloth after her master. Not seeing much other option, I ran to catch up.

"Grandfather, wait," I puffed. "Where are we going now?"

"Don't you know?" he asked in typically enigmatic fashion, as he stopped to turn his lighthouse-beam gaze upon me.

"No, of course I don't." I was already out of breath. "I wouldn't have asked otherwise."

He started walking again at a slightly more reasonable pace. "Well, where do *you* suggest we should go? Who do your instincts tell you we should be talking to next?"

I had a good think about it. "Clem- Fello- Cor-" I began, hoping to see some reaction on his face to tell me I was on the right path, before settling on, "George?"

"Very good. We'll pass through the kitchen on the way to see whether the staff saw anyone upstairs yesterday, though I very much doubt it. I really only mentioned the idea to make your mother feel better about your father's arrest. Then, after that, we're heading to London."

CHAPTER THIRTY

Grandfather was most insightful in his prediction. None of the maids had seen anything unusual the previous morning. George had been up there of course, as his room was a little way along from my parents', but he'd been downstairs immediately after Maitland was shot and we still couldn't say for certain where the crossbow had been fired from. It felt to me as though we'd wandered into yet another cul-de-sac.

On the bright side, we came across Todd reading one of his adventure novels in the kitchen. We gave him his commission for the day and he escorted us to the garage.

"Marvellous!" Grandfather yelled as soon as the barn doors were open and he was able to survey his impressive collection. "Of course, I read so much about them in pamphlets and magazines before I purchased each one that I feel I know them all intimately."

"Should I crank up the Silver Ghost, Milord?"

Like a child on Christmas morning, my grandfather's gaze was darting around the wonders he beheld. Swaying slightly from one foot to the other, he held one hand up in his chauffeur's direction.

"Not so fast, young man. This is a moment to savour." He walked up to the Rolls and gave the 'flying lady' bonnet ornament an affectionate pat on the head, before continuing on down the alley in the middle of the barn. His eyes grew wider as he approached his red Alfa Romeo Targa Florio.

Todd whispered to me in a reverent tone. "I heard that the Aga Khan drove an Alfa RLS and said it was 'one of the most excellent cars' he'd ever driven."

I made an impressed cooing sound, though I couldn't quite remember who the Aga Khan was.

As the sporty model wasn't what he was looking for, my Grandfather moved on. He passed a comparatively sensible black Mercedes and a stunning white Talbot-Darracq drophead coupé then paused to consider a Matchless motorcycle and sidecar. I have to say, I was relieved when he kept walking. But it was when he ran his fingers along the bonnet of the next car that he really came to life.

Looking back at us over his shoulder, he yelled, "Crossley Bugatti! This is the one."

Todd was quick to point out a flaw in his plan. "It only has two seats, Milord. May I suggest the Talbot?"

Grandfather did not look happy but whipped his hand through the air in reluctant acceptance and Todd got to work preparing our chariot. Delilah was very excited by the noise of the engine roaring into life and ran around in circles with her tail wagging.

"I'm sorry, old girl," her master said, "but I'm afraid you'll have to stay at home today. London is no place for a creature like you."

Delilah must have understood each and every word he said as she immediately lay down on the ground in the middle of the barn and looked glum.

"Well, don't be like that. It's not my fault that the English capital isn't fit for a dog. Take my word for it; you'll be much happier here."

Delilah did not look convinced as we climbed into the Talbot. We got halfway out of the barn but the faithful retriever wouldn't budge. Grandfather leaned over Todd to honk the horn and that clever dog pretended she hadn't heard and stayed right where she was. In the end, he got out and carried Delilah to safety, for Todd to ease the car outside. Even then she insisted on following us right to the gatehouse, barking unhappily the whole way.

Sadly for me, my seat that day was even more cramped and bumpy than the Aston Martin's had been. In fact, *seat* is rather an ostentatious term for what was essentially a compartment for me to fold my body into. The dickey seat placed me right in the back of the vehicle where the boot should have been. It was loud and cold and I got hit a number of times by stones flying up from under the tyres. At least I'd thought to grab some goggles this time though.

To begin with, Grandfather was full of the joys of spring, even if it did start raining as soon as we passed Woking. He was clearly enjoying the luxury of being driven around in such… well, luxury. I noticed however that his mood changed as we got closer to our destination. From my pauper's throne, I could see that his face was like a barometer and grew increasingly dark and gloomy in direct proportion to our proximity to London. It rather reminded me of Sherlock Holmes in 'The Adventure of the Copper Beeches'. While Holmes fears the degeneracy of the countryside, Superintendent Edgington apparently disapproved of the sins of the city.

It was all very green and pleasant as we drove past Hampton Court and around Richmond Park but then London sneaked up on me without my expecting it. As soon as we crossed Putney Bridge, the grand edifices of the capital reared up in front of the car. For a Surrey boy, born and bred in the country, I can tell you it was a real thrill.

By the time we arrived in Knightsbridge, Grandfather looked like a haunted man. Were there ghosts around us that only he could see? Perhaps his decades on the force had left a permanent stain on every street in London. I could only imagine the horrors he'd encountered there over the years and would have to ask him what he had been thinking, just as soon as he looked a tad less... murderous.

We drove past the Natural History Museum and Harrods department store and soon pulled up in front of George's building. Wasting no time, the engine had barely come to a stop when Grandfather pushed his door open and jumped from the vehicle. He paused on the pavement to look up at the terrace of white-fronted townhouses, before striding up the steps of the property to hammer on the front door.

"What's your business here?" the porter answered in a brusque East London accent once the door had opened a fraction.

Lord Edgington's eyes narrowed. "I'm here to see George Trevelyan."

The bald, beige-faced man looked unintimidated by our arrival and sniffed long and loudly through the crack in the door. "Are you expected?"

In order to communicate quite how great an inconvenience this conversation was to a man of his eminence, Grandfather did not look at the porter as he replied, but stared along the busy residential street, as if he had far more significant issues to concern himself with.

"I telephoned an hour ago, but there was no answer."

The porter popped his head back inside the building to consult... I have no idea what, before opening the door to let us pass.

"Apartment 1B," he called after us. "And don't go dirtying the walls. They've only recently been painted."

We huffed our way past the officious chap and along his sparkling corridor. I was tempted to leave fingerprints on the glossy dado rail, but I'm not that cruel.

"George," Grandfather boomed, after we found the right door. We didn't have to wait to enter as it was slightly ajar. "Are you in here? Are you decent?"

"Yes, yes!" a voice called back from the end of the dark hall. "Quite decent by most people's standards." He let out a laugh, which more or less confirmed that my cousin was sozzled.

We followed the sound and came to a rather modern living room. It was all Mackintosh furniture and Liberty print fabrics. Well, it was modern compared to Cranley Hall where the most up-to-date feature was a Gainsborough landscape that a long dead ancestor had commissioned and which now hung in one of the pokier guest bathrooms.

"Grandfather, what a joy to have you here!" George intoned. "And you brought your lapdog Chrissy along with you. How wonderful."

Do you remember what I said about my affection for the pariah of the family? Well, I'd changed my mind by this point.

He was sitting on a long white sofa which, judging by the blankets and pillows strewn across it, had doubled as his bed the previous night. It was only twelve noon but the smell of spirits was thick in the air and a couple of bottles lay toppled on the carpet at his feet. I had to wonder whether he'd started drinking early or finished late.

"George," my grandfather replied in a murmur, but, before he could say anything more, our host recommenced his sunny performance.

"To what do I owe this unexpected pleasure? Let me guess, you're here to accuse me of matricide again. Or perhaps you've brought good news and Mother isn't dead after all and it was all a hilarious trick."

Sitting on the edge of the elongated pine coffee table, Grandfather cut straight to the point. "We know what you were doing with Maitland and young Adelaide on Saturday night before the toast. So, I'm going to ask you once more, what is your connection to Horatio Adelaide and for what reason did he send you to the ball?"

I believe the force of this opening roll of the dice must have struck George rather firmly between the eyes. His head wobbled on its perch for a moment before finding equilibrium, as though my grandfather's words had sobered him up.

"You'll have to excuse me," he said. "I'm having a moment of déjà vu. Didn't we already discuss this whole matter? I believe I already informed you that Horatio Adelaide and I play golf together, nothing more, nothing less. I've heard people say that he's something of a rotter, but all I can tell you about him is that he's got a fine handicap and puts me to shame with a one-wood."

He let out a short, high laugh, like the first whistling note escaping from a kettle.

"You're smarter than this, boy." Grandfather was not amused. "You know what your golfing chum was willing to do to Maitland when he wouldn't pay up. What do you think will happen when you're no longer useful to him?"

It seemed as though the message was finally penetrating George's thick skull. He licked his lips from side to side reflexively before responding.

"I appreciate your concern, I really do. But you needn't worry. I have an understanding with Horatio and I won't get myself into the position that Maitland was in."

"As uttered every gambler in history," our grandfather snapped and George peered down at the inch of gin which remained in the bottle on the floor.

Feeling that I might have something to contribute for once, I started in on a question of my own. "Why did Maitland owe so much money? His family are well off, they have a lovely house and servants and all that sort of thing. How did he become involved with Adelaide in the first place?"

George took five seconds to decide whether he wanted to cooperate, sighed and gave in. "They have a nice house for the moment, but they won't for much longer if Adelaide has his way." He looked up at the ceiling and shook his head. "You know, people think I'm such a cad for going to the horses once in a while, or dropping a few hundred pounds at a Saint James's club, but nobody worries about the Maitlands and Walters of this world. No one criticises the bankers and brokers who gamble with the wealth and welfare of the people whose lives depend upon them."

I followed up my question with another. "So Maitland invested poorly then?"

"Ask your father. He might be scraping through this mess, but I can't imagine he's doing a great deal better himself."

I thought about where my father was just then – locked in a cell or enduring another of Inspector Blunt's interrogations – and my skin prickled.

My Grandfather took over. "Young Adelaide said that Maitland had owed his father money for years. How could it have gone on for so long without any of us knowing about it?"

My cousin released another cold burst of laughter. "I thought you would have worked that out by now. After all, you know the kind of business that Horatio Adelaide is involved in." He paused to allow our grandfather a moment to consider this.

"Maitland was investing Adelaide's money? Making his ill-gotten gains look respectable through the markets?"

George gleefully extended one finger towards us. "Right first time, Grandfather. And that was fine when times were good, but when the war hit and the stock exchange was closed, Adelaide made a loss which he was not willing to bear. Maitland spent the last decade trying to recoup the money and Horatio finally ran out of patience."

The atmosphere in the room had changed. I was suddenly nervous listening to George's story. There was darkness to everything he said, like he couldn't care less what had happened to our uncle and perhaps even his own mother. This was all just business to him, and I was determined to take him up on it.

"So Horatio Adelaide had you poison the champagne and, when that didn't go as planned, you murdered Maitland with the crossbow." I admit that I should have waited for Grandfather to draw his own conclusions. In my defence, I was caught up in the moment and, as George kept shuffling in his seat like he couldn't wait to get away, it seemed like a sensible suggestion to make.

"Ha! No, of course not." Turning to address the old man, George's whole demeanour brightened. "You'd better watch this one, Grandfather. He's been reading too many racy stories and thinks the worst of everyone."

"Actually, I'm rather partial to Charles Dickens!" I replied in a haughty tone which did nothing for my standing in the discussion.

"Chrissy, dear boy. I didn't kill anyone." The temptation had got too much for him and he lunged for the nearest bottle, uncorked the stopper and poured the last traces of clear spirit down his throat. "Horatio sent me to warn Maitland that if he didn't make up the money that Adelaide had lost, he'd be taking the family home."

Grandfather held his gaze on his eldest grandson for five ticks of the carriage clock. "Are you absolutely sure of this, George? You honestly believe that the Adelaides played no part in the murders?"

When my cousin replied, the arrogance had drained from his voice. "Well, as far as I know. Horatio's no fool, after all. His business would only suffer if he started killing off members of the ruling class willy-nilly."

I was trying to judge for myself whether he was speaking the truth, but it was so hard to say for certain. Still, there was one chink in his argument that I had spotted. "What about Marmaduke? Why did you beat him black and blue?"

He straightened up then and, like my geography master when explaining the effects of erosion on British coasts or listing the different types of soil, he raised his hand and counted off the fingers.

"For three clear reasons actually. First, I knew it would strike fear into wimpy old Maitland – though, I admit, I got a little carried away with the gangster role I was playing. Second, I know that Horatio has little patience with his son, and was only going to be grateful that I'd given Marmaduke a thrashing." He paused then and turned his head to one side, his eyes on me alone. "And third, I'd heard the little blighter boasting that he'd given my favourite cousin a black eye at school and I didn't like it one bit."

I wanted to believe him, I really did, but there was something holding me back.

"Well, that was admirable behaviour, no doubt," Grandfather replied with a sarcastic note in his voice. "But you should have told me all of this yesterday. Why string it out for so long?"

George stood and wandered over to the window. He pulled a slim box from his pocket and lit a cigarette before answering. "Because, in case you haven't worked it out yet..." He made us wait, sucking the smoke into his lungs and then letting it back out again in a single, perfect ring. "...I don't always do what's in my best interest."

CHAPTER THIRTY-ONE

The journey home was a depressing one. The rain fell like a blanket over the car and it was all right for Grandfather and Todd under the drophead roof, but I got positively drenched in the back, all squashed up in my dickey seat.

I wasn't the only one feeling blue either. Grandfather had left George's flat in a foul mood. It was hard to say what was going on in his brilliant brain, but something had upset him. I couldn't shake the feeling that we'd gone too softly on George. He may have come up with a good story to spin us, but could we rule him out of the enquiries so quickly? He was a charmer and, as my mother always said, charmers weren't to be trusted.

Crossing the river and entering Surrey made me feel slightly more positive but it did nothing to brighten up the clouds above me and I shivered all the way home under a waxed leather tarpaulin. I half wished Delilah had come with us as, even if she'd have taken up the remaining inches of space, she'd have kept me nice and warm.

Back at Cranley, Grandfather launched himself from the Talbot without another word. Perhaps he'd forgotten I was even there, as we hadn't spoken since leaving London. Todd drove me round to the garage and I noticed that Cora's car was parked beside the house. I remained in the back seat, pondering the conundrum we were faced with, as the chauffeur wiped the raindrops off the bonnet.

"Todd, you've waited on Grandfather from time to time over the years," I said when my thoughts had got me nowhere. "Do you think he's..." I struggled to choose the right words. "Well, do you think he's *all there*?"

Todd dropped the soapy sponge into its bucket and laughed at me. "Yes, Master Christopher. I think of all the people I've had the honour of meeting in my life, Lord Edgington stands as the brightest and best. Even when he was shut up in his rooms, he spent every day consuming literature, scientific journals and world news. I wouldn't worry too much about him on that score."

I pulled the tarpaulin off me and wished I hadn't as it burst the humid bubble I'd been trapped within.

"Thank you," was all I could think to say.

He picked up a chamois leather and looked at me like he was expecting something more.

"Would you mind jumping out?" he asked, when I failed to catch his meaning. "Only I need to close up the boot and give it a polish."

I didn't feel like returning to my room, and it was too wet to go back to the woods, so I went for a turn around the house to think. I find that walking often helps clear my mind and stimulate the senses. An old house like Cranley Hall comes in handy for such pastimes when the weather is bad too. I went all the way from the kitchen to the far end of the east wing as I considered the facts of the case.

There were so many questions left unanswered; *who was the murderer?* for one! And before I could answer that whopper, I'd have to fill in some holes first. The issue my grandfather kept returning to was why the killer would have only poisoned Fellowes but not killed him. The obvious reason was a lack of time or opportunity. Perhaps he'd run out of cyanide, after dumping so much of the stuff in the champagne. Or perhaps it was due to the fact that, whilst people don't seem too fond of the Cranley family, the kind-hearted murderer was unwilling to knock off an innocent butler.

Of course, Fellowes was a puzzle in himself. He was an ex-convict whose murky past Grandfather had kept hidden, even after Inspector Blunt revealed his criminal record. And I couldn't see that Fellowes saving the old man's life twenty years earlier was enough to prove he hadn't played a part in the poisoning. It was all a bit too convenient; leaving the drinks room like that for the killer to lace the champagne.

Grandfather had gone far too easy on Cora too. What if she'd been working with her beau to steal the inheritance from the rest of us? The two of them in cahoots would have found it easy to silence Maitland with the crossbow, even if Fellowes was laid up with a dicky stomach. Yes! That had to be it. If he'd handled the poison, perhaps he'd breathed in the molecules of it and made himself sick. That sort of thing was always happening in the spy novels that Albert read, rogue substances getting into the population and creating havoc.

Had I just solved the murders where the great Lord Edgington had failed to? It seemed awfully likely, but I couldn't present the case to him until I had more evidence. I sat down in the petit salon to think things through, then had to get straight back up again a moment later as I knew what was required.

"Yes!" I said out loud as I strode down the corridor in the west wing. And, as such positive affirmation motivates me, I said it a few times more. "Yes! Yes! Yes!"

"Master Christopher, are you all right?" It was lovely Alice. She'd stepped out of the silver room to see what the fuss was about.

I was so sure of myself right then, that I might well have asked that beautiful specimen to marry me. Perhaps luckily, I went with a far subtler, "Indeed. And all the better for seeing you."

"Oh, Master Christopher, you do like to tease." She shook her head and returned to her duties, apparently oblivious to the romantic overture I'd made.

I carried on towards the servants' quarters, but instead of taking the narrow stairs down to them, I went to the kitchen and out through the tradesman's entrance to skirt around the side of the building. I felt just like Richard Hannay in 'The Thirty-Nine Steps', I was a spy on a mission; a wronged man searching for answers.

I didn't have to creep too far to reach the tiny window of our butler's quarters, from where I could listen in on his conversation with his lover. To be honest, I had to wait quite some time to get to anything juicy. They talked about the rain, Cook's complex culinary abilities, whether Fellowes's tummy was on the mend or not and, in great and lengthy detail, what he would eat once he was back to one hundred per cent.

It was cold out and, though I could cower against the building to avoid the worst of the perpetual downfall, large drops occasionally splashed down upon me from the edge of the roof. It was enough to make a spy give up and go back inside!

My commitment to the investigation held out though and, while I did get a little sleepy at one point, my watch finally bore fruits.

"You mustn't worry so much, Reg," Cora told him and I wish that I hadn't got distracted by a rather affectionate robin who had landed down beside me. "The old man adores you. And, though I may say so myself..." She let out a rather wicked laugh just then. "...he's putty in my hands!"

Fellowes joined in with the laughter and I heard a kissy noise that turned my stomach. The two of them were thrilling in their crimes and the deaths of my aunt and uncle.

"All I'm saying is that we don't want to do anything to compromise our position."

I heard the bed springs flex then and imagined that my scheming second cousin was cuddling up to her partner. "You're such a worrier, Reg. Just stay calm and everything will turn out fine."

There was some more smacking of lips and I felt a bit guilty for listening into such a private moment, then remembered they were most likely murderers and didn't feel so bad.

As they enjoyed their time together, I processed the evidence against them once more. Fellowes was the one with primary access to the champagne. He'd left his post unnecessarily – I'm sorry, but butlers aren't generally granted kissing breaks in the middle of an important function – and he even lied about hearing the gardeners call his name when first challenged on the issue.

Cora on the other hand, stood to gain more than any other person without a glass of champagne. Though her elderly grandmother was the next in line to the family fortune, she was Clementine's only direct heir and would easily have gained control of the inheritance. With Fellowes help, Cora must have planted the cyanide in the bottle. Which means that Maitland spotted them together and he was about to tell us when she shot him dead from the armoury, only to use the sleepy old woman as her alibi. As my parents descended to find out what had happened, the not entirely incapacitated Fellowes nipped upstairs to plant the crossbow. It all made sense!

I'd answered Grandfather's big outstanding question for certain now. All the pieces had fallen into place and so I let out another triumphant, "Yes!"

"Chrissy?" Cora asked through the window. "Is that you out there?"

I swallowed hard, feeling dreadfully silly. Richard Hannay would never have made such an amateurish mistake!

"Um, yes. It's me." I searched through the winding corridors of my brain for something to explain why I was outside their window, in the rain, whilst they were in bed together. "I… You see… There was a robin out here. Awfully friendly chap. He's gone now, but I wasn't listening to your conversation. I promise."

CHAPTER THIRTY-TWO

Despite this minor setback to my otherwise sterling detective work, I returned to the relative warmth of Cranley Hall. I couldn't decide whether to head back to my room to update my notebook on my findings, or search out Grandfather to reveal the terrifying truth I had discovered. In the end, the choice was made for me.

"Chrissy," the old man's voice boomed out of the ballroom as I passed.

Until now, there had been chairs blocking the entrance, which the police had put there to stop anyone contaminating the crime scene. Of course, if anyone had the authority to barge through them it was former-Superintendent Edgington. When I looped back and stepped inside, he was standing in the middle of the room, apparently in a daze.

I didn't like to say anything as he looked so distant that I was afraid he was sleepwalking and I know how dangerous it can be to wake a somnambulist. I read a newspaper article once about a woman in East Grinstead who beat her husband to death with a chair leg after he attempted to wake her. I wouldn't be trying that.

It turned out, though, that Grandfather wasn't sleeping at all. He glanced around the ballroom inquisitively, as though deciding what new furnishings to buy. Furthermore, he wasn't alone. I hadn't spotted him at first, but Todd was standing near the French windows and Halfpenny was sitting beside the door to the grand salon, looking bored.

"One moment, Chrissy," Grandfather told me. "We're working through something. I'll explain when I can."

Just then, dear, sweet Alice bustled past me from the corridor. She was apparently quite drunk all of a sudden.

"Excellent acting, Alice." Grandfather beat his hands together in appreciation. "Really quite remarkable stuff."

"Thank you, Milord," she replied in a voice that was as melodic as any Celtic harp.

"Stay in character, though. I need to maintain the atmosphere if we're going to work this thing out."

I was surprised to see Cook appear in the doorway, pushing a drinks trolley with a host of champagne flutes on board.

"I'll put these over here shall, I, Milord?" she asked, as she came to a stop near her employer.

"Jolly good, Cook."

To complete the tableau, the two gardeners came in from the hall in the slow, apologetic manner they adopted whenever Grandfather was present.

Our host looked about between his staff. When no one else joined us, he explained, "We're a couple of suspects short. Marmaduke Adelaide remained outside on the terrace, whilst my dear sister-in-law was asleep in one of the neighbouring rooms."

It was at this point that I finally realised what was going on. They were re-enacting the events of Aunt Belinda's last moments on Earth.

Grandfather stepped forward to direct. "So, we all took a glass."

Todd, the two gardeners, Alice and Halfpenny – who were standing in for our suspects – seized their glasses from the trolley and Cook mimed the pouring of the champagne.

"No, not like that, Cook," Grandfather admonished. "Fellowes had already poured out the glasses in the drinks room by this point. In fact, you can go back to the kitchen if you're busy."

"Perfect," she replied with a grin. "I'm making a cottage pie for supper and I must get on."

"Your own recipe?" Grandfather enquired, sounding quite excited.

"That's right. Beef and peanuts."

"Delightful! Off you pop then."

After our seasoned chef had left the scene, the old man turned his attention to Todd. "Right, at this moment, I was making my speech, but Belinda didn't wait for the toast to drink her champagne and it was soon after that-"

Todd clutched his neck and, wandering back towards the row of chairs at the side of the room, collapsed with a noisy imitation of a death gurgle.

"No need to be quite so graphic, thank you, Todd." My grandfather's moustaches scrunched together in disapproval.

Unperturbed by the critique that his employer had provided, Todd bolted upright on the floor. "Actually, Milord, this doesn't make any sense. I can't be Belinda."

His concentration broken once more, Grandfather let out a huff.

"And why's that, my man?"

"Because I was there on the night." Todd spoke as if the significance of this fact should be wildly apparent. "If I'm Belinda, who's playing me?"

Grandfather rolled his eyes to the ceiling. "Yes, that's an admirable point, Todd. But we're mainly focussed on the suspects to the murder here. As fine a job as you did behind the bar, I think we can manage without a stand in. Now, if it isn't too much trouble, be a good chap and die."

Todd gave a cheerful smile, emitted another stomach-churning noise from deep in his throat and collapsed once more.

Grandfather continued with the re-enactment. "So, George rushed over to his mother, we all thought she had imbibed a little too freely and then…"

He came to a sudden halt. Looking about at the various players, he was whispering something to himself, but I couldn't work out what it was. We waited expectantly for him to reveal what he had discovered. Instead, he peered around the room, spinning slowly on the ball of one foot.

"No, it's no good," he finally declared, after everyone was tired of holding their positions like statues and our dead body had opened his eyes several times to see what was going on. "I appreciate your help, but you can all go back to your regular duties. I shall seek you out again if anything else occurs to me."

"We have every faith in you, Milord." Old Halfpenny, who has always been a bit of a bootlicker, bowed low before ushering the others out of the room. I had no doubt that he was enjoying his role at the top of the household staff in Fellowes's absence. From what I'd heard in the servants' quarters, it didn't sound as though he would maintain this lofty position for much longer as Fellowes was clearly on the mend.

Whether or not Grandfather had learnt anything from this piece of theatre, yet another clue to our culprits' guilt had clicked into place in my brain. Seeing the events unfold for the second time, I remembered Cora claiming that, having taken her time to check her appearance in a mirror, she entered the ballroom to find that the toast had started. But on both the night of the ball, and now in Grandfather's re-staging, she had been the first of the two to appear. So why lie?

I'll tell you why! Because their whole story from beginning to end was one elaborate concoction. There was no opportunity for anyone else to poison the champagne because Fellowes was the poisoner all along. Cora made sure that the job was in progress before running along to the ball to be seen there when the supposed killer was supposedly doing the deed!

Gosh! My skills of deduction had improved beyond recognition. What an incredible job my grandfather had done training me in such a short time. He'd still shown signs of his famous abilities, of course, but, in his dotage, he was simply too trusting. He'd been taken in by Cora and Fellowes's innocent act, but I refused to be so easily led.

CHAPTER THIRTY-THREE

Once the others had left, I was at a quandary over how to present my discoveries to Grandfather. Luckily, he made it easy.

"What is it that I'm missing?"

It was the perfect moment to reveal the truth, but discretion is the better part of valour and all that, so I had to phrase it diplomatically. "Don't blame yourself, Grandfather. It's not your fault that you haven't found the killer."

He looked a little confused. "Finding the killer isn't necessarily the problem. It's in piecing every scrap of evidence together that things get complicated. I could prove to you that several of our suspects had the means and opportunity to carry out the killings. And I have no doubt that the evidence I have already assembled would be enough to convince a jury, but there are still so many question marks and contradictions to account for."

His answer had knocked the wind out of me a little and I posed a question of my own. "Oh yes?" I tried to sound cool and disinterested, as though I weren't checking to see whether he'd worked out something that I'd failed to. "Like what for example?"

His answer came out in a torrent as he zipped about the room, retracing the steps of our suspects at the ball.

"For one thing, we don't know what Maitland saw on the night his sister was killed." I thought, *I do,* but I let him continue. "There's also the question of how the killer managed to plant the crossbow in your parents' bedroom without being caught after the second murder." Transparently obvious! "And why he only put Fellowes out of action temporarily instead of sending him to the mortuary."

His erratic journey came to a stop at the place where Aunt Belinda had breathed her last, and he threw his arms in the air in frustration. "I don't even know for certain why my children were killed. Most investigations begin by focussing on the victim, but I've been so set on the idea that this whole thing came about because someone was after my money that I've ignored the basic tenets of police work."

He crashed down in the nearest chair and buried his head in his hands. I felt awful for him and realised that it was my job to help him along to the solution. Perhaps I'd never tell him that I'd discovered it first. He could have all the glory and I'd enjoy the satisfaction of making an elderly chap feel less bleak about the world.

"Why don't we go back to the beginning and think about everything we know about Belinda, Maitland and our suspects?"

He didn't look up at me immediately but, when he spoke again, his voice was calmer. "That's a grand idea, Christopher. Really, top notch."

"Why don't you start with Cora and Fellowes?" I suggested, as subtly as a fox.

He was up on his feet and back to his old self, but instantly brushed aside my idea. "No, no. We've already ruled them out. That would just be a waste of time."

I felt like screaming. Of all the stubborn, pig-headed people I'd ever met, he had to be the worst!

"Let's start with Belinda as you suggested before." He breathed in to steel himself for what he was about to do. "Though we believe every glass of champagne was poisoned, the killer might have predicted that she would be the first to drink. So, why would anyone want her dead?"

"She wasn't the most popular person in the family and she'd been jealous of me for helping you prepare the ball when..." I never finished that sentence as I realised that it might well implicate my father in the crime.

Luckily, Grandfather had his mind on other things. "No, it has to be something bigger. You're right that she was unpopular. Belinda had the most impressive skill for making enemies. Even my staff couldn't stand her. But she wasn't close enough to anyone outside the family to warrant murdering." It was odd to hear him speak of his daughter in such unfavourable terms. "If anyone had something against her, it was George."

A thought sprang to mind. "You're right. We know that Belinda had stopped paying her son's debts. Perhaps he was seeking revenge."

Grandfather stroked the long, white hair on one side of his jaw. "Yes, and I have to say, I wasn't entirely convinced by what your cousin had to say for himself. You were right about George, he's not the kind soul I believed him to be. He assaulted a sixteen-year-old boy and, though he might claim that he was sticking up for you, I do not believe it for one moment. We know he would gain from the death of his mother, that there was no risk of him drinking the poison after he dropped his glass and that he is in debt to a potentially dangerous adversary."

I was carried along on the wave of his ratiocination and almost forgot about my own infallible theory. "So you're saying he's our man?"

He thought for a moment then shook his head. "No, it's not enough. We haven't found a shred of physical evidence to link him to either of the murders and I think it would be a stretch for him to have poisoned Fellowes, unless he was working with an accomplice."

"Then what about the Adelaides?"

"Nope. That's a dead end, I'm sure of it. As George told us himself, Horatio Adelaide has spent the last three decades keeping his distance from violent crimes. It wouldn't make sense for George to kill anyone on his behalf."

It was good to see him recover his vigour and I urged him on once more. "It seems like you've ruled him out then. So that's one down. And Clementine surely can't have been involved."

He turned away from me abruptly and marched from the room. I was rather tired of chasing around after him, and positively fed up of my supposed mentor ignoring my ideas, but I followed him anyway.

"Haven't you learnt anything from me, Christopher?" he shouted down the hall. "We can never rule out a suspect until we have concrete evidence that they were in no way involved."

I drew alongside him as he stepped into the library. "But you just did the very same thing with Cora and Fellowes!"

"Yes, but only because I have concrete evidence that they were in no way involved."

I groaned then as, even by our family's standards, he was becoming eccentric.

I had to wonder whether he'd slept at all the night before, as the room we'd entered was covered with scraps of paper. There were hundreds of the things, taking up every inch of carpet, floorboard and desk and I had to walk over them to sit down in my usual armchair. I took a peek at the notes around me, but the handwriting was practically illegible.

I continued to lay out the evidence. "Great-Aunt Clementine is a thousand years old and can barely look after herself. She surely wouldn't have had the physical or mental capacity to carry out such an elaborate scheme."

His distaste for his sister-in-law flared up and he let out a snorting laugh. "Ha, that's just what she wants you to believe!"

I really felt like waving the white flag at this point, but responded all the same. "You can't mean that, Grandfather. Didn't you see how grubby she was when we went to her house? She was covered in dirt and the place was an absolute pigsty. I really don't think she could have been involved."

"Prove it!" the belligerent old man declared, in a rather school-boyish manner.

"I'm sorry?"

"You heard me."

I tried to think of some *concrete evidence* to rule out his far-fetched theory but failed. "I can't prove it," I had to admit. "There's no way to say she's undeniably innocent."

"Exactly!" He sat down rather proudly on the overlapping notes on his desk. "Do you understand what I'm saying now? We can't rule out anyone until we *can* rule them out. And that's been the problem with this case from the beginning. Too many suspects, too many avenues of thought. Even Maitland, may God rest his soul, can't be excluded altogether from the investigation."

He rushed over to me like an arrow from a bow, upending his filing system as he went. "There were sixty guests walking around on Saturday night and I haven't even been able to eliminate my loony old sister-in-law! That's how confounding this case is."

"Very well. Next suspect. What about my father?" I asked, unsure whether I wanted an answer. "You might as well go through everything we've got on him too!"

"If you insist." He smiled sympathetically before delivering the evidence. "Walter hasn't been doing well in his work. In fact, he's had to borrow money from me on a number of occasions. But then half of our suspects are in debt to someone and it's still only circumstantial evidence."

"The crossbow isn't," I replied, finding myself in the odd position of acting as the prosecution in my father's mock trial. "It was found in his room which itself overlooked the spot where Maitland was shot."

Grandfather hesitated. "Yes, but Walter wouldn't have left the murder weapon right there for the police to find it. And, as your mother pointed out, though he's hunted with a rifle all his life, do you really think he could shoot from that distance with any accuracy?"

This at least presented me with some small relief as my Grandfather became occupied by another tangent in his thoughts. "Our killer is an opportunist; Walter is an out-and-out planner. The killer couldn't rely on the fact that Fellowes would leave his post, but they must have been aware of who the drinks he was serving were intended for."

I jumped in with a thought of my own. "So that means they were present on your birthday when you told us about the bottle of champagne from your wedding."

"That's right. Which sadly only rules out young Adelaide, and George could have told him. But it's clear the killer decided on his course of action that day. He prepared or bought the cyanide, carried it along to the ball, then waited for the opportunity to strike. Perhaps if Fellowes hadn't abandoned his post when he did, our culprit would have found another way to achieve his goal."

He leaned back on his haunches before continuing. "That notwithstanding, and though I believe the police will show there was poison in every glass of champagne, I can't overlook the feeling that I was the main target. It was *my* speech and *my* celebration in *my* house after *my* decade-long hermitage."

I smiled to myself then, thinking that I really had filled in a good ninety per cent of the outstanding holes in the case. Well… perhaps seventy-five, but I was almost entirely certain of the culprits and decided to prod him in the right direction.

"Of course, if Fellowes was working with another of our suspects, he could have-"

"No, no. That can't be it." Becoming weary from crouching for so long, he awkwardly stood back up and walked around the centre of the room in a circle. He cut a trail through the scraps of paper, like a child kicking up autumn leaves. "But it does raise that same question of why he was poisoned."He came to a stop and gazed at the notes before rushing over to search for one on his desk. "My only theory was that… Now, where did I put it…? There it is. Yes, the only thing I came up with was that our assassin had no qualms about killing two members of the Cranley family but couldn't bring himself to murder an innocent bystander. That still doesn't tell us why he wanted

Fellowes out of the way in the first place though."

I'd got caught up in his manic energy and offered an answer. "Perhaps the poison didn't act fast enough. Perhaps the killer planned to get rid of Fellowes in order to access the champagne, but he only got sick much later."

He paused long enough to consider this. "Not a bad suggestion, Chrissy. But as the killer knew to use a fast-acting poison in the champagne, surely he'd have found a similarly potent toxin to deal with the butler." He thought for a moment. "No, it simply has to be something that Fellowes saw on the night of the ball."

"But we spoke to him, Grandfather. Even before the police arrived, we asked him what he'd seen when he left the drinks room and what was happening outside. He was with Cora and they heard my father running up the steps above them, but there was no one else on that side of the house. George, Maitland and Marmaduke were on the terrace beside the ballroom. Fellowes didn't see anything."

He looked at me then like I'd said something incredible. "You little genius!" He shook his head in disbelief and, for a moment, I was worried he was mocking me. "You brilliant boy, I could hug you!"

Before such an awkward outcome could arise, we were interrupted by an unexpected visitor.

"Good afternoon, Milord."

"Fellowes!" Grandfather raced over to greet his supposedly faithful retainer. "How wonderful that you're up on your feet again."

It was painful to see the old man immediately charmed by that wretched character. Whatever instinct my grandfather possessed for judging the angels and demons of a person's nature had been neutralised by Fellowes's skilful machinations.

The butler's brow was creased and he sent a glare in my direction, before replying in a sycophantic tone. "Thank you for your trust and support, Lord Edgington. I can't say how much it means to me."

"Good man, good man." Grandfather rubbed his hands together and shifted his weight from side to side, as though he didn't know what to say next. "I'm sorry to spring this on you, considering what you've just been through, but I have to invite some guests over this evening. Tell the staff to be prepared. We've another party to plan."

CHAPTER THIRTY-FOUR

Despite my best attempts to save his blushes, Grandfather clearly wouldn't listen to what I'd discovered. He was committed to his plan for the evening and so we headed to the petit salon to invite our guests.

"George?" the old man asked but didn't wait for a reply. "I need you to be here by nine o'clock and bring young Adelaide with you."

"Why should I?" I heard him grumble down the line. He'd clearly been asleep when the telephone rang. "I've only recently returned from my ancestral backwater. Why would I want to go back so soon?"

"Because if you don't, I'll change my will and leave everything I own to Battersea Dogs Home!" He slammed the telephone down on its hook and, with a satisfied smile on his face, stroked his long white beard. "If someone had spoken to your cousin like that a decade ago, he might not be the disaster that he is today."

With George crossed off his list, he informed Great-Aunt Clementine's staff that he'd be sending a car to pick her up for dinner. It was a widely known fact that the old thing was always up for a party, so we didn't imagine any resistance on her part. Cora was still on the property and so, with these arrangements made, there was only one suspect left to include. Straightening his back regally and sucking his stomach in, Grandfather needed to ask his enemy for a favour.

"I'm telling you that if you bring Walter Prentiss to my house this evening, I'll hand over the killer."

Inspector Blunt's tone was so gruff and aggressive that I struggled to work out what he said in reply.

"IF YOU £*+> $%&* %-& FOR ONE SECOND THEN, I'LL $%&* £%*!\…"

Grandfather was not intimidated. "What harm can it do, man? You can bring as many officers as you like and leave Walter in irons for all I care. He's not likely to escape."

The scratchiness of the line decreased as Blunt replied in a marginally less agitated manner. "Fine, but I'll be watching you, Edgington. Don't go getting any funny ideas."

"Well, that set me straight," my grandfather barked back. "I can promise you this, Blunt, by the end of the evening, you'll be thanking me."

The inspector let out an oddly witch-like cackle. "I look forward to you proving me wrong."

Grandfather put the phone down but stayed rooted to the spot, peering off through the window at the dramatic black sky. "What a very unpleasant man he is."

I, on the other hand, was a very cowardly man. I knew that my lovely old grandfather was setting himself up for ridicule, and should have grabbed him by the arm and made him listen to reason.

Instead, I meekly enquired, "Grandfather, are sure you want to go through with the meal this evening?" The least I could do was check.

His eyes became tiny slits and I knew how all those criminals he arrested must have felt being interviewed by the steely Superintendent Edgington. "I've never been more certain of anything in my life." There was a definite, unspoken *why?* in his voice which I felt I had to answer.

"I just thought you might prefer to do things quietly, instead of making a big performance of it."

He leaned on the telephone table, as if the effort he'd already undergone was too much for him. "That's where you're wrong, my boy. It may sound petty, but any chance I get to show up that repugnant inspector is very much worth taking. Now, fetch your tailcoat as this evening's soiree will be a white tie event."

He nodded with his usual military air and marched off to get ready. I did as instructed and, a little while later, was the first to arrive in the large, airy dining room. I was convinced that the evening would not go to plan and sat waiting for the others in a fog of nerves, as Halfpenny laid the place settings around me.

If nothing else came from the dinner, at least I got to see my father again. After a day in a cell at St Mary-Under-Twine police station, he was in a sorry state. His normally perfect hair was bedraggled, his clothes were somehow stained and he looked like he hadn't slept in days. Two constables escorted him into the room, with the diminutive inspector hurrying along after them.

"Walter, you poor thing," my mother pronounced, when she arrived in the dining room moments later. Dressed to the nines in her best crimson gown, she positively sparkled as she ran over to him.

"Um, stand back please, madam." Blunt lunged to place himself between my parents. "That is a prisoner whose hair you are currently stroking. As far as I'm concerned, he is not here in his role as your husband."

The inspector hadn't opted for irons and shackles at least, but set the two constables to guard the door. Once my mother had apprehensively sat down beside my father, the veteran officer retreated to an alcove to watch the proceedings.

George, Cora and Great-Aunt Clementine were the next to arrive and took their places alongside me, but there was no sign of Marmaduke.

"Grandfather won't be happy you came alone," I whispered to George, in an attempt to be discreet.

"Oh, do be quiet, Chrissy." Any charm that he'd displayed that morning was absent once more. "Just so you know-"

He didn't have to finish his statement as, at that moment, a tall, heavily set man with arms like tree trunks and legs like Nelson's Column barged into the room to sit in Grandfather's chair at the head of the table. He had wavy red hair and wore a flamboyant suit of thick, purple damask. He looked like a well-dressed boxer, which wasn't far from the truth.

"Good evening, ladies and gentlemen." His deep, booming voice was exceedingly well-polished but had a distinctly arrogant undertone. "My name is Horatio Adelaide. Lord Edgington and I go back years. I'm sure he'll be happy to see me."

There was a murmur of disapproval from the other diners, as the identity of the intruder became apparent. Apparently oblivious, my schoolmate's father looked about the room as though he was considering purchasing Cranley Hall.

Grandfather must have had a spy planted to tell him when all the guests had arrived as he appeared forthwith. He paused on the threshold as he took in the unusual congregation. I thought he might react to Horatio Adelaide occupying his seat but, instead, he nodded cheerfully and walked to the far end of the table.

"Welcome everybody, I'm so glad you could come."

CHAPTER THIRTY-FIVE

Lord Edgington was clearly looking forward to his second social event of the season, but would make us wait for the highlight of the evening.

"We have some important matters to discuss, but first, we must dine together like old friends."

He spread his arms out in front of him and Fellowes walked forward to whisk the domed silver covers off two dishes in the middle of the table. They held a selection of fine continental meats and smoked salmon, and there were more plates laid out with rich pâtés and hors d'oeuvres. It was quite the treat to start the meal with and almost compensated for the no doubt unconventional nature of the forthcoming courses.

Grandfather took his seat and Halfpenny immediately served him an assortment of cold cuts.

Blunt jumped down from the windowsill he'd been perched on, like Zacchaeus from his tree. "Excuse me, but I didn't come here this evening to watch a bunch of toffs stuffing their faces."

"You're right," his former colleague agreed. "I would much prefer it if you joined us. There are provisions for your men too, if they so wish."

There was a spare seat at the table and another area already laid out in the petit salon for the constables. Grandfather looked back innocently at the inspector who was clearly torn over the best answer to such a tantalising offer. He peered at the culinary offerings which spanned the length of the table and then back to our patient host.

"You're trying to pull the wool over my eyes! Well, let me tell you, you can't butter me up, so don't even try."

I could understand entirely why he'd say this. Wool and butter, of course, should never meet.

My grandfather remained calm. "There is no obligation, Blunt. I simply considered that you might like to break bread with us."

Blunt thought a little longer and his two constables exchanged glances, obviously hoping they'd get a chance to sample Cranley Hall's offerings.

"I'll sit down," he eventually replied, as if he were doing us a great favour. "But I won't eat anything."

"Jolly good!" Grandfather watched as the petulant little man took up the spare place at the table and his officers happily dashed from the room.

There was silence as we started eating. Clearly no one felt we should make eye contact and we stared down at our plates. Knives screeched against porcelain, our servers rushed about with drinks and condiments, but no one spoke until Grandfather broke the silence.

"How nice to see you after all this time, Horatio." He glanced across at the once disreputable criminal with a truly welcoming expression.

"And you, Lord Edgington." The man smiled on half of his face. "It seemed right that I should come here in my son's stead, given that you will all be talking about him." There was a challenge buried in his words but Grandfather refused to be baited and the conversation petered out once more.

Being a Cranley, I imagine that I have lived through more awkward dinners in my life but I certainly can't think of an example. I expected some rabble-rousing from George or a little entertainment from old Clementine, but they were as meek as my mother and Cora, both of whom looked like they'd rather be having a tooth removed than participating in this uneasy performance.

The main course was served and everyone regarded Cook's oddly triangular pie, attempting to work out what on Earth she had produced. The hush that had fallen over us had an eerie quality to it by this point and the only attempt at communication was an occasional command to the staff, issued in an apologetic whisper. Eyes darted up from the meal and then back down again and I had to imagine that everyone was wondering the same thing; *am I going to be the one he pins the blame on?*

Well, practically everyone. I knew that I was in the clear and was busy dealing with the knowledge that this whole sorry show could have been avoided if I'd had the courage to tell Grandfather who was really responsible for the killings. Just as I thought I might scream out my confession, the old man threw in the towel... or his napkin at least.

"Very well, that's enough." He balled it up and, rising from his seat, flung it across the table to land in a heap in the centre. "I thought we might have one last civilised evening together before going through the particulars, but this is even less pleasant than a lifetime behind bars. It's high time I put you out of your misery." He paused to watch the reactions of those assembled.

Despite his previous claim to the contrary, Inspector Blunt had filled plate after plate with food. He was the only one who continued tucking into the pie, even after grandfather called order. Horatio was smiling, his eyebrows raised in perpetual enquiry, Clementine had finally come to herself and was humming a pretty melody and the others wore anxious masks in place of their regular features. I took particular notice of Cora who, as well she might, remained stunned into nervous silence.

To break the tension, Grandfather spoke again. "I requested your presence here this evening to reveal that the person who stole my children from me is-"

"No!" This single word echoed about the room and forced every last person there, from insignificant Halfpenny the footman to chirpy Great-Aunt Clementine, to turn in my direction. Slowly, reluctantly, but seeing no other option, I rose to my feet. "Or rather... I mean..."

Now that I had started, I couldn't quite remember what I wanted to say. Grandfather's thick brows had closed in on one another to make one long, prickly bush on his forehead. It was a look of both curiosity and judgement and the pressure it loaded upon me somehow sparked me into life.

"I mean to say that, Grandfather and I have been investigating together and, as the novice in this case, he has offered me the chance to present my findings." I was talking nonsense of course, but the curiosity in him won out and he sat back down to listen. "My aunt and uncle were murdered for the oldest reason in the world."

"Jealousy!" my father uttered in a bitter tone and I felt a little horrid for contradicting him.

"Money!"

"But Cain killed Abel because of-" he began, before my mother put her hand on his and I continued.

"By putting cyanide in the champagne that had been given to my grandparents on their wedding day, which the whole family knew would be served at the spring ball, the killer had a chance to wipe out my entire family and ensure that this estate would pass on to her."

There was some speculative mumbling as I said this, and I realised that I'd rather blown the big reveal I was building up to. "I'm talking of course about Lord Edgington's great niece, Cora Villiers. The granddaughter of his only brother, Arthur, who died before he could inherit this estate, therefore denying Cora her family birthright."

I allowed this scandalous announcement to blow around the room and luxuriated a little in the excitement it had provoked. My partner in crime-detection looked less enthusiastic, but I'd known that would be the case and had to keep going.

"Such a dastardly plan was the only way to obtain my grandfather's significant wealth and it was hatched with great skill. From the beginning we knew she was lying about what happened on the night of the ball, but this was explained when we learnt of her love for a butler in the employ of Cranley Hall. Reginald Fellowes, the man who has been serving us this evening."

A few eyes turned to Halfpenny, who was pouring gravy at that moment and now wore an uncomfortable look on his heavily lined face.

"No, sorry, not him," I had to explain. "The other one."

Heads flicked to the shadows by the door where Cora's despicable accomplice stood listening. He shot me a stare that could have toasted bread, but I wasn't scared now. Finally revealing the truth had rewarded me with confidence, and I took a moment to soak in the atmosphere.

Unsurprisingly, Cora looked yet more distraught as she processed the knowledge that her one-way ticket to the hangman's noose at Holloway Women's Prison was now confirmed. Inspector Blunt was all ears (and eyes for that matter). He was hanging on my words, and I could tell he would do the right thing and arrest the scoundrels when the moment came. Grandfather still wasn't giving anything away, but softly tapped the table in front of him.

I understood his implication and began to lay out the evidence. "Fellowes told us that he had opened the champagne only to swan off with his young lady in the gardens, but this would have deteriorated the quality of a fine wine, and what faithful butler would do such a thing? This was the first point which made me suspicious, but there was more to come. Much more!" I was trying to sound dramatic but ended up with a far too diabolical tone, like the villain in a Christmas pantomime.

I cleared my throat and continued. "Cora ensured that the champagne was spiked, then returned to the ballroom just before

Grandfather made his toast. Only, the two plotters didn't get their stories straight in advance and their accounts of these events were vague and hazy. Cora claimed to have gone back to the party after her boyfriend. Fellowes said he'd heard a voice through the drinks room window, but Cora never mentioned calling up to him."

This was my first major piece of evidence and it had the effect I was hoping for. Blunt raised his chin, clearly impressed by my powers of observation. Mother and Father even looked a little proud of me.

"Cora?" George murmured, sounding oddly proud. "You devil!"

I didn't let him break my concentration. "When Belinda sampled the champagne and died before the rest of the family could drink, Cora and Reggie's nefarious plan came to nothing. It was not enough to murder one heir to the family fortune if there were another ten waiting in the wings and the two desperately scrambled to cover their tracks."

I paused then, knowing that my killer blow was still to come. Thanks to my excessively sympathetic nature, I almost felt sorry for poor, doomed Cora. But, as the old saying goes, he who seeks revenge digs two graves … No, wait, that doesn't quite capture it. Maybe, money is the root of all evil? Either way, she'd made a terrible mess of things.

"My uncle Maitland had caught the two of them together on the night of the ball and so he was the next to die. I have to give the murderers credit for what they achieved. They came up with a mechanism to distance themselves from their crimes which almost fooled the great Superintendent Edgington – the scourge of London criminals for half the Victorian age. Unluckily for them, we finally got to the truth."

My grandfather himself sat listening impartially. That serious expression was still on his face and his eyes drilled a hole through my head. I could tell he still didn't believe what I had to say and so I raced to finish.

"You see, far from contradicting the possibility of his guilt and providing him with an alibi for the second killing, it was Fellowes's apparent poisoning which gave me the evidence I needed." Another big pause, as I felt I deserved a moment of glory. "That's right, our loyal servant poisoned himself!"

This was the discovery which had changed everything for me.

George, Mother, Clementine and, well, pretty much everyone in fact let out an astonished gasp. Emboldened by my success, I was just about to hammer my point home when Grandfather interrupted.

"Wait, wait, wait!" I bet he wished he'd kept hold of his napkin to throw it down dramatically just then. "I'm afraid I have to interrupt you, Christopher. You've got it all wrong."

CHAPTER THIRTY-SIX

Our eyes locked onto one another's, but I wasn't giving up so easily.

"I'm sorry, Grandfather, but they're guilty as sin. You couldn't understand why the killer used one poison for the family and another for your butler, but that was because it was never meant to kill him. Not only did it make us assume his innocence, it gave Cora – the expert archer – an alibi at the time that Maitland was shot. Think about it for one moment. I saw her running from the armoury immediately after he died, what if she hadn't been visiting her sickly beau but, in actual fact, was the person who'd pulled the trigger?"

In the end, it wasn't my grandfather who contradicted me, but his old rival.

"Hold on there a second, son." Blunt raised one finger enquiringly. "But what exactly do you think your uncle saw them doing before your aunt died? You haven't explained that."

"They killed him because…" These interruptions had injected any amount of doubt into my mind and I struggled to get my thoughts in order. "Because… Well, he must have caught them with the poison, mustn't he?"

The inspector made a clicking sound with his cheeks. "Nope. I interviewed Maitland Cranley on the night of his sister's murder and he didn't say anything about Miss Villiers."

When Grandfather spoke, his voice was far kinder than I could have hoped. "If Maitland had caught the killer in the act, he would have told the police immediately."

"But I heard them talking this afternoon, Cora said that you were putty in her hands and Fellowes told her he didn't want to do anything to jeopardise their position, I swear-"

"I was talking about my job here at Cranley, you eavesdropper," the butler interrupted, sounding more than a little sore that I'd accused him of a double murder. "I was worried about being fired after your grandfather found out about my relationship with his great-niece!"

This response cut a hole through me (and my argument) and I fell back into my chair. My theory, which had seemed so solid just moments earlier, now lay in pieces. The certainty that I had possessed had deserted me and I had to wonder how I could have got it all so wrong.

My grandfather addressed the party to cover my embarrassment. "Ladies and Gentlemen, I offered my assistant on this case a chance to present his own, independent solution and I think we can agree that he made an awfully good job of it."

No one seemed very impressed by my attempt. George rolled his eyes and knocked back his wine, Clementine was singing 'Daddy Wouldn't Buy me a Bow-Wow' and trying to get my father to join in and Cora had broken down in tears to be comforted by her loving (and not the slightest bit murderous) partner.

"I will now reveal the true circumstances that led to my son and daughter's tragic deaths," Grandfather continued. "You see-"

"I'll tell you *the true circumstances* that led to their deaths," Blunt interrupted, his voice full of disgust as he mimicked my grandfather. "Walter Prentiss murdered them!" He let the accusation bounce from wall to wall before laying out his case. "Your son-in-law is up to his eyeballs in debt and decided that the only way out of it was to access the money you've been keeping to yourself like Silas Marner all these years."

Such a highbrow literary reference was rather unexpected coming from a man like Inspector Blunt. Not that I thought that at the time. Right then, I was thinking, *how dare you say such things about my father!*

"Circumstantial evidence at best, Blunt," Grandfather told him. "I would hope you could do better than that."

The little man leaned forward into the light of the electric chandelier and his hairless dome glistened as he anticipated his response. "How about the crossbow in his room? The room which just happened to overlook the scene of the second murder?"

"Were there any fingerprints on it?" My grandfather had fired a shot across the inspector's bow and I could tell there was more to come.

Blunt wrinkled up his nose. "Well… no there weren't none, but that doesn't mean he wasn't involved. Just means he wore gloves, don't it?"

Grandfather adopted a loftier tone, which was only ever going to infuriate his adversary. "Like Christopher, you've made a good attempt at making the evidence fit your theory, but it's not enough. The crossbow under Walter's bed was not the murder weapon for one thing and the only reason that my son-in-law left the party was to escape his insufferable mother."

My father gasped. "How on Earth did you know that?"

"Anyone who's spent five minutes in the presence of that woman could have guessed."

Blunt wore a chastised frown but wasn't giving up. "Typical toffs sticking up for one another. I tell you now, you won't get away with a cover-up."

Grandfather was well armed with his reply. "It's no conspiracy, man. Just eat your pie and listen to what really transpired."

George let out a whistle and, despite the fact our butler had his arms around the man's cousin, he motioned for Fellowes to fill his glass. Like a spider spinning a web, Horatio Adelaide had been biding his time, carefully listening to each new piece of information. His moment had come to pounce.

"And what about my boy?" he said, as if this was a key piece of the puzzle. "Why has no one mentioned Marmaduke in the proceedings?"

Grandfather let out a huff of laughter. "Are you putting your own son forward as a suspect, Horatio? Really, that's low even for you."

Adelaide folded his powerful arms across his chest. "I'm merely trying to ascertain the facts. That boy of mine has been running wild for years, so I'd like to confirm that the version of events he described was the truth."

"But why would he have killed anyone?"

The former gangster took a deep breath, as if what he was about to say would be difficult to get out. "I have given Marmaduke every advantage in life, every possible luxury, and yet he has grown up to be the very thing I feared that I myself would become at his age. The boy is a brute. He enjoys nothing more than inflicting pain on others and, if you tell me he was responsible for the murders, I will believe you and remedy the situation myself."

I was trying to imagine what the man was implying when Grandfather answered him. "Marmaduke was an unlucky bystander in more ways than one. I've spoken to him and can honestly tell you that he is no brute. He is merely a sixteen-year-old boy who has never learnt right from wrong. He's not the first person I've known with such an issue and he won't be the last." His eyes flicked over to George, who raised his glass sarcastically in reply.

Horatio wasn't convinced. "But he was in the vicinity of both crimes and couldn't tell me exactly what he was doing during either one."

Grandfather shook his head despairingly. "That's probably because he lives in crippling fear of you and didn't want to admit that he'd had his head slapped about by the man whose care you'd put him under." He was shouting by now and leaned across the table to drive his message home. "Spend some time with the boy, show him that you care about him – rather than accusing him of murder – and perhaps he won't be so wild."

The fact that my grandfather could find such compassion for a hopeless soul like Marmaduke surely suggested where my excessively sympathetic nature came from.

Horatio Adelaide turned away in disgust but stayed right where he was. Like everyone, he was eager to discover what had really happened the previous weekend at Cranley Hall and, like everyone, he was about to find out.

Grandfather raised himself up to his full height and pulled the cuffs of his sleeves down so that there was not the faintest crease visible on his long silver coat. "Now, if no one else wishes to put forward a theory, perhaps I can begin."

CHAPTER THIRTY-SEVEN

"Though my grandson Christopher may not have reached the right conclusion, he spoke any amount of truth in the case he presented to us. I believe that my daughter Belinda and my son Maitland were murdered for money. Well, money and the oldest reason in the world; jealousy."

After the slew of chattering interruptions, Grandfather was easing in to his tale. All eyes were upon him. The only sound was his sonorous voice, which sailed through the still air like music from a gramophone.

"Had everything gone to plan, I wouldn't be here today to speak to you. In fact, half the people in this room and most of our immediate relatives would have been wiped from existence." In one mechanical movement, his eyes flicked to his eldest grandson. "But not you of course, George. You were lucky enough to avoid that possibility when your glass of champagne conveniently slipped from your fingers."

My cousin did not seem intimidated by the arch look our grandfather gave him. "Oh, yes, that's me. Lucky old George Trevelyan!"

Grandfather gave a sad laugh and continued. "I have to say that there were elements to this case that had me truly baffled. My assistant Christopher must have concluded that it was my old age which held me back, but, in fact, this was one of the most perplexing and contradictory murders I've come across."

I was so caught up in his story that I barely took the time to notice that he'd read my mind again. Of course, I no longer thought he was a foolish old man. I was willing to believe he was an absolute genius. The fact that I had somehow helped him reach his conclusion was the real miracle.

"There were certain questions which I simply couldn't get beyond. For one thing, as we've already heard, it didn't make sense that our killer would happily murder a whole family – men, women and children alike – but stop short of getting rid of a witness to their crime."

He picked up a knife from his place setting and waved it through the air as he spoke. "Christopher came up with a number of interesting solutions for why the poison that Fellowes ingested gave him little more than a dicky tummy. He wondered whether an insufficiently strong toxin had been administered in the hope of incapacitating

Fellowes and leaving the champagne unattended. I steered him away from such thinking and then, in front of you all this evening, my grandson described how Fellowes could have consumed some weak dose of poison himself to throw us off the scent.

"While I considered these two possibilities early on, it is wonderful to see that Christopher's young mind could function almost as efficiently as one with my years of experience."

George scoffed at this and gave me a wry look. There was a brief moment of silent tension, which was broken by Great-Aunt Clementine taking up her song.

> **"Daddy wouldn't buy me a bow-wow! Bow wow!**
> **Daddy wouldn't buy me a bow-wow! Bow wow!**
> **I've got a little cat,**
> **And I'm very fond of that,**
> **But I'd rather have a bow-wow**
> **Wow, wow, wow, wow."**

Inspector Blunt looked impressed once more by her vocal skills, but Grandfather was less appreciative. "Thank you, Clemmie, old girl. I do always enjoy your performances." His voice was soaked in sarcasm, like a Christmas pudding in brandy. "Now, if I may continue…"

Clementine tilted her head in humble acceptance, as though she were a famous opera singer ceding the stage to a promising ingénue.

"Having been acquainted with my butler since he was a child, and for reasons that it is not my place to go into, I knew that Fellowes was no murderer."

Still comforting his *petite amie,* Fellowes signalled his appreciation with a silent nod. Though Cora herself had stopped crying, she let out the occasional whimper as my grandfather continued his explanation.

"This knowledge reduced our list of suspects, but the killer's identity still eluded me. While Belinda's death could be seen as a failed attempt to snatch Cranley Hall, which George, Clementine, Cora and several more distant members of the family would have benefitted from, Maitland's murder, moments before he was about to reveal a key piece of evidence, was another conundrum which I couldn't at first solve."

He paused then and turned to address the inspector, who was

the only one still eating. "Blunt, I imagine that you ran tests on the champagne and found cyanide in both the bottle and every glass which Fellowes poured?"

"That's right," he said through a mouthful of potato and beef.

"Not a single glass was missed?"

The little man nodded and shovelled a forkful of green beans into his mouth.

Grandfather's moustaches bunched together confidently. "As I concluded, Belinda's murder was not targeted specifically at her, and so the possible motives were once more reduced. However, I was still stuck with the question of why the killer went on to murder my son and poison my butler. The obvious deduction was that the two men had witnessed something around the time of the first murder, but Fellowes swore that he hadn't seen anything that would have made him a target."

He wore a mournful look as he gazed around his audience. "I must have run through a thousand solutions in my head, but it was Christopher who finally showed me what I was missing. I was obsessed by the idea that Maitland had caught sight of the killer on his way from the terrace to the ballroom, but if that was the case, why hadn't he told the police? Neither my son, nor my faithful retainer knew the identity of their assailant and yet they were both targeted. In Maitland's case, he was merely a stooge; his murder was a smokescreen to distract from more significant evidence. But it was what Fellowes *didn't* see that made him a target.

"When Belinda died and my world felt like it had disintegrated beneath my feet, I imagined a scenario so completely void of sense that I put it out of my mind until this afternoon. There was a solution to the crime that felt logical to me but would have involved such planning and vitriol that I didn't want to believe it possible."

His voice faltered. "I can see now that we haven't been investigating a murder, so much as eliminating every last possibility to confirm that the one which seemed impossible really was correct. There is a person sitting at this table who has spent years plotting to destroy me and take Cranley Hall for herself."

I noticed my father seize hold of his fork then and grip it in his fist, like a condemned man before his last meal. Cora let out a pained cry and, as if by prior arrangement, the room fell quiet for Lord Edgington to reveal the truth.

"Clementine, as I've already mentioned, I've always enjoyed your performances, your little songs, your eccentricities. When exactly did you take on this role?"

Great-Aunt Clementine's face bloomed into life, as if she was happy to be asked such a question. Instead of responding, she started in on another verse of her song.

> **"We used to have two tiny dogs,**
> **Such pretty little dears.**
> **But Daddy sold 'em 'cause they used**
> **To bite each other's ears."**

"You can play the fool all you like, woman," my grandfather continued in a wrathful tone. "It's been standing you in good stead for years, but I know that you're guilty. You've never forgiven me for taking your husband's inheritance. The opportunity to wipe out my family in one go was too good to resist. When that failed, you killed Maitland in order to frame Walter, who you'd spotted in the petit salon just before you put the cyanide in the champagne. You knew that no one would suspect a mad old lady. You're so much like a ghost these days that we barely notice you floating about the place and that was the perfect cover."

If Clementine had heard his accusation, she didn't let on.

> **"I cried all day: at eight each night,**
> **Papa sent me to bed.**
> **When Ma came home and wiped my eyes,**
> **I cried again and said..."**

Grandfather was not distracted and continued laying out the evidence against his sister-in-law. "Of course, you were doing all this for Cora, not yourself. She's the one who would inherit Cranley if you got caught or died. So you weren't about to murder the man she loved now, were you?"

She wouldn't give in, but continued her whimsical act, like a naughty child who won't admit to a mistake. "Daddy wouldn't buy me a bow-wow! Bow wow!"

210

His voice rose with his anger. "When we came to your house to speak to her, Cora mentioned that she keeps no secrets from you. You knew all about her relationship with Fellowes and no doubt encouraged her to tempt him outside on the night of the ball." Cora let out her sharpest note of the evening then, which served to confirm Grandfather's theory. "But there was a problem. When Fellowes returned to the house, you weren't asleep in the petit salon where Christopher and Walter had previously noticed you. He saw no one, and you were afraid that the police would latch on to this fact, so another person had to suffer."

"I'd rather have a bow-wow, wow, wow, wow, wow." The confidence had gone from her voice and she finally looked up at her inquisitor.

"There were any number of substances which could have done the job. Though, from the floral adornment to your dress that night, I assume that you crushed delphinium seeds in the whisky you poured Fellowes when the inspector called us together in the smoking room. The house was swamped with the darned flowers after Christopher ordered so many to decorate the ball."

Grandfather cast me a brief glance then turned his attention back to the killer. "With the amount of time you once spent tending to your gardens at Langford House, I dare say you learnt a fair bit about horticulture and even pharmacology. Enough to extract cyanide from greengage stones, at least. Everyone knows that apple pips contain amygdalin, but those innocent-looking plums in your garden are many times deadlier if prepared correctly.

"But poisoning Fellowes was a fruitless act; I'd already spoken to him before he got sick. If anything, it provided me with the evidence I needed to prove your guilt. Though I didn't see the significance at the time, delphiniums cause irritation to the skin and you blackened your fingers when you extracted the seeds. Again it was Christopher who had spotted the grubby marks when we visited you the following day."

All eyes jumped to Clementine's hands and, in a moment of self-consciousness, she hid the now dark bruises beneath the table cloth.

"And I have to give it to you, shooting Maitland certainly threw me off your trail. I'm sure that the years you spent taking archery classes with your granddaughter made you a whiz with a crossbow and I should have considered you more carefully. Instead, I delved into Maitland's life, his debts, dalliances and dilemmas, but it could have been anyone you shot out there. You didn't care who you hurt, as long as we couldn't trace the murders back to you. You killed Maitland and poisoned Fellowes just to cover your trail."

He allowed the words to linger and we watched as Clementine searched the room for someone to defend her.

Her granddaughter would not be that person. "How could you, Grandmother? How could you be so evil?"

My mother was just as shocked. "How could you possess so much hatred for your own family?"

"I…" Clementine screeched, but the sound faded out again just as abruptly.

Grandfather hadn't finished. "You went all those years without your mask slipping, but you made a mistake. By pushing Walter as the culprit when we spoke at your house, you were too alert, too aware of what had occurred on the night of Belinda's death for the rest of your mumming to hold true."

He stopped for a moment and looked almost impressed by her. "If you'd simply planted Walter's cigar ash in the armoury and hidden the second crossbow beneath his bed before you murdered Maitland, I might have believed your ruse. But you pushed your advantage and gave yourself away. So, I'll ask you again, for how long have you been playing the part of the helpless old lady?"

The cycle of emotions she'd been going through had reached an unexpected conclusion. She jutted out her chin, sat up in her chair and was suddenly a different person. "Oh, I'd say I've been at it for about a decade. I found that people were so quick to dismiss an old widow that I could get away with all sorts. In fact, it started not so very long before your dear wife Katherine died." In the light of the chandelier, a malevolent glint sparkled in her eyes.

I gasped then as a realisation settled within me. There were no more surprises to come; Clementine was our killer and she was entirely unrepentant for what she'd done. I turned to my grandfather to see the look of horror on his face. He gripped the edge of the table as though he could no longer support his own weight. His utter dejection was mirrored in Cora's, but neither said a word. The reality they were facing was too terrible to bear.

"But why?" George managed to ask on their behalf, before his jaw fell slack.

"Tell us!" I whispered, my voice shaking.

Clementine's gaze hadn't left my grandfather and the corners of her mouth turned up proudly. "You took my whole life from me and so I took your wife from you. I put a little aconitine in dear Kathryn's tea one day, when she oh so generously came round for a visit. She was back at home with you when her symptoms began and almost dead by the time the doctor could diagnose a heart attack. I poisoned the woman you treasured and you, the great Superintendent Edgington, suspected nothing."

Her words had silenced the room once more. I had never witnessed such contempt. The only comfort I could find was that, one way or another, the wretched creature would die in gaol.

"I thought that my retribution was complete when you retreated from the world, but alas you would not stay dead." As she was speaking, she pulled her glass of wine close to her. I failed to realise her purpose but my grandfather saw it immediately.

"Fellowes, stop her!" He shouted and the butler shot forward to wrestle the glass away.

Her conceited attitude had dissipated and she let out a doleful cry. "No. Let me die!"

My mother gripped the old woman's bony wrist so that a small paper sachet, of what I had to assume was cyanide, dropped from her grasp. She looked at her aunt in disgust and delivered her staccato response one condemnatory word at a time. "You deserve no such mercy."

"I didn't steal your life from you," Grandfather took a step forward to direct his comment at Clementine. "My brother's death was a tragedy and I'm sorry that my parents were so old-fashioned that they wouldn't allow his widow and child to inherit this place. But you went from being obscenely wealthy to only filthy rich and that doesn't excuse your contemptible actions."

"I was humiliated!" A single tear appeared in the corner of Clementine's right eye. "Thrown off the estate that should have passed to my child. Out of sight and out of mind, we were abandoned by your family to rot. You treat your darned dog better than that, so I did what I had to for the sake of my granddaughter."

Cora stifled her sobs and delivered a stinging rebuke. "No, you didn't! You murdered three people and poisoned the man I love for your own petty jealousies." She brushed her short fringe from her face to fix her once beloved grandmother with a reproachful stare. "I hope that the pain you caused reflects back upon you for the rest of your days."

With this bitter proclamation, the room came to life. Grandfather collapsed back into his seat, Inspector Blunt called to his constables and my mother and father embraced, the relief palpable as it flowed between them.

When the officers clapped my murderous great-aunt in handcuffs and escorted her from the room, there was no joy to be found in her fate. A great evil had befallen my family, which no punishment could make up for.

CHAPTER THIRTY-EIGHT

I was quite honestly overwhelmed by everything that I'd seen. I sat right where I was as my companions cried and commiserated. Blunt did not thank us for what we had discovered, or apologise to my parents for arresting the wrong suspect. Instead, he made a begrudging nod of recognition in my Grandfather's direction before following his subordinates from the room.

Horatio Adelaide was the next to leave. Looking as though he still had his doubts, he approached the old man and said, "Lord Edgington, I very much enjoyed the evening and have a feeling we'll cross paths again before long."

My grandfather could not find it in himself to reply but bowed his head solemnly and the enigmatic character made his way out, followed by my cousin George.

"Must run, Grandfather," he said with a confident smile. "I'm eager to discuss a business arrangement with old Adelaide, but I've had a wonderful time." He delivered the remark with all his usual flippant charm, then frowned for a moment before sidling off.

Fellowes thanked the old man several times for all he had done. Cora, her makeup a runny mess, embraced her great-uncle and apologised keenly for her grandmother's actions. And then it was my parents' turn.

"I don't know what to say, Daddy," Mother began.

"I do." My father had regained his usual quiet authority and his clothes even looked a little smarter somehow. "You saved me. Ten hours in a police cell was enough to last a lifetime. Thank you so much for getting me out."

"We'll be here until tomorrow morning if there's anything you need." Mother's voice wavered and she hastily bustled her husband from the room before her tears could break loose.

I enjoyed a moment of silence but then my father rushed back inside and I thought he might actually hug me. I needn't have worried.

"Chrissy," he said and I could tell how difficult it had been for him to get this much out. "I should thank you too. I know you didn't catch the killer but you gave it a heck of a good try and..." Such enthusiasm did not come naturally to him. He cleared his throat and concluded his appraisal with an outstretched hand and a few final words. "And, well… I'm really rather proud of you."

I was practically speechless by this point and couldn't do much more than accept the offer and shake his hand. He patted me on the shoulder and ran off after Mother with some of his energy restored.

My grandfather and I were finally alone and the atmosphere in the room changed once more. He hadn't said anything since he concluded his testimony and now sat staring at the sparkling crystal droplets which hung from the chandelier.

I wanted to say something to make him feel better, but I knew there were no words that could repair the damage that had been done. I watched as he pursed his lips together and breathed in deeply, his prodigious moustache moving a fraction as the air whistled past it.

I realised something then that had taken me far too long. My grandfather had been so focussed on the investigation that he hadn't let his emotion for the loss of his children cloud his judgement. Now that it was over, every imaginable feeling came rushing at him. Anguish and misery, pain and relief bombarded him and, sitting just a few chairs away, I felt it too.

He folded his arms on the table in front of him and rested his head there. I thought about putting my arm around him or thanking him for all he had taught me, but I knew this was something for which he needed no assistant. Softly pulling back from the table, I made my way from the room and went to tell the staff not to disturb him.

I'd already missed a day of school after the bank holiday and decided one more wouldn't hurt. I slept in the next morning and, once I'd said farewell to my parents, spent the afternoon in the sunny gardens, throwing a ball to Delilah and looking out for woodpeckers. I didn't dare visit my grandfather, though there were a million things I wanted to ask him as I wiled away the time, dreaming of the summer holidays and coming up with a list of adventures we could have.

I had my supper in the kitchen. Cook and Alice seemed most impressed that I'd helped to catch the killer, and everyone speculated over what Fellowes might do now that his illicit love affair was common knowledge. Todd offered to drive me back to school the following morning and it was with a mix of sadness and excitement that I accepted.

Alone in my room that night, I had trouble sleeping. My head was filled with all the evidence I'd overlooked and I wrote up my case notes so that, were I ever to be in such a situation again, I might learn from my mistakes. Point number one was…

Never underestimate the elderly!

It wasn't just my embarrassing failure that stayed with me, I was still recovering from the vicarious thrill of assisting my grandfather's investigation. My head, like my notebook, was crammed full of so many disparate thoughts and ideas, it's a wonder that I ever fell asleep.

The morning eventually arrived, however, and, after passing up the offer of one final breakfast from Cook and packing my few transportable possessions into my Gladstone bag, I headed off to find Todd.

"Good morning, Christopher. Do you mind if I walk with you?" Grandfather was in the garden waiting for me as I stepped outside. I didn't really think anything of it at the time but he had his silk top hat and his amethyst cane with him which he'd carried at the ball.

As a good alumnus of Oakton Academy, I tried to keep my emotions in check and not show how much this meant to me, but… well, I failed rather miserably.

"Oh! Grandfather you came to see me off?" I positively launched myself at him and gave him the biggest hug I could manage. "I was worried I wouldn't see you before I left."

If this had been almost any other family member, I've no doubt they would have gone running for a doctor to find out what was wrong with me. But then, my grandfather wasn't quite like anyone else.

"I couldn't let my trusty assistant go without saying goodbye." He patted me on the arm and I finally pulled back from him.

"Are you feeling…" I searched for the right word, but apparently it didn't exist. "…better?"

He spun on the spot in the direction of Todd's garage and I padded along beside him.

"I'm not sure that I'll ever feel better about the murder of my wife and two children, but I'm feeling…" It was his turn to run dry. "… alive, at the very least."

"That's jolly good," I said, sounding more like my stony father than I'd intended.

I'd been considering some of the finer points of the case since our killer had been revealed and there were so many things I wanted to ask him, but wasn't quite sure where to begin.

"What a sumptuous day and what a beautiful world we live in!" He looked up at the sky as he spoke and even in this jubilant proclamation there was a mournful note.

"Grandfather, would you mind explaining something?" As the now experienced assistant to a famous detective, I decided this sounded a little weak so quickly made it right. "I mean, I understand most of what went on over the last few days but there are a few minor details I'd rather like refreshing in my mind."

His wonderful white moustache curled upwards. "Of course, dear boy. What exactly would you like me to *refresh*?"

This was the thing I couldn't quite put my finger on so I went with, "Well, why don't you start from the beginning, and I'll tell you if we get to any parts that you can skip?"

I think he saw through my subterfuge, as he laughed before replying. "Very well. We'll start with the ball, shall we?"

"Or your birthday even?" I suggested as our feet crunched along the gravel path in front of Cranley's west wing. "There's no sense doing things by halves."

"That's so true." He paused to collect his thoughts. "Rather foolishly on my part, at a meeting with my every living relative, many of whom would be happy for me to meet my maker, I mentioned the fact that I would be opening a bottle of 1872 Veuve Clicquot champagne. Perhaps even more significantly though, I revealed that I had a lot more living to do and the woman who, as it turns out, had murdered my wife was not too keen on this outcome. Old Clemmie even spent the night here to plan her attack – passing off her supposedly accidental extended visit as the folly of her faltering mind."

I was just about keeping up with him until this point, though I already had one question. "How can you be so sure that's what happened?"

"I can't, but it's what I'd have done if I were her. Planning is paramount!" He continued straight on with his summary as if I hadn't interrupted. "With her groundwork laid, she waited for the night of the ball. She arrived with Cora and would have encouraged her granddaughter to attract her boyfriend's attention while she had a nap behind the door in the petit salon, where you and, fortuitously your father, could attest to her being. If she'd merely returned to where she'd been sleeping, no one would have noticed her absence and she would have got away with her crime. I have a feeling that the temptation was too great though and, having spiked the champagne, she tiptoed off to the terrace to watch me die."

We had reached the steps up to the ballroom, and fell into silent thought for a moment, which I soon broke into. "One thing I never understood is why there weren't any fingerprints on the bottle. We know that Clementine wasn't wearing gloves as she wouldn't have hurt her hands otherwise."

"She didn't need to touch the bottle to put the poison in it, Fellowes had already removed the cork and so she simply poured the cyanide inside. Perhaps she thought that wearing gloves would have drawn attention to her, but a white-tie ball is one place she could have got away with it."

His voice rose theatrically as he made this supposition, but there were more facts to deliver and he didn't get distracted for long. "I imagine that this was when she got the idea to incriminate your father. Maitland was killed merely to confuse the investigation. I fell for her trick and falsely assumed he had seen something when he hadn't. With Clementine's testimony Walter became a prime suspect, but your uncle's death also forced me to pay more attention to George and the Adelaides. She did an awfully good job of muddying the waters and, I have to admit that I took far too long to consider that she was involved."

We had been rocketing along the path but Grandfather came to a stop all of a sudden and looked out across the great lawn towards the lake. "It was really rather ingenious what she did to Maitland. With the first killing, she'd been banking on the fact that no one would suspect an old woman. If she'd managed to kill us all but got caught, it was Cora who would have inherited everything anyway. With Maitland, though, she came up with a clever trick."

This was the part of the case where I'd really got lost and I was glad he was about explain it all. I just hoped I wouldn't have to ask him to speak more slowly or repeat everything twice.

"There were two crossbows in the armoury and she had all the time in the world to hide one under your parents' bed while they were at breakfast, at least an hour before Maitland died. After that, all she needed was a quiet moment while your uncle was on his morning walk to set up in the armoury and TWANG! The bolt pierced poor Maitland's heart and he died in my arms. In many families, such a crack shot would have narrowed down our field of suspects. Sadly, George and your father had grown up hunting, Fellowes is pretty handy with a pistol and I knew that Clemmie had done plenty of archery back when Cora was at school. In fact, the only person it would have ruled out was Maitland himself – who couldn't hit a cow with a carbine at point blank range. Perhaps that's why she chose him as her target, or perhaps she would have killed whoever walked into her sights.

"Clementine closed the window to make it look as though your father had shot down from the floor above. It was simple enough for her to take your father's cigar ash from the smoking room too and plant it in the armoury. And though only an incredibly stupid criminal would have been smoking as he carried out a murder, I'm sorry to tell you that I couldn't rule out your father's guilt for some time."

I suppose this meant my grandfather had lied to me, but I didn't hold it against him. "That's okay. I know you only kept quiet to save my feelings. He was a suspect like anyone else and, without you, he'd still be in a cell."

It was his turn for a question. "Did you spot the moment when Clementine gave Fellowes the poison in his drink after the ball?"

"Oh... Um, not exactly, but then she's an awfully clever old thing."

"Well, quite!" His smile grew and he humoured me by explaining. "She'd camouflaged the moment nicely; making a big song and dance of pouring out the whisky for everyone when Blunt called us in to the smoking room. It was only after I was certain that she was the killer that I reconsidered that moment and worked out what she'd done."

He turned then and we recommenced our gentle stroll across the grounds. I was in no hurry to leave.

"It's bizarre when you think about it," I reflected. "I suppose she was desperate after her plan to murder the family failed. If she hadn't tried to cover it up, we... or, rather, *you* might never have caught her."

He walked a little more briskly, as if encouraged by my words. "It's often the way with criminals; given enough time they incriminate themselves. But desperate is the right word for that wretched woman.

She didn't give a damn what happened to her. She was driven by revenge, even after all these years."

The conversation died out then. I considered that this would be the moment to reveal my whole-hearted adoration of our housemaid, but another more pressing issue came to mind.

"I'm very sorry about Grandmother," I told him in little more than an awkward mumble. "I was only young when she died but I have the most wonderfully happy memories of her."

We'd arrived at Todd's garage and he stopped before entering. "Thank you, my boy. My Katherine was a truly good person – about as far from my despicable sister-in-law as you can get." He regarded me with great warmth and put one hand on my shoulder. "She would have been immensely proud to see you growing into such a fine young man."

I probably blushed like a red apple then, as I'm not entirely accustomed to compliments from members of my family. I didn't manage to get a response out, in fact, before Grandfather said, "Actually, you wait there one moment," and disappeared into the barn.

I stayed where I was until Todd threw the double doors open for my grandfather to come roaring out astride his Matchless Model H motorbike. Its sidecar was a pale grey to match the long leather coat he'd put on and Delilah was already inside.

"Fancy a lift to school?" He threw a helmet in my direction. I've never been very good at catching things and it slipped through my hands and fell to the ground.

Apprehensive, but encouraged by his warm words, I cautiously climbed into the sidecar. Delilah looked a little put out that I was taking up her spot, but she soon settled down on my lap, her long tail wagging.

Grandfather put his gloves and helmet on, and wrapped his fingers around the handlebars "Despite the circumstances," he began, with a melancholy air, "it's been a pleasure working with you, my boy. And I don't want it to end here."

He started the motor and we rolled along the gravel path. I clung onto the frame of the sidecar, in case he drove anywhere near as fast as on our first excursion together.

"I told you before, Chrissy. There are so many adventures I still wish to have and I'd like you there alongside me." He looked at me then, expecting a response. Even though we were only going five miles an hour, I wished he'd keep his eyes on the road. "What do you say? Are you game?"

I was obviously flattered and couldn't think what else to say, so nodded profusely.

He bellowed out a laugh as we pulled onto the main drive. "Fantastic! I knew you wouldn't let me down."

My helmet restricted the view, but I could tell that he was grinning. He looked back at the road and I felt rather wonderful about the world. Despite far too many dead relatives and one diabolical old lady, life was just grand.

"I've always wanted to have a go on one of these things," Grandfather said and I suddenly didn't feel so positive.

"You mean you've never ridden a motorbike before?"

"No, but I'll soon learn!" He revved the engine and sped away up the drive with a mischievous look on his face.

"Wait, Grandfather. I think I'd rather walk." We pulled onto the road and he immediately accelerated. "Grandfather, let me out!"

THE END (FOR NOW. . .)

Read

LORD EDGINGTON'S NEXT ADVENTURE

absolutely **free**...

Download your free novella at
www.benedictbrown.net

"LORD EDGINGTON INVESTIGATES..."

The second full-length mystery is
available now at **amazon**.

ABOUT THIS BOOK

This book is special to me for a number of reasons. I wrote it for my father, Kevin, who is surely responsible for getting me into crime fiction in the first place. Dad died in 2014 having already suffered with Alzheimer's for fifteen years. He had long since lost the ability to read, but carried a book with him wherever he went and talked about them as special treasures he had to keep safe.

As Mr Kevin Brown died aged seventy-four, I thought it was rather fitting to start this book on Lord Edgington's seventy-fifth birthday. It almost felt like I was writing a fantastical sequel to Dad's life. Except for the silvery hair and love of nice suits, my father was nothing like Lord Edgington. He was born in an absolutely miniscule house in South London, close to where my family still live. His parents were Alice, who had come over from Ireland to find a job as a domestic worker, and Harry, an engineer who, by all accounts, was extremely Victorian in his parenting. Despite having a father who communicated no affection to him, my dad was the kindest, most affectionate man I've ever met. I once went into our local bank and the manager introduced me around to all the staff as 'Kevin was simply the nicest customer we have.' When Dad died, there was standing room only at the funeral and people we hadn't seen for thirty years turned up. My mother made everyone laugh with the eulogy, my brother made everyone cry, and there was even some dancing – but that's another story.

My father was, and still is, very much loved, so this is for you Dad. I hope you get a kick out of having your very own country house mystery.

The stories which we tell in my family – from both the Welsh and Irish/English sides – influence everything about my writing. Dad's mum made notoriously inedible meals (in my mother's words, "she could even overcook salad") and so her influence is there in both the young maid, Alice, and the eccentric cook. I'm glad to say that my family are nothing like the Cranleys. On the plus side, we rarely plot against one another, though, less positively, we also lack their sprawling estate and car collection.

226

Cranley Hall is based on a number of houses my history teacher mother dragged my brothers and I too when we were kids. If you'd like to see a similar Neo-Palladian estate, take a look at Chiswick House in the west of London or Woburn Abbey in Bedfordshire. The house on the front cover is Wollaton Hall in Nottinghamshire, which is a truly stunning Elizabethan property (and has doubled for Wayne Manor in the Batman films). It doesn't quite fit the architectural style of Cranley Hall, but it's difficult to find images which you can legally use for book covers and my wife Marion has worked wonders to make it look just perfect.

There are two songs included in the book which I did not write. 'Daddy Wouldn't Buy Me a Bow Wow' was written in 1892 by English songwriter Joseph Tabrar and there is even a Toulouse-Lautrec painting of a famous singer performing it. And 'Come, Gentle Night!' was a poem written by Clifton Bingham, which the popular English composer Edward Elgar set to music in 1901.

I chose the name Cranley as it's a place which existed once but no longer does, so I thought it fitted rather nicely. The village now known as Cranleigh in Surrey changed the spelling of its name in the 1860s to avoid confusion with the nearby town of Crawley. I think it's a funny story and so I brought Cranley back to life in approximately the same place. In my book, Cranley Hall and the village of St Mary-Under-Twine are located in the, also fictional, Hundred of Edgington. Starting in the middle ages, a 'hundred' was a division of a larger area, like a borough or district today. I recently discovered that my home town of Wallington once had its own hundred which covered a large swathe of Surrey and South London, so I borrowed the largely forgotten term to give The Marquess of Edgington an ancestral estate. History is a fascinating thing and I've enjoyed combining different elements to create the book you've just read.

THE "MURDER AT THE SPRING BALL" COCKTAIL

If anyone would like to make the 'Hanky-Panky' cocktail, which that versatile chap Todd mixes for Marmaduke, the recipe is:

> **1 1/2oz (45 ml) dry gin**
>
> **1 1/2oz (45ml) sweet vermouth**
>
> **2 dashes Fernet-Branca**
>
> **A dash of fresh orange juice**
>
> **And orange peel to garnish**

The cocktail was created by Ada 'Coley' Coleman, the first female head bartender at the Savoy Hotel in London's famous American Bar. During her twenty-two-year tenure from 1903 to 1925, she served countless famous figures including Mark Twain, Marlene Dietrich, Charlie Chaplin and the Prince of Wales, and estimated that she had served one hundred thousand customers and poured one million drinks by the time she retired.

The Hanky-Panky itself was created for the actor Charles Hawtrey. When Coleman whipped him up the drink one night, he described it as "the real hanky-panky" and the name stuck.

A word of warning, if you go to the Savoy and order the vintage Hanky-Panky, it costs an eye-watering £120 ($165). Ouch!

ACKNOWLEDGEMENTS

It turns out that writing and researching a historical novel takes rather a lot of effort. So many people have helped me get the tone, plot and language right for this book and I've spent months with my head in an old dictionary or searching through etymological websites. So a big thank you to Douglas Harper who started **etymonline.com** and Jonathon Green for creating **greensdictofslang.com**. Both are invaluable and truly fascinating resources and I love learning about language and its mysterious roots and routes.

Thank you as always to my wife and daughter for inspiring me and giving me a reason to write, to my family for reading my books and my crack team of experts – the Hoggs and the Martins (**fiction**), Paul Bickley (**policing**), Karen Baugh Menuhin (**marketing**) and Mar Pérez (**forensic pathology**) for knowing lots of stuff when I don't. Thanks to my fellow writers who are always there for me, especially Pete, Suzanne, Rose and my friend Lucy Middlemass, who taught me so much over many years.

Thank you, many times over to all the readers in my ARC team who have sought out every last anachronistic word and typo that I missed. I really couldn't do it without you. I hope you'll stick with me, Izzy and Lord Edgington to see what happens next…

Rebecca Brooks, James Woodworth, Ferne Miller, John Vaudrey, Craig Jones, Melinda Kimlinger, Deborah McNeill, Emma James, Mindy Denkin, Namoi Lamont, Katharine Reibig, Linsey Neale, Sarah Brown, Karen Davis, Taylor Rain, Brenda, Christine Folks McGraw, Terri Roller, Margaret Liddle, Esther Lamin, Tracy Humphries, Lori Willis, Anja Peerdeman, Liz Batton, Allie Copland, Kate Newnham, Marion Davis, Adelia Hammond, Tiana Hammond, Tina Laws, Sarah Turner, Linda Brain, Stephanie Keller, Linda Locke, Kathryn Davenport, Another Kat, Barb Hackel, Sandra Hoff, Karen M, Mary Nickell, Vanessa Rivington, Darlene Riggs and my mum, Laraine.

If you're looking for a modern murder mystery series with just as many off-the-wall characters but a little more edge, try **"The Izzy Palmer Mysteries"** for your next whodunit fix.

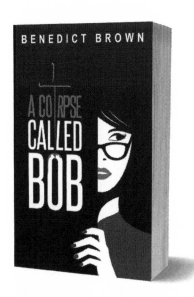

"A CORPSE CALLED BOB"
(BOOK ONE)

Izzy just found her horrible boss murdered in his office and all her dreams are about to come true! Miss Marple meets Bridget Jones in a fast and funny new detective series with a hilarious cast of characters and a wicked resolution you'll never see coming. Read now to discover why one Amazon reviewer called it, ***"Sheer murder mystery bliss."***

ABOUT ME

Writing has always been my passion. It was my favourite half-an-hour a week at primary school, and I started on my first, truly abysmal book as a teenager. So it wasn't a difficult decision to study literature at university which led to a masters in Creative Writing.

I'm a Welsh-Irish-Englishman originally from **South London** but now living with my French/Spanish wife and presumably quite confused infant daughter in **Burgos**, a beautiful mediaeval city in the north of Spain. I write overlooking the Castilian countryside, trying not to be distracted by the vultures, hawks and red kites that fly past my window each day.

When Covid 19 hit in 2020, the language school where I worked as an English teacher closed down and I became a full-time writer. I have two murder mystery series. There are already six books written in **"The Izzy Palmer Mysteries"** which is a more modern, zany take on the genre. I will continue to alternate releases between Izzy and Lord Edgington. I hope to release at least ten books in each series.

I previously spent years focussing on kids' books and wrote everything from fairy tales to environmental dystopian fantasies, right through to issue-based teen fiction. My book **"The Princess and The Peach"** was long-listed for the Chicken House prize in The Times and an American producer even talked about adapting it into a film. I'll be slowly publishing those books over the next year whenever we find the time.

"Murder at the Spring Ball" is the first book in the "Lord Edgington Investigates…" series. The second novel, **A Body at a Boarding School** is now available and there's a free novella if you sign up to my **readers' club**. If you feel like telling me what you think about Chrissy and his grandfather, my writing or the world at large, I'd love to hear from you, so feel free to get in touch via…

www.benedictbrown.net

Made in the USA
Monee, IL
16 October 2021